STOLEN

A KIERAN YEATS MYSTERY

LINDA J WRIGHT

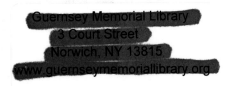

Published 2018
Printed in the United States of America
First Edition
ISBN 978-1-7323593-0-7
E-ISBN 978-1-7323593-1-4
Library of Congress Control Number: 2017930398

Cover Design by Word-2-Kindle

For information, contact:

Cats Paw Books
630 Hickory Street NW
Suite 120-119
Albany, OR 97321
catspawbooks@mail.com

For Sheila Crandles

Acknowledgements

M ANY PEOPLE, WHETHER they know it or not, helped bring this book into being. Some helped a lot, some helped a little, and if I've neglected to mention anyone, I'm sincerely sorry.

Thank you to my editors Katherine Forrest and Christine Cassidy. Every author needs a good editor, and I had two. Thank you to my beta reader Jac Lambert, who told me where the book worked and where it didn't. Thank you to my excellent proofreader and partner, Martha. Thank you to the amazing Derek Murphy at creativeindie. com, for his generosity about all things indie publishing. And thank you to Word-2-Kindle for their beautiful cover design.

Thank you to three poets whose work has enriched my life and informed my writing: Mary Oliver, whose poem "Praying" Kieran mentions in Chapter 1; former Oregon Poet Laureate William Stafford, whose poem "Choosing A Dog" is displayed on the wall of the Sanctuary in Chapter 12; and Ben-Hur Lampman, former Oregon Poet Laureate and associate editor of The Portland Oregonian, whose poem "Where To Bury A Dog" Kieran recalls in Chapter 25.

And finally, what can any of us say to all the animals (some of whom are pets) who die every day in traumatic, painful, often unnecessary experiments in researchers' labs. Thanks? Sorry? We all ought to be ashamed. And, like the fictional Kieran Yeats, perhaps we need to become speakers for the living.

About the Author

L INDA J. WRIGHT is a Canadian citizen. Born in Ontario, she grew up in a military family, and spent part of her childhood in Europe. She lived in Victoria, British Columbia, before moving to Oregon, where she now lives with her partner and their spoiled rotten cat. In the 90s, she was awarded three California Arts Council Artist-in-Residence grants to teach fiction writing to GATE high school students and won a California Association of Teachers of English Excellence Award for those classes. Writing as Lauren Wright Douglas, she won the Lambda Literary Award for Best Mystery for her second novel. *Stolen* is her eleventh novel.

An animal rights advocate, Linda has been involved in animal welfare for nearly 30 years. In 1990, she founded the rescue organization The Cat People, and served as its first President. Since then, she has served on the Boards of several animal welfare organizations and has been a consultant to dozens of animal rescue/welfare groups. In 1999 she was part of the team that rescued Keiko the orca (the real Free Willy) and rehabilitated him in Newport, Oregon, setting him free off Iceland. She continues to advocate for animals through her writing.

MONDAY

Chapter 1

Abarrage of door-pounding jolted me out of sleep. I cracked an eye open and read the time on my bedside clock . . . 3:48. What the hell? Who comes pounding on your door at three in the morning? I grabbed my sweats from the floor, my .38 from the closet, and hurried out of the bedroom.

Dressing clumsily in my enclosed back porch, I apologized to my feral, Vlad, who cackled at me from his perch in the rafters. Mindful of the fact that over the years I've irritated more than a few people, I eased open the door and padded quietly through the not-quite-spring grass to the front of the house, soaking my socks.

Peering through the screen of rhododendron bushes, I saw a small, skinny kid on the front porch give my door another couple of whacks. Hardly an intimidating sight. Maybe grabbing my gun had been a bit of overkill.

"Kieran! Open the door!" the kid yelled.

"Hey, knock it off!" I said, coming around the corner of the house. I was cold, hung over, and ticked off. And I had a headache the size of Newfoundland which the door-pounding had not improved.

"It's Jen," a small voice answered. "And I'm sorry for the racket."

The kid stepped into the light cast by the streetlamp: a small, slender girl of about thirteen, hands jammed into the pockets of a black leather jacket, teeth chattering. My goddaughter Jen, who should have been home in bed where all kids are at three in the morning. A bicycle stood propped against the porch railing.

"What's up?" I called, thoroughly mystified at this middle-of-the-night drama.

"Why aren't you answering your phone?" she wailed.

"My phone? It's in a bag of rice. I dropped it in a sinkful of water. Jen, what are you doing here?" A spider of fear walked across the back of my neck. "Is everything all right?" Dumb question. Of course everything was not all right.

"My life is ruined," Jen said. "Apart from that, everything's all right."

☙

I sat at the kitchen table with Jen, waiting for her to talk, feeling guilty for yelling at her. My portly grey cat Trey sat on the table between us, regarding Jen with fierce intensity – the feline equivalent of worry. "It's okay," I told Trey, patting his head. The coffeemaker burbled on the counter behind me. I had hopes that a large infusion of caffeine would nudge my sluggish brain out of neutral where it now idled.

"You're not pregnant, are you?" I asked Jen, a sudden awful thought occurring to me.

"Kieran, I'm only thirteen," she exclaimed in horror. "I haven't even started, well, you know . . ." she trailed off in evident embarrassment. "And by the way, you missed my birthday."

Yeah, well, I had undoubtedly missed a lot of things over the past little while. I was in a depressive funk. My own March Madness. And I had lied to Jen about my phone. It wasn't in a bag of rice. It was in my bedside table drawer, powered off. I simply didn't want to talk to anyone. Through the murk of my hangover and headache, I tried to focus in on what Jen was telling me. But it was not making much sense.

"The cats at Wild At Heart," I said, repeating what she had told me on the way into the house. "They're gone. All eleven of them. The cattery's empty. They've . . . disappeared."

"Yes!" she yelled, fists clenched, evidently wanting to strangle someone. "And Norma Carruthers is going to kill me. She'll do worse than kill me. She'll never hire me again. She'll think this is all my fault."

To her credit, she was not blubbering. She wasn't a crier. But she was clearly pretty damned upset.

I got up and poured coffee for myself. Deciding that Jen was too young to start a caffeine addiction, I put a mugful of water in the microwave and made instant cocoa for her. "Drink this," I said firmly. "And maybe take your jacket off."

She nodded miserably, pulling off her jacket and hanging it over the back of her chair. Underneath was a black T-shirt featuring the head of a snarling tiger. I got it. She was a precocious thirteen-year-old in her first year at a new school. She was telling the world she was a tough kid. But right now she was a scared-to-death kid.

"Take a deep breath, kiddo. Just tell me what happened."

She looked up at me, lips pressed together, dark eyes huge with fear. "I fell asleep with my earbuds in, listening to my iPod," she said. "My music assignment. We're supposed to re-imagine an opera and my friend Donovan and I chose the rock opera *Tommy*. I recorded what we've done so far and I was listening to it." She looked furtively into the corners of the kitchen as if goblins might spring out and grab her.

I took a few swigs of coffee. A little less about the re-imagined opera and more about the cats would be swell. I told myself to be patient. Let the kid tell the story in her own way.

"Norma's gone to Ottawa for a cat show," she explained, calming down a little. "She hired me to stay in the house and look after the cattery for a few days. I've been dropping by after school for about two weeks, working with a kitten from the latest litter. He's small and, well, a little timid. Norma wanted me to give him some extra attention. Build up his confidence so he would be more adoptable." She ran a hand through her messy, short dark hair, making her spikes even spikier.

"You're staying at Norma's for a few days . . . what about school?" I asked her.

"It's spring break, Kieran," she pointed out acerbically.

"Oh yeah, that. Okay, you were taking care of the place, and last night you fell asleep. When you woke up, the cats were just . . . gone?"

"Yes!" she said miserably. "Something told me to go downstairs and check on them. The cage doors were all standing open, and the cages were empty. Empty!" A note of panic edged into her voice.

This was certainly odd, but maybe there was a simple explanation for it. "Now, don't get mad at me, but you're sure, right? You looked and they aren't just . . . somewhere else in the house, you know, playing, or hiding, or sleeping?"

She gave me a withering look. "It's a *cattery*, Kieran. These aren't pets. Well, some of them might be later, but not now. They don't play in the house. The cattery is nice and homey, you know, sofas and cat trees and all that. But they go back in their cages at night. They're valuable animals. Pet quality Bengal kittens sell for a thousand to fifteen hundred dollars apiece. Show quality Bengals sell for up to five thousand dollars."

It took me a moment to process this. Fifteen hundred dollars for a kitten? I paid less for my Karmann Ghia's reconditioned engine. "Yeah, that's valuable all right. And they didn't get out?"

She looked at me incredulously, eyes wide. "You mean out of the *house*?"

Obviously I was not doing a good job with my questions.

"No. No way," she said firmly. "I put everyone in their cages and made sure the latches were closed. I've done the same thing dozens of times." She looked at me in what was clearly panicked horror. "You do believe me, don't you?"

"Of course I believe you," I said loyally, but dammit, part of me, well, doubted. This was too screwy. "I'm just trying to figure out what happened."

"What happened is that I went to sleep and the cats disappeared and it's my fault."

"No, it's not your fault. From what you're telling me, you didn't do anything wrong. But something happened when you were asleep. The only thing that makes sense is that someone got in and took the cats."

Jen said nothing, hunched miserably over her cocoa.

"Right?"

She shrugged. "Yes. No. I guess so. But how? How would anyone get in? There's an alarm system."

Oh, brother. This called for another large swig of coffee. C'mon brain, wake up. "And the alarm didn't go off?"

"Nope. I would have heard it. And it was set when I got up to check the cats. No one could have gotten in the house. I was the only one there." She began to babble. "People will think I did it. Or at least I had a hand in it." Her eyes pleaded with me. *Please believe me, Kieran*, they seemed to say.

"Well, you didn't do it and you didn't have a hand in it," I reassured her. "That's that. It must have been someone else."

She nodded, studying the depths of her cocoa mug. Then she looked up at me. "Kieran, will you try to figure out what happened? Where the cats went and who did it? How to get them back? You know, take this on like, take it on as a case? I mean, you're an animal crimes investigator. This is the kind of thing you do, right?"

I groaned. Yeah, sure, this was what I did – investigate crimes involving animals – but I was not quite at my best. Hadn't been for a couple of weeks. I'd fallen down the rabbit hole of my annual depression again, which for me meant listening to minor-key music, reading my famous forebear William Butler's poetry, and drinking too much Method and Madness Single Malt Irish Whiskey.

Jen must have misinterpreted my silence. "I know what you charge," she said in a small voice. "I can pay you. I have a savings account."

"Oh, Jen," I said. "It's not the money." Although she had a point. I charge five hundred dollars a day plus expenses. A thousand up front. Ah yes, my time was so damned valuable. After all, someone has to reimburse me for those hours taken away from bad poetry and good whiskey.

"Then, what?" she asked. "It's that you don't believe me, isn't it?"

Clearly sensing Jen's distress, Trey butted her under the chin, then turned to regard me with slit-eyed accusation.

I felt small, mean, ashamed. Yeah, part of me didn't quite believe her. But another part, a miserable, self-indulgent part, just wanted to be left alone to brood. "*C'mon Kieran, help the kid out*," an interior voice that I identified as my better half urged me. "*And figuring things out, using your brain, might even haul you out of the Slough of Despond. You're an investigator. So why not investigate?"*

"Okay," I heard myself say, hoping this wouldn't turn out to be one of my more regrettable decisions. "I'll do it. Try to figure things out. Okay."

Chapter 2

B ENGAL CATS, I discovered by Googling, have retained much of the appearance of their jungle heritage. Originally bred by crossing the Asian Leopard Cat with a Domestic Shorthair (how that had been managed I couldn't imagine), Bengals were now bred together, leaving the Asian Leopard Cat as only a distant memory in their genetic past. Modern Bengals have rounded ears, large eyes, a long and powerful stride, distinct facial markings, and beautiful spotted bronze coats. Apparently, they also have some of the same behavioral characteristics of their wild forebears: only people who can keep up with this high-energy, athletic breed ought to consider adopting them, Google explained. Hmm. Wild At Heart's Bengals were described by Norma on her website as being sweet-tempered and loving as well as beautiful. Indeed they were lovely.

Another cup of coffee and a much-needed shower had rendered me approximately human and I had even donned real clothes in celebration of my renaissance: a pair of tan cords and a cream wool turtleneck. A quick check in the bathroom mirror both reassured and surprised me that I did not quite look the wreck I felt as the result of my descent into *desuetude*. I saw a woman with short, wavy dark hair that needed cutting, grey eyes, and a mouth that did not smile often enough. Oh, there were perhaps a few more frown lines between my eyebrows, but who was counting? After all, I was approaching middle age. I'd soon be forty. I snorted. Middle Age . . . that sounded like some dismal British hamlet, just down the road from Girlhood-Under-Bridge and not quite as far as Lesser Dotage.

Forcing my thoughts back to the problem at hand, I asked myself, so who stole the Bengals? Figure that out, get them back, and Jen was off the hook. Unless Norma had been the object of a cruel prank, the solution ought to be a simple matter of *cui bono* – who stood to benefit from the crime. Then I could nail him or them, and bring the Bengals home. Well, there were a host of questions to be answered first, not the least of which was how the hell anyone could have gotten in without tripping the alarm.

I laced my fingers behind my head and sat back in my chair, realizing that I was becoming intrigued by the Bengals' theft. Which was good. Because I needed a Rubik's Cube of a distraction. I needed something that would keep me from my annual bout of perseveration concerning the case that had driven me from the Crown Counsel's office, a precedent-setting animal law case: Her Majesty The Queen vs Owen Mallory, heard before Justice Patrick O'Rourke, argued by Ms. Kieran Yeats, newly-minted Senior Counsel for The Crown.

Ah, hubris.

I'd never argued an animal law case before – indeed the penalties for crimes against animals were so ludicrously lenient that they didn't merit arguing. But this case was different. Parliament had just enacted a new set of sentencing guidelines for crimes against animals: a maximum of five years instead of the token six months that had been on the books for decades. At last Parliament had realized how out of step it had become with current societal values. This was to be the pioneering case that affirmed our country's condemnation of those who engaged in animal cruelty.

So what went wrong? Nothing. The investigative work was thorough; my arguments were unassailable; the judge was more than sympathetic.

The crime? Well, it was, in a word, horrendous.

One March several years ago, a man named Owen Mallory moved in with his girlfriend Gianna Brock and her three Pugs – Ziggy, Pasha and Mr. T. But in the course of one short month, Pasha was dead, Ziggy was seriously injured, and Gianna was traumatized. The report obtained from Ms. Brock's veterinarian by detective Alexander MacLeish of the Oak Bay Police Department chronicled a litany of horrors perpetrated upon the two Pugs. Between them, they had suffered blunt force trauma, chemical and electrical burns, hemorrhages, a separated retina, a collapsed lung, fourteen rib fractures, perforation of the thoracic cavity . . . and on and on. The unemployed Owen Mallory, having nothing but free time on his hands, must have dedicated himself to this torture, I argued. Justice O'Rourke, appalled, agreed.

Owen Mallory was sentenced to the maximum prison time the newly rewritten law allowed: five years. He was also ordered to repay Gianna Brock $5,741 in vet bills; $311 for an autopsy of Pasha; $1,100 in lost salary for veterinary visits; $1,550 for moving costs to put herself in "a safe and secure place away from him" as she put it; and $2,700 in psychotherapy costs. Mallory was ordered to pay in monthly installments of $350.

Additionally, Justice O'Rourke found the crimes against these animals to be so "chilling", as he wrote in his judgment, and the suffering "so severe and protracted" that he prohibited Owen Mallory from "owning, having custody or control of, or residing on the same premises as an animal or bird for a period of twenty-five years." Lastly, Mallory was placed on three years' probation; ordered to perform 150 hours of community service that did not involve animals; prohibited from contacting or coming within 200 meters of Gianna Brock; undergoing psychiatric treatment for anger management and domestic abuse issues; prohibited from ever owning a weapon; and required to give a DNA sample.

So Justice was served, right?

Wrong.

Within six months following his conviction and incarceration, Mallory hired a new lawyer and mounted an appeal, based on the discovery of "fresh evidence". His new attorney argued that the fresh evidence demonstrated that Pasha's injuries and death were from falls down the stairs due to a medical condition. What the hell? This sure sounded bogus to me. I did not argue for the Crown on Mallory's appeal – appeals cases are argued by different Crown Counsel personnel – so I never got a chance to examine the evidence. After a short trial, Mallory's sentence was overturned, and he was released for time served – six months. I was infuriated. Why the hell had we bothered? His new attorney also succeeded in slicing almost $4,000 off his restitution order and dispensing with the community service requirement and the psychiatric treatment. The only small victories left the Crown were the pet prohibition ban, the keep-away order, the firearm prohibition ban, and the DNA sample. I don't know how much comfort Gianna Brock took from that quartet.

And whereas Gianna, her mother, and I had celebrated the night after Mallory was sentenced, I hadn't had the guts to contact them after the appeal and his release. I imagined they felt that I, as well as the law, had let them down. Why hadn't I called, or emailed, or texted them? I was a coward. I felt guilty and ashamed. I felt like slinking out of town, tail between my legs.

But another feeling came to displace shame, or at least to take up residence with it: betrayal. I got rip-roaring drunk the night of Mallory's release. And I quit the Crown Counsel's office the next day.

You see, I was heartbroken. My beloved, the law, had jilted me. How dare she? Fifteen years of my life had been devoted to her. And for this? To have a case where I could have been a pioneer, could have made a difference, snatched from me through no fault of mine? I brooded. I drank immoderately. I bathed irregularly. I ate seldom and unwisely. I shut off my phone. I was becoming more and more unhinged, and I knew it. Wasn't it Euripides who said: "Those who the gods would destroy, they first make mad?" I was halfway there.

Eventually, though, common sense prevailed. I didn't, as the kids say, just get over it. No, I just put the whole bundle of feelings somewhere to be dealt with later. I got out of bed, showered, dressed, shopped for food, cleaned my house, apologized to my cats, and decided to look for work. But work guided by something inspirational that Justice O'Rouke had written in his judgment. He wrote: "A person who abuses a child always runs the risk that the child will overcome his fear and report his suffering. The abuser of an animal has no such concern. So long as he commits his abuses beyond the reach of prying eyes, he need not fear that his victim will reveal his crimes.

Tragically, in this case, it was only in death that Pasha found her voice to identify the nature of hers and Ziggy's torment, and the identity of their tormentor."

I read and re-read that paragraph many times during my dark night of the soul. Pasha's voice, alas, had been heard only in death. Therefore, I, as her champion, could only act as speaker for the dead. Somewhere in those late-night hours of too much drinking and too little sleeping, I made a decision. I would work for animals *before* they met a fate like Pasha's. I would no longer serve the law, justice with a capital J. Instead I would serve those whom the new laws were intended to benefit but all too often continued to fail – animals. I would listen to the Pashas and Ziggys and act for them. I would be both listener and speaker for the living, wherever that decision might take me.

That decision had taken me into the world of animal advocacy, and sometimes into cases involving tremendous animal cruelty and neglect, but I never regretted my decision. At the end of the day, it felt so much better to have intervened on behalf of a living animal than to have argued in court for justice for a dead one. And Norma Carruthers' eleven missing Bengal cats could certainly use my help. Someone needed to advocate for them.

But here I was, poleaxed by depression again. Would the damned Mallory case never loosen its grip on me? My therapist Margaret believed it would, pointing out that it was the unfortunate co-incidence of Pasha's death and Mallory's early release from prison that sandbagged me every March. The repetition was certainly getting old. Feeling grumpy, I got up to pour another cup of coffee, resolving to evict Mallory from my mind and invite the Bengals back in.

Jen had been pretty damned lucky, I thought. If it hadn't been for the earbuds and her music, she might well have heard the thieves at work, come downstairs, and gotten seriously hurt. I didn't doubt for a minute that anyone who had designs on many thousands of dollars worth of exotic cats would have given too much consideration to whacking a kid who appeared in the middle of the crime.

As if thought had conjured her, Jen appeared in the kitchen doorway.

"I had a shower, too," she announced. "I heard you up." She jammed her hands into the pockets of her jeans. "I called Norma in Ottawa."

"How did that go?" I asked. That phone call must have been hard, but she had done the right thing. She hadn't come asking me to be the one to break the bad news to her employer. I was proud of her.

Jen shrugged, looking down at her sneakers. "Okay, I guess. At least she didn't yell. I thought she would. She just sounded . . . horrified. Sad. She said she would come back early. Tomorrow in fact." She raised her eyes to mine. "I told her that you were an animal crimes investigator. That you were on the case. Was that all right?"

I winced. Yup. I was on the case all right. "Sure. What did she say?"

"That you should call her later today. After she had a chance to let all this sink in. I texted her number to your phone. Is it working?" she asked. "I forgot about it being in a bag of rice."

I cleared my throat guiltily. "Erm, yes, it seems to be okay now." In fact it was charging in my office as we spoke.

"Jen, I was thinking . . . let's go back to Wild At Heart before I take you home. I'd like to look things over. We can stop by McDonald's for breakfast."

She brightened a little. Apparently breakfast at the Golden Arches was still a favorite with young people. Ye gods, I knew as much about teenagers as I did about the denizens of the Marianas Trench.

"And I'd better call Mac. He can meet us at Wild At Heart. This needs to be reported to the police." Jen didn't look very enthusiastic. "You know that, right?"

"I know, I know," she said impatiently. "I talked about that with Norma. It's just that . . . how many people am I going to have to tell this story to? It makes me feel stupid. And awful."

"Maybe just one more," I said, trying for the right tone with her. I hoped soothing would work.

"You said I didn't do anything wrong, but I feel like I did."

Trey came to stand between us, skewering me with that accusing look again, clearly Jen's champion. *Feline ingrate,* I thought at him. *Just wait until you want to snuggle in bed tonight.*

"I don't mind talking to Mac," Jen said sadly. "He's a friend. I just mind that he'll probably think I had something to do with it. After all, he's a cop. Isn't it his job to suspect everybody?"

Alexander MacLeish was a detective in the Oak Bay Police Department, having worked his way up through the ranks from constable. No more lurking behind lampposts on Oak Bay Avenue for him, waiting for unwary tourists from Moose Jaw to leave their cars too long in the yellow zones. Mac and I had been friends for many years. Our promotions came in tandem, his to detective, mine to Senior Counsel. He'd been my investigator. Together we'd shared the satisfaction of seeing his canny investigations and my stellar arguments put away wife-beaters, rapists, and child-molesters. And when we stumbled, we'd shared our disappointment over pitchers of beer at the Oak Bay Marina Snug.

"The police don't always suspect everyone," I told Jen reasonably. "But, c'mon, kiddo. I'll get my phone and we'll take off."

∾

We loaded Jen's bike into the back of my Karmann Ghia and headed for Beach Drive, taking the coast road north. The sea was cobalt today with a few whitecaps frosting the wave-tops, the sky powder blue and cloudless with a scoured-clean look to it. The Karmann Ghia's heater tried bravely to warm our feet, but I zipped my jacket a little higher, familiar with my car's caprice. Ah spring. As the old song says, I hadn't seen a crocus or a rosebud or a robin on the wing. Where were those storied harbingers of hope anyhow?

My phone rang as we were just north of Cordova Bay.

"Yeats," I said.

"So you are alive," my friend Anne said. "I've only called you twelve times in the last little while."

"My phone was disabled," I fibbed. "But see? Persistence paid off. Thirteen is obviously your lucky number."

"Hmm. Want to come to dinner on Saturday and explain your absence from the world? I'm making risotto. Val and Tonia are coming."

I consulted my empty social calendar and, finding no conflicts, agreed. "You said the magic word."

"Come about six," Anne said. "You could bring wine. It will be nice to see you, Kieran. And I've invited someone else, too," she said mysteriously.

"You're not trying to hook me up again, are you?" I asked in alarm.

"Who says the latest hooking up efforts will be meant for you?" Anne teased.

""Yeah, touché," I said. "My solipsism is showing. Sorry. Just so you keep firmly in your mind that I'm temporarily *hors de combat.*"

"Got it," Anne said. "See you Saturday."

"You know you're not supposed to talk on the phone while you're driving," Jen said primly.

"Uh huh. Another of my bad habits which you shouldn't emulate, kiddo," I told her.

After a moment, she asked: "Kieran, do you think you and Anne will get back together? As . . . you know."

"Hmm, well," I equivocated, a little surprised at her question. "Probably not. We're pretty good friends, though. Why do you ask?"

"I just wondered," she said.

I doubted that Jen was "just wondering", so I waited.

"Kieran, when did you know you were gay?"

Aha. Her real question. Anne had just been an entrée into what was really on Jen's mind. Somehow I wasn't too surprised. I possessed pretty good "gaydar" and it had been pinging about Jen for some time now.

"Hmm," I said, wondering just how much to tell her. "When did I know? Well, when I was just about your age. Thirteen. She was a girl in my class at school."

"Yeah? What happened?" Jen asked.

"Well, I fell in love. Like that corny old song says: my heart stood still."

When Jen said nothing, I wondered if I'd said too much. Or too little. What the hell. I stepped into the silence. "Of course things don't always happen like that, though," I hastened to reassure her. "I imagine for everyone it's different."

"Uh huh," she said quietly, lost in thought.

We drove along in silence for a bit longer, then I tiptoed into my question: "Is there someone in your life you'd like to tell me about?" I asked gently.

"Well, maybe," she said, clearly struggling. "I . . . it's hard to explain. Maybe later. Right now, though, I just wanted to know when you knew. And if you thought I was too young to know."

"No, I don't think you're too young." I didn't want to pry, but I wanted to leave the door open. "I'm always here if you want to talk," I said. "I promise to keep my phone and the sink far apart in future."

"Okay. Thanks," she said, nodding. Clearly the subject was closed for the time being.

We drove along in silence and I realized that I hadn't had a chance to talk to Jen, really talk to her, for some time. While I'd been busy brooding, and she'd been busy at school, time was slipping inexorably away. She'd turned thirteen, an important milestone for a young person. Dammit, I loved this kid. I really had to do better.

Suddenly Jen turned to me and asked: "Do you believe in God, Kieran?"

I figuratively bit my tongue, holding back my true thoughts on the matter, which would begin with: "Hell, no," or "Are you kidding me?" I searched for an answer that I thought a thirteen-year-old would find useful. Maybe the subtext of her question was why God allows bad things to happen. That was a good question, in light of the present circumstances.

"If I had to say, I would say that my belief is a work in process," I tap-danced.

"Okay, but where are you now? In the process, I mean?" she persisted.

Okay, Kieran, cough it up. "Um, well, no, I don't believe in God. Not the God with the long white beard perched on a cloud on the ceiling of Michelangelo's Sistine Chapel, holding his index finger out to Adam."

"Then, what?" she said after a moment.

"Well, I'd have to say I do believe all this," I gestured out at the shoreline and the ocean, "was created. That it didn't happen by chance."

I looked over at Jen to find her regarding me intently. Crap. I hoped I was saying the right things.

"If it didn't happen by chance, and if God didn't do it, then who did?" she asked.

I cleared my throat. "Well, maybe it isn't a who so much as a what."

"You mean a thing? Like an alien?"

I had just opened my mouth to further expound on this theory when, suddenly, right in front of my windshield, about a dozen Canada Geese just *appeared*, gliding downward at a steep angle. It was as if pieces of the sky had fallen. To my amazement, we did not hit any of them, and I gasped. My windshield all but kissed the last goose's tailfeathers as they swooped down to land near a pond off to our right.

"Omigod!" Jen called out, turning to look as we sped by. "Oh, wow! I thought we were going to, like, drive right into them."

"Me, too," I said, loosening my death grip on the steering wheel. "Want me to go back around so we can see them?"

"Yes!" Jen exclaimed.

I turned my car around on the empty road and drove back to where dozens and dozens of Canada Geese were arranging themselves beside a little pond. "Aren't they beautiful?" she said with the amazed passion of a poet . . . or a teenager. We contemplated the geese in shared silence.

Thinking back to Jen's question about God, I had an idea. An idea produced by the geese.

"Kiddo, about God . . ." I said.

"Yeah?" she said.

"I'm going to text a poem to your phone when I get a minute. It's by a wonderful poet named Mary Oliver, and it's called "Praying". I think you'll like it. She writes about the natural world – deer, geese – and that flock of geese appearing as they did just now, and your question about God suddenly put me in mind of the poem. In it she says that anything in the natural world can be a doorway."

"A doorway?"

"Yeah. A doorway into thanks."

Huh," Jen said, clearly thinking this over.

"She says if we are silent, and just wait by the doorway, another voice might speak to us."

"Wow," said Jen, evidently moved. "Like maybe God's voice."

"Maybe," I said. "According to Oliver, we don't have to do anything special. Just pay attention."

"That's why you turned the car around, isn't it?" she asked me. "So we could go back and pay attention. I get it."

After a few minutes, I glanced over at Jen. She was looking off into the distance, lost in thought. I hoped I had said something useful. I'd text her the poem, and maybe it would pique her interest. Maybe she would Google other poems by Oliver. They were certainly thought-provoking and I didn't think Jen was too young for such thoughts. We turned into the McDonald's parking lot. Thank heavens. If the drive had been longer, maybe Jen would have wanted to know how I'd voted. A trifecta of religion, relationships and politics, all before breakfast.

"What do you say, kiddo?" I said. "Breakfast is on me. You can have an Egg McMuffin and *two* orders of hash browns. I'll have to rein myself in at one, however. My ageing arteries might never recover otherwise."

Chapter 3

Wild At Heart was a big, grey stone-fronted two-story house in a pocket of others just like it, slightly north of the Oak Bay Marina. There was no identifying sign, nothing to proclaim it any different from the other houses in the neighborhood. The oak trees on the lots were tall, the homes well set back from the street. Some had brick or stone fronts, some were Tudor-inspired, which I found a deplorable architectural affectation, but overall the effect was pleasing. A well-established, quiet neighborhood. All is well here, the vibe said. No one was out and about yet this morning, which I found odd. Where were all the dog-walkers? Trotting behind dogs was Victoria's chief suburban pastime. Mac's car, a blue Bronco, was in the driveway, and I pulled in behind it. Jen got out of my Karmann Ghia and gave me only one spooked-horse look, before marching past Mac's car to the front porch.

"Hang on a bit," I called to her. "Let's see how Mac wants to do this." When she looked at me quizzically, I told her, "It's a crime scene, remember?"

Mac got out of his Bronco, folding a stiff-looking eight by eleven piece of paper, and tucking it inside his tweed blazer. A tall, burly, fair-haired, blue-eyed Scot in his late forties, he was one of the few people I allowed to kiss me on the cheek, which he did now.

"Mary and I have missed you, Kieran," he said, peering at me inquisitively from the thicket of his eyebrows. "She'd like to make haggis for you one night soon."

I'm sure I blanched. Haggis was not high on my culinary hit parade, although I had never quite summoned the nerve to say so to Mac's wife. "I'll look forward to it," I replied evasively. Did I look pale and wan, I wondered? Here were two old friends within thirty minutes of each other offering to ply me with food.

"Jen, you remember Mac, don't you?" I said as Mac and I joined her on the porch.

She nodded miserably.

"So you've had a break-in and a wee theft, Kieran tells me," Mac began, evidently having decided to soft-pedal this with Jen.

Jen looked as though she would like to disappear. "Yes," she said in a small voice.

"Well, you can tell me all about it," Mac said. "I'll take a report. No need for you to come down to the station. I'll have Burglary contact Miz Carruthers when she gets back. Right now, though, why don't you open up?"

Jen nodded, stuck her key in the front door lock and opened the door. Immediately a beeping noise sounded from the wall to our right. "The alarm," she explained, stepping inside. Mac and I followed her into a small foyer. "The keypad is here. You have fifteen seconds to disable the alarm." She reached to her right and the beeping noise stopped. "Oh," she said quickly, "I touched it. Do you want to take prints? Have I spoiled things?"

Mac smiled. "No. I can't see the thieves thoughtfully setting the alarm on their way out the front door."

Jen slumped, evidently miserable. "I can't even see how they got *in*, let alone got *out*. I just don't get it."

Mac winked at her. "That's what we're here for, Kieran and I. Between us, we'll figure things out." He took a small notebook and a pen out of an inner pocket of his blazer.

I winced. Oh sure. My figuring-things-out skills were not exactly in full flower today. Still, it was necessary to project a seemly confidence. I tried.

"The front door . . . is it the only door on the alarm system?" Mac asked Jen.

"No," she said. "There's another door, too. A sliding glass door, in the cattery."

"Will you show us?" Mac asked.

"Through here," Jen said, leading us from the front hall toward a room separated from the rest of the house by a door with extra heavy screening.

"Norma doesn't want the kittens running around in the main house, getting into trouble when they're little. So they stay in here. The adults, and the kittens when they're older, can be underfoot in the house. It's good for them to be with people. And they like to watch movies in the evening," she said. "Just like they would do in a home once they're adopted. But everyone goes back into the cattery at night."

The cattery was a huge, bright, cream-painted room with a vaulted ceiling and a bank of six oversized stainless steel cages against one wall. On the floor were two black and red patterned Oriental carpets. Against the wall opposite the cages were three sofas upholstered in a sturdy-looking multicolored tweedy fabric, with red throw pillows. Four three-story cat trees, each with a carpeted box for a base, a central upright wound with sisal, and a top platform with sides, were spaced against the walls of the room between the sofas. A skylight, plus a set of sliding doors leading to sunroom on the deck, made the space exceptionally light and airy-feeling, as did a set of clerestory windows on the wall above the sofa. There were hooded litterpans discreetly placed here and there in the room, as well as small litterpans in the cages. Amazingly, there was no odor.

"You were a good housekeeper," I told Jen. "No litterpan smell."

"A big space," Mac said. "Miz Carruthers must have converted the garage as well as the original master bedroom."

Mac walked through the cattery and stopped at the sliding glass door. Just outside the slider, attached to the house, was a large sunroom containing several wicker chairs sporting comfy-looking bright blue cushions. Nothing but the best for those Bengals, I thought. He tapped the glass of the sliding door and turned to Jen. "So this is the other door on the alarm system?"

She nodded.

"What about the door out of the sunroom onto the deck?" He pointed through the sunroom.

"No. It's not on the alarm system. Just the slider."

He flipped up the latch on the sliding door, opened it, and went out into the sunroom. I followed him. A clear glass door set in one wall of the sunroom led outside onto the deck. There was a lock in the door's handle and the key was in the lock.

"Does Norma always keep the key in the door like this?" Mac asked.

Jen nodded. "Yeah. She keeps the door locked and the key in the lock like that to remind her not to brainlessly open the door, she says. There might be cats in the sunroom. She doesn't want anyone to run out."

Mac nodded. "Logical." He tried the door. It was indeed locked.

Coming back inside, he latched the sliding door to the sunroom, and smoothed his moustache.

"What else is on the alarm system, Jen?

"Three downstairs windows," she said. "One in the living room, one in the dining room, and one in the kitchen."

"Do you check them all at night before you turn in?"

She nodded. "Yes. All of them. Even though I've never opened any of them. I'm a little paranoid, I guess. These cats are worth a lot of money. And besides," she shrugged, "if one of the windows had been accidentally left open, say by Norma, I couldn't arm the system."

Mac nodded thoughtfully. "What about the high windows, there?" he asked, pointing to the clerestory windows.

"They don't open," she said.

"All right then," he said. "Let's look at the rest of the room."

There was a small office space at the end of the cattery opposite the sliding door – an oak rolltop desk, a bookcase, and a filing cabinet. Over the desk, on the wall, hung a large monthly dry erase calendar for March, with notations made for cat shows and vet visits. A black and silver phone sat on the desk. "Norma's office," Jen explained.

Mac pushed the rolltop up. Inside was an array of pigeonholes stuffed with paper, envelopes, pens – the usual clutter of an office contained in a small space. "No computer," he said, raising an eyebrow.

"She took it with her," Jen told him. "It's a laptop."

"Hmm," Mac said, looking around once more. "There must be cat carriers. Where are they stored?"

Jen opened a door beside Norma's desk and switched on a light. "In here. Along with jugs of litter. This is just a big closet with shelves. Oh," she said in alarm, "there were five black soft-sided carriers. You know . . . the kind that have mesh inserts so the cats can see out. But they're gone."

I looked inside the closet. There were three medium-sized teal-green hard plastic carriers stacked one on the other, half a dozen jugs of scoop litter, and an unopened bag of Evo cat kibble. That was all.

"Norma must have used the other two hard-sided carriers for the cats she took with her to Ottawa," Jen said, "but all the soft-sided ones are gone. That's how the thieves carried the cats out, isn't it?" she said indignantly.

"How many cats were here?" Mac asked.

"Eleven," Jen said, tight-lipped. "They must have doubled them up, two cats to a carrier . . . maybe three kittens in one. But why did they take only the soft-sided carriers?" she asked Mac. "The hard plastic ones are bigger. The cats wouldn't have been so crowded."

He sighed. "All good questions, young lady."

We peered into the closet as if we might find clues in its dim interior, then Mac reached in and flipped off the light switch. "Jen, are your things still here?"

She nodded.

"Why don't you go get them. I want to talk to Kieran."

Jen eyed him suspiciously, then left us. Mac watched her go, then turned back to me.

"I have to say I'm a little stumped," I told him. "Nothing brilliant is occurring to me. There are only two doors into this place, they're both on the alarm system, and they were both locked. The alarm system was armed. There are only three windows that open and they were locked, too. Yet, eleven cats, stuffed into five nifty mesh-sided cat carriers disappeared last night. I'm thinking teleportation," I said. "Beam them up, Scotty."

"This is certainly a puzzler," he said. "But maybe this will help."
He reached into an inner pocket of his blazer and took out the folded
sheet of paper I had seen him reading earlier. "Have a look at this."

I unfolded the paper. At the top in large black letters it read:
HAVE YOU SEEN ME? I'M MISSING. Underneath was the photo
of a half-grown German Shepherd, with a phone number at the bottom of the page. "Someone's dog is missing," I said. "I'm sorry. But
how is that helpful?"

"It's not just this dog who's gone missing, Kieran. Every flier
is different. A German Shepherd, two beagles, a Schnauzer, a yellow
lab . . ."

I sighed. "Mac, maybe I'm particularly dense this morning," I
said, "but I don't see what a couple of missing dogs has to do with the
theft of cats from Wild At Heart."

He rubbed his eyebrows thoughtfully, looking past me in the
direction Jen had disappeared, clearly not wanting her to hear what he
was about to say.

"There was a case like this a few years ago, up-island," he said.
"The case fell under the RCMP's jurisdiction. I know the chap who
headed the so-called investigation and he's a bit of a lazy sod. At the
end of the day it was deemed, ah, expedient to write the missing pets
off to coyotes."

"Okay," I said, puzzled, waiting to see where Mac's story was
going. "I gather you didn't think much of the police work?"

"I did not," he said forcefully.

"How were you involved if it was the RCMP's jurisdiction?"

"Mary's sister lost her terrier to those so-called coyotes," he said.
"It fair broke her heart. That's when I took an interest in the investigation. I did a little research and found that coyotes hadn't been spotted
in that neighborhood for years."

"Go on."

"There were two waves of animal disappearances in that community," he said. "Over twenty pets vanished from about a seven-block
area in the space of a weekend. Then there was a lull. In the lull, the
RCMP talked to some of the owners of the missing pets, concluded in
a stroke of brilliance that coyotes were to blame, wrote a perfunctory
report, then got busy with other things. A week later, six or seven pets

disappeared from Going To The Dogs, a doggie day care operation on the other side of town."

"And the RCMP's conclusion?"

"Coyotes again," he snorted. "The back gate at Going To The Dogs was found open. The RCMP contended that that the owner had been negligent and left the gate ajar, whereupon coyotes entered the yard and carried off the dogs. Perhaps even the same slavering beasties whose taste for blood had merely been whetted the week before," he said.

"Sounds a bit far-fetched to me," I said.

"Indeed," Mac said. "One of the RCMP constables was a family friend. She shared the discouraging details of the investigation with me. We both believed that these coyotes were of the two-legged variety. As well, we believed that the same thieves who carried off Mary's terrier and her neighbors' pets carried off the dogs at Going To The Dogs." He sighed. "It would offend my theory of coincidences to believe anything else."

"Ah yes, MacLeish's Theory of Coincidences." I smiled. "I believe it goes like this: There Are No Coincidences." I wasn't certain I agreed with this theory, but decided this was not the time to express my reservations.

Mac shrugged, looking a bit embarrassed. "Ah well, sometimes I can be a wee bit too dogmatic. No pun intended. However, to believe anything else about the vanishing animals would be to defy reason. I did a bit of checking. Apart from the occasional wandering dog who was subsequently found, no animals were reported missing either before or after the two-week period in which the so-called coyote predation took place."

"I guess the coyotes moved on," I said sarcastically.

"Apparently so," he replied, frowning. "So what do I really know? Only that the RCMP dropped the ball, which outraged and saddened a lot of people in that community. And until I saw the fliers on the telephone poles this morning, I'd pretty much forgotten about that case. I was assuming that the theft of the cats here at Wild At Heart was a one-off. But over the years, I've been impressed by patterns. The missing animals in this neighborhood, the missing Bengals . . ." He broke off.

"You think they resemble the thefts up-island," I said, finishing his thought for him. "Substitute Wild At Heart for Going To The Dogs and they're nearly identical. And Oak Bay sure doesn't have many coyotes. Of the four-legged kind."

Mac looked over his shoulder as we heard Jen in the front hall. "Let me take Jen off your hands," he offered. "I have to be in court in a bit, so it's no trouble to drop her at home. There's a number at the bottom of the flier," he said. "You might want to call it. Neighbors here must have gotten organized as soon as they realized their pets were missing because it's the same number on all the fliers." He frowned, dropping his voice. "I can't help you with this, though. I wish I could."

"You can't? Why not?"

"I'm up to my ears in this bloody epidemic of bootleg fentanyl. All the jurisdictions are. We're drowning in a tide of this damned drug coming in from China. Through the postal service, no less! Addicts who think they're just getting their usual heroin hit are dying because their heroin has been laced with contaminated fentanyl. Sorry," he said ruefully. "I'll pass on to you whatever information I still have in my files. That's about all I can do, I'm afraid."

"Hey, I'm grateful for any help," I said. "One of the pet owners may well have seen something pertinent. I'll call the number."

"Call which number?" Jen asked, coming to join us in the cattery. "I put my stuff in the front hall. What's up?"

"Mac's going to run you home" I told her, folding the flier into fourths and putting it in my jacket pocket. "I have to make a phone call."

"It's a lead, isn't it?" Jen said eagerly. "Mac's helping and he knows something!"

"Maybe," I told her.

"Call me this evening, Kieran?" Mac asked me as we all walked to the front door. "I can give you that additional information."

"Can't you guys tell me *anything?*" Jen asked, evidently frustrated.

"Let's see how this pans out," I said evasively, not knowing how in hell I was going to handle my inquisitive thirteen-year-old employer. Well, I'd figure that out.

In the meantime, I thought I'd better make a phone call about a German shepherd . . . and a Schnauzer . . . and a yellow lab . . .

Chapter 4

MID-AFTERNOON FOUND ME parked at the verge of a tiny fir-rimmed lake just north of U Vic, eating a tuna sub sandwich, drinking coffee, and thinking. I had several hours to kill. I'd called the phone number on the flier Mac had given me, identified myself as an investigator working for Norma Carruthers, and was told by a tearful-sounding woman named Mara Riordan that there would be a neighborhood pet owners' meeting just before dinner. Was there any way I could attend, she wondered? Of course, I said, determined to anesthetize myself to the mingled hope and pain in her voice. Apart from passing on a few tips about how to find lost pets, what could I do for Mara and her neighbors? I had hopes of my own – that someone in that neighborhood had seen something that would make my finding the Bengals easier. So I assured her that I would attend the meeting and sternly told myself that I would not be moved by the pet owners' distress. The meeting was still some hours away, so that gave me time to make a few more phone calls.

The first call was to a number which, in the past, you would never find in any directory – paper and ink, or online. Edgar Poe, my go-to-guy for hacking, had bragged to me for years that there wasn't a database anywhere safe from his prying. I believed him. He'd done me many good, albeit illegal turns. Now, he had a website for crap's sake, a logo, and a business motto. Now he was Poe Enterprises, his logo was a glaring, ruffled raven perched atop a computer, and his business motto was "Nevermore." Cute. And whereas in the not-so-distant past he had been a night creature – up when ordinary people were down – he had morphed into, well, a nine to fiver. Poe Enterprises now had a phone answerer, a swanky suite of offices downtown, and actual employees, although I imagined those employees were all former hackers who, like Edgar, had suddenly seen the light.. Whatever the reason for their metamorphosis, Edgar and his merry band now performed cybersecurity for some of Victoria's top tech companies. He had become depressingly conventional. I used to imagine him a vampire bat, flitting into a closet at the first blush of dawn, wrapping himself in leathery wings, hanging by his toenails in the crepuscular gloom until dusk. Alas, nevermore.

"Edgar, are you on phone duty today?" I asked in amazement when he answered.

"No, sweetie," he said. "The system recognized your number. I picked up because I always have time for old friends."

Old friends, hmmf. I hadn't yet had to hire Edgar in his new respectable incarnation, and I didn't know what to expect. In the past, his services were only performed after an aggravating back and forth charade in which he feigned overwork, I flattered and pleaded, and we finally agreed upon a price that he vowed would impoverish him. Sometimes when negotiations became truly tense, we traded insults and speculated upon each other's parentage. Negotiating with Edgar in the past had felt like being nibbled to death by piranhas. I wondered what the new dynamic would be.

"I can only give you a minute, though," he said. "An entire hospital will go dark unless my associates and I can repel a ransomware attack."

Ah, this I understood. Master Poe was still full of himself.

"You always were such a busy guy," I falsely commiserated. "And talented, too. But really, Edgar, this will only take a jiffy. For someone of your talents, that is."

"Hmmf," he said, clearly mollified. "Well, maybe . . ."

I decided to cut to the chase. "I need you to hack into an alarm company's records for me. I want to see the last couple of days. Armings, disarmings, whatever you call them. When the doors and windows were opened and closed. And I need to know which ones. Can you do that?"

"Well, I *could*. But that isn't really the sort of thing I do anymore. And as I said, I *am* rather busy."

In the past, this was where I was expected to beg. I sighed, and slipped into my role as supplicant. "I know you are," I said soothingly, "But this would be child's play for you. Or one of your associates."

"Welllllll . . ." he hedged.

"And I can pay extra." Ah, the magic word.

"All right, all right," he agreed. "For old time's sake."

I told him the details, and after we had agreed upon a price that I felt would impoverish *me*, I slipped in the knife. "And I need this by tomorrow." I cut off his spluttering. "I really do, Edgar. Lives may depend on it. E-mail me with the information. And, yes, go ahead and charge my VISA card."

How times had changed for Edgar, I marveled. Once a free-wheeling devil-may-care hacker, he'd now become a buttoned-down businessman. And what had wrought this change? Shrewd opportunism, I thought, brought about by Victoria's changing economic profile. Formerly Canada's backwater, a sleepy little outpost frequented, as the wags put it, by the newly wed and nearly dead, the city had become tech heaven. There are now more than a thousand tech companies operating on the island, and their combined efforts have added over four billion dollars to Canada's economy. Tech had become Victoria's ascendant employer, leaving government and tourism in the shade. Downtown was unrecognizable from a decade ago; realtors were in a swoon of excitement; and, predictably, parking spaces were nonexistent. Heck, we're Silicon Valley north . . . and damned proud of it. Even tiny companies like Poe Enterprises were flourishing. If Edgar really did have, as he asserted, a hospital as a cyberclient, he was doing well.

I drank a little more coffee and gazed out over the lake. Spring wasn't quite upon us here on the island, but at least we weren't up to our fetlocks in frozen gunk, as those in the east surely were. I lived in Toronto for most of my adult life, and March in Toronto is marked by cairns of beige snow on the city streets, and grim-lipped, winter-weary folk dancing around them. Remember these lines from Ezra Pound's parody of that ancient poem to spring?

Skiddeth bus and sloppeth us,
An ague hath my ham. Sing Goddam.

Indeed, my daily trek from the subway to my office was just like that. Brrr. I recall those eastern winters still.

But I carry with me a better memory: the memory of when I first came to Vancouver Island. It was on a business trip while I was still living in the east. I left Toronto on a winter day so cold the snow squeaked when you walked on it, and landed in Victoria in the middle of the night. My flight didn't have a jetway, and when I stepped outside the plane into the open air, my nose was flooded with such a profusion of moist, *living* smells that I stood there with my mouth open in amazement. I recognized cedar and pine, the smell of damp earth, and something that smelled unbelievably like roses. My God, I thought, awed, this in the middle of January? But there was something else, something tangy and unidentifiable, something indescribably exotic like an operatic *leitmotif.*

I was horribly disappointed that the windows in my hotel did not open, and hardly slept in anticipation of the next day when I could rush outside and enjoy all those smells. I remember falling asleep praying: "Please, no snow." I needn't have worried. As I stood in the hotel lobby the next morning, waiting for the sun to come up, I realized with a thrill that the ocean, or a tongue of it anyway, was right *there,* right outside the hotel. I was so excited I didn't wait for dawn. In the grey half-light, I ran down a little path through the hotel's rose garden to the sea. And as I reached the ocean's edge, the sun came up over the towers of the city behind me, turning the waters of the bay to rippled gold. A line of Gerard Manley Hopkins' poetry popped into my head:

The world is charged with the glory of God; it shall shine out
Like flaming from shook foil.

And suddenly I was sobbing my head off – an overdressed easterner making a fool of herself in the gardens of Victoria's most expensive hotel. Hardly an auspicious beginning for a love affair.

It had taken me awhile, and some disentangling, to move west, but when I did I went back to Vancouver Island, to Victoria, and the little hamlet of Oak Bay on the southernmost tip of the island. Roses don't bloom here in the winter, but you can smell cedar and pine any time you like. And that mysterious something, that olfactory undercurrent that my eastern nose couldn't identify two decades ago is now something I take for granted. The smell of the sea.

The longer I lived here, the more smitten I became with the island and in a fit of exploration one weekend, I even drove up to its northernmost point – Cape Scott, 140 miles north of Victoria. It gave me a spooky feeling to know that north of the cape lay . . . nothing. Only open ocean.

These days, however, I'd been exploring a little closer to home, discovering lakes, and I'd become particularly fond of this one. Today an errant breeze ruffled the lake's surface, putting me in mind of a piece of blue watered silk I'd seen once in a fiber art gallery. But there was another reason I came to this lake, a reason quite apart from its undeniable beauty.

Finishing my sandwich, but saving one piece of crust, I got out of my car and walked towards a flat-topped boulder not far from where I was parked. There, on the boulder was a small, shiny metal bead. Laughing, I put it in my pocket and exchanged it for the bread crust. A raucous cawing came from a fir tree overlooking the boulder, and I looked up.

"Hey, Crow," I said.

More cawing.

"Come eat," I called, backing off, "and thanks for the bead."

A crow with a thumbprint-sized patch of white feathers on his throat swooped down to land on the boulder. Putting one foot on the bread crust, he regarded me with bright black shoebutton eyes.

"Yeah, I know, peanuts would have been better," I told him. "However, the cupboard was bare. I have them on my grocery list, though. Hold a good thought."

He fluffed his feathers. Crows are so damned smart – he probably understood every word I said. And sometimes crows give people gifts in exchange for food. I don't know if all crows do this, but Crow does. And he didn't do it right away. I had been coming here for several weeks, eating sandwiches and dropping bread crusts out my car window for whichever starving avian might want them before I noticed that one crow in particular – one with a small white patch on his throat – always met my car and landed on the asphalt beside the driver's door as if waiting to have lunch with me. After I read about the little girl in Seattle whose backyard crows gave her gifts, I wondered: would Crow do the same? So I started leaving my bread crusts on a nearby boulder, and one day a shiny gum wrapper was waiting for me. I laughed out loud that day. Crow didn't always leave me gifts, but he did more often than not. And I was very grateful to him.

"Bread is the best I can do today," I told him. "Maybe peanuts tomorrow. Better take your tidbit and fly away home now." I walked to my car, swigged the last of my coffee, tossed the cup into the garbage bag behind my seat and, when I turned back to the boulder again, Crow was gone. As was my bread crust. I smiled.

I took a last look at the lake, ascertained that all was well, then wheeled out of the parking lot. I had some serious questions about animal theft, and the thought of waiting until this evening to talk to Mac made me itchy. Patience was not my long suit. I thought I might know who could supply me with some answers.

Chapter 5

NINTH LIFE'S STAR had ascended over the years I had been associated with them. From a ragtag group of protesters, they had blossomed into one of Canada's premiere animal advocacy organizations, championing various animal rights causes, including pressing for an end to cosmetics testing on animals. The group seemed poised to bring off this important victory, as the Cruelty-Free Cosmetics Act had passed its second reading in Parliament just this past winter, and was due for its third any day now.

Amazingly, the Ninth Lifers still had a presence in the same modest brown house in James Bay, not far from downtown Victoria. Their main office was in Ottawa, but apparently they considered Victoria their home. I had called ahead, so I was expected.

As I parked in the driveway behind a black Prius, the front door opened and a small woman with curly light brown hair and dark eyes, dressed in jeans and a blue denim shirt, came out onto the porch: Alison Bell, Ninth Life's director.

"Kieran!" she said in evident delight, holding out her hands. "I was so happy to hear from you. How long has it been? Months and months, I'm afraid."

I took her hands and we hugged. "A few months," I agreed. "You folks have done well. I hear about you on the news now and then. The progress you've made with the cruelty-free cosmetics act is really something."

"Well, we're not out of the woods yet," she said. "We have a friendly Senator to thank for pushing Bill S-214. It's aggravating and discouraging that even the European Union has banned cosmetics testing on animals, yet we lag behind. It will take a change in the legal status of animals from things to sentient beings, I'm afraid. That made the difference in Europe. Ah well, c'mon in."

"Ian!" she called to the back of the house after we were inside and she had hung up my jacket. "It's Kieran Yeats."

A slender young man with a dark wing of hair that fell over his forehead came from the kitchen, a flowered apron tied around his waist. "Hey, Kieran," he said, smiling broadly. "Excuse the apron. I'm baking bread. I do it when I'm anxious."

"Anxious?" I scoffed. "You? The intrepid Ian Burns? The last time I saw you we were both up to our knees in manure, concluding the investigation at that ill-named Happy Cows Dairy up north."

He shook his head. "Yeah, that was awful, all right. But we put the damned place out of business, didn't we? Happy cows indeed," he snorted. "I'm not sure any cows are happy living to be milked. But at least those wretched animals got moved to someplace clean and safe where they can eat grass and look at the sun."

"By the way, I love your apron." I teased.

He blushed. "Oh, that. Yeah, well, we're meeting with members of an animal activist group called Open The Cages. They have some radical ideas they want us to consider for our newest battle: making a dent in the awful business of animals used in research labs. Specifically experiments and research that use companion animals – cats and dogs. We want to make use of their ideas, but we have to tone them down somehow. They're more, um, militant that we are. That's not our style any longer. We've pretty much become a lobbying organization. We press for legislation." He snorted. "Logic, common sense, and compassion do not represent as big a stick as the law. As you well know.

"Anyhow, we'd like to utilize OTC's ideas, and we're hoping that discussing things over dinner will be more productive than just sitting around chewing the fat. Also, we've invited a woman named Susan Chu to join us for dinner. She's a partner in an island PR firm called Idea Magic. They were the ones who came up with the dynamite newspaper and TV PSAs for the anti-cruelty cosmetics campaigns we ran several years ago. So we hope we can get everyone working together. And we have a few bottles of local wine that ought to really help or really hurt." He grinned at me. "Excuse me. I need to get the bread. Come in and sit down."

I sat at one end of a rust-colored sofa and Alison came to sit at the other. "Thanks for agreeing to see me," I said. "I figured you folks would have some ideas about the missing Bengals. I confess to being stumped."

"Animal theft," Alison said, brows drawn together in thought. "We do have a file on this," she said in a businesslike manner. "Ian's going to bring it in. And the people we're meeting with have had a lot of experience with animal theft. I want to tell you before we start though, that, apart from this being a horrible and heartbreaking crime, the chances of recovering stolen animals are not good."

My heart sank. "Shit, Alison."

Ian, minus his apron, came and sat in an armchair to my right, putting a fat manila folder on the coffee table. "Did you tell Kieran she's up against bunchers?" he asked Alison.

Alison shook her head. "I was just getting to that."

"Bunchers?" I asked. "I haven't had any cases involving bunchers. I confess to not knowing much about them. But, really, aren't they pretty much of a bad joke? People who cruise neighborhoods at night and nab pets? And then what . . . sell them? To whom?" They looked at each other and I suddenly realized that Norma's Bengals might be in serious trouble. Trouble which I knew very little about. I took a deep breath. "Go on."

"Bunchers are scum," Ian said flatly. "They break people's hearts. They're opportunists who prey on the fact that people don't realize they shouldn't leave their pets outside unattended. And they thrive because providing animals for research or education is lucrative. It's doubly disgusting, because it's organized crime sanctioned by the government."

"Wait," I said. "The Bengals were stolen because some government researcher needs subjects?"

"Maybe," he said. "Or a private facility conducting tests needs them. Or a university teaching institution using cats and dogs for vivisection." He paused, and I felt sick.

"Animal theft is provoked by either spite or profit," he continued. "By spite, I mean someone gets sick of Fluffy digging in their flowerbeds for example, or Rover barking his head off all night, and just removes them from the neighborhood. Sometimes they're taken to a shelter, sometimes they're dropped off in the country. But those are not the acts of bunchers. That kind of thing is done out of pure cussedness, by pissed-off neighbors.

"Ordinarily I would say that exotic cats like the Bengals were stolen for simple resale and you would probably find them in a couple of days on Craigslist or Kijiji. But from what Alison told me about the theft of the Bengals, plus the theft of the Oak Bay neighborhood pets . . . well, we've talked it over, and we just don't see the two kinds of thefts as being coincidental. We could be wrong, but we think the likelihood is that all the animals were taken by bunchers. They may not even know how valuable the Bengals are. They're may just be filling their quota."

"Taken by bunchers." I felt stupid. Plainly there was a hole in my experience. Why didn't I know more about this? If it had been anyone other than Ian and Alison telling me about this, I might not have believed them. Maybe this was the "'more information" that Mac had alluded to when he said we'd talk this evening.

"And these guys are paid well enough to induce them to do this? Steal people's pets?" I asked.

Ian grimaced. "Yeah, they are. By their standards anyway. They get paid so much for cats, so much for dogs. And even more for certain dog breeds like beagles and golden retrievers. In fact, some in-demand breeds net them eight hundred dollars per animal."

"Dammit, Ian. I got my cat Trey back in the Dark Ages when he was liberated from an experiment in my university's Psychology Department. So he was someone's pet that a buncher got paid for stealing?"

"Probably," Ian said.

"I can't believe this still goes on," I said heatedly.

Ian looked apologetic. I had to remind myself not to kill the messenger. "Yeah, it does. The animals stolen in Oak Bay may well end up in labs. Sorry."

I tried to fight down a rising tide of panic. "How does this work, anyhow? My brain kind of shut down a few minutes ago."

"This makes all of us crazy," Ian said grimly. "This is how it goes. A researcher gets funding for a particular project that needs cats or dogs. Or a teaching institution needs animals. Or a product testing lab needs subjects. So they contact the guy a little lower on the food chain – the animal dealer, the guy who actually buys the animals for them. And even though animal dealers are supposed to be prohibited by law from using bunchers, all too often they do. Animals provided by bunchers – stolen pets – are cheaper than, say, animals seized from the pound or bred specifically for research."

"So the dealer contacts the buncher," I said.

"Right," Ian said. "And the buncher looks around, sees that nice, peaceful neighborhood in Oak Bay where people let their pets out, and . . . takes them."

"Just like that?"

"Yeah. Sometimes they need to use persuasion: food, females in heat, snare poles, nets. On the other hand, sometimes pets are so damned friendly they'll jump in a car with anyone. Bunchers have been known to grab dogs out of the backs of pickups or cats in carriers waiting in the car at vets' parking lots. They once grabbed eight dogs out of the back of a dogwalker's van in Toronto."

"Jesus. Then what?"

"Then the buncher takes the animals to, oh, an isolated location and squeezes them into crappy runs or cages until he has a 'bunch'," he said bitterly. "Typically the animals are housed in filthy, crowded conditions with inadequate food or water – the buncher doesn't want to have to expend too much money or energy looking after them, doncha know. Then, after he has his quota, he contacts the guy who hired him – the animal dealer – and the dealer takes them on to the research lab. Oh, the dealer might have to house them for awhile also, in similar shitty conditions, but eventually they go on to the labs. "

"Where are these labs?"

Ian shrugged. "At pharmaceutical companies, or universities, or private testing facilities . . . or even labs run by our wonderful federal government. Some aren't even close by. In our files we have accounts of animals transported over hundreds of miles. We learned of one case where cats and kittens were driven by truck over a thousand miles to the lab that wanted them. " He smiled wryly . . . a smile that was in no way in a real smile. "And you know how much cats like road trips."

I turned to Alison. "Okay. I get it. I have to break this chain by finding the animals before they leave the buncher's . . . cages, place, location, whatever."

"Yes. That's pretty much the only chance," she said. "Once they pass out of the buncher's hands into the hands of the animal dealer, it'll be too hard to trace them. That's when retrieval becomes . . . unlikely. The people at OTC have been through this before. I think they can tell you more about the timeline and so on."

"But you said earlier that the chances of getting the animals back were not good."

"They're not," she said. "But not good is not the same as impossible. You're very persistent. And ingenious. That's why people hire you. I think you can do this. Find the animals."

Shit. No pressure. "Have you opened that wine yet? " I asked Ian.

He shook his head. "I'll go get it," he said. "And three glasses. We could probably use some right now."

"And the Bengals got swept into this, how?" I asked Alison. "The bunchers scoped out the neighborhood and just stumbled onto the cattery? How did they even know it was there? There's no sign saying Wild At Heart. And the Bengals disappeared from an interior location, the Oak Bay pets from their yards. How did the bunchers pull off the Bengals' theft?"

"That's the question, isn't it?" Alison said.

Ian put three glasses on the coffee table and poured wine. "It's a Pinot Noir from Cherry Point Winery, up-island," he said. "Even though it's before five, the sun is over the yardarm somewhere. Cheers."

"Cheers," I repeated mechanically. Well, now I knew. Odds were the cats had been taken by bunchers. As had the neighborhood animals. Mac was right: there were no coincidences. Well, I still had to find them. Knowing about bunchers, and the labs for which the bunchers provided animals, just made the theft more horrific.

The doorbell rang.

"It's them," Alison said, looking meaningfully at Ian. "Olga is aggravating, but the animal world needs her energy and passion. And she's a very provocative writer. So try not to yell when she gets confrontational. Remember, it's not us she's mad at. Oh, Susan might be here as well."

Ian took a big swallow of wine. "Not to worry. I'll be good."

Chapter 6

I SAT WRAPPED in thought while Ian answered the door. I heard his and several women's voices – the OTCers and Susan Chu had arrived simultaneously, I guessed. Alison turned to me.

"Olga may really ruffle your feathers," she said ruefully. "She's hot. Impatient. Accusatory." She continued: "What Olga doesn't get is that change comes incrementally. Profound, deep-down, bedrock change is an intellectual and affective marathon, not a sprint. We're asking people to radically alter their lifelong ways of thinking about animals and we can't bludgeon them into it. Hearts and minds don't get changed that way. Anyhow, before we get into arm-wrestling with Olga and Ellen – and Ellen is much more reasonable than Olga, thankfully – I'm hoping you can get the information you need and be on your way. Not that you aren't welcome to stay for dinner, but you told me you have to go meet with the owners of the stolen pets."

I groaned. "I do. And I'm not looking forward to it. I'm sure there'll be much wailing and gnashing of teeth. Heck, I'd be wailing if it were *my* pet who had been stolen. I'm not good with people's distress."

"Olga, Ellen, Susan, this is Kieran Yeats," Ian said, escorting three women into the living room. "Kieran is an animal crimes investigator who's been hired to find some stolen cats and dogs. Alison and I are hoping OTC can give her the benefit of your experience with this."

Olga marched to the armchair vacated by Ian, Ellen leaned against the fireplace, and Susan took an armchair at the other end of the coffee table..

"Here!" Olga announced dramatically, dropping a small stack of fliers on the coffee table with a flourish. Tall, strong-looking, longish blonde hair tied behind her head, she put me in mind of a Nordic *Asynjor*, a fearsome avenging deity. She pushed her blue plaid shirt-sleeves up above her elbows and frowned at us all fiercely.

Susan looked at her noncommittally, then took a pair of glasses from a pocket of her khaki photographer's vest. Retrieving one of the fliers from the stack on the coffee table, she began to study it.

"Stolen cats, hmmf," Olga said to me with a pitying shake of her head. "Kieran, right? Well, you might as well kiss them goodbye. Want to know how many pets – dogs and cats – perished in labs last year? Thirty thousand cats and fifteen thousand dogs . . . and that's in our country alone. In the US? Easily ten times as many. This is how your stolen cats will end up." She peeled a flier off the top of the stack and tossed it at me.

IMAGINE GIVING YOUR BODY TO SCIENCE WHILE YOU'RE STILL IN IT

Beneath the bold print heading was a photo of an orange cat behind the bars of a laboratory cage, fur greasy and disheveled, a flat black silver dollar-sized *something* glued to the top of his head, wires leading out of it, eyes screwed closed in evident pain, mouth open in a cry. I felt like throwing up. This was indeed a bludgeon and I couldn't see it changing anyone's heart or mind.

Taking a firm grip on my anger at Olga for dismissing my search before it had even started, I tossed the flier back onto the coffee table.

"All this . . . *research* on animals is so much crap," Olga told me heatedly. "I call B.S on it. Total B.S. It's useless. A useless waste. The director of the National Institute of Bloody Fucking Health admits that animal experimentation is a goddammed boondoggle. Researchers drank the Koolaid decades ago, and they continue to drink it."

"We're working to change that," Alison told her reasonably. Ellen, a sensible-looking brunette, nodded. Evidently she'd had to weather Olga's monologues before.

"Do you know that *researchers* cured cancer in mice decades ago?" Olga continued, hardly pausing for breath. "But they can't translate their work into any effective treatment for humans. That doesn't stop 'em, though. They just go on killing mice. Eighty million last year alone." She skewered me with an accusing glare.

Hell, why me? I hadn't killed any mice lately.

"The goddammed senselessness of all this animal slaughter is enough to make you puke. Why, there's a researcher at a very prestigious university who has been killing golden retrievers for over three decades. Three decades! Doing the same experiments on muscular dystrophy again and again. We've learned nothing about the disease from him. But he's published over thirty research articles on it. How nice for him. His dogs can't eat properly, they're choking on their own drool, they can't stand up, they're in pain, but he keeps getting grant funding. He –"

"Okay, Olga," Ellen said wearily, giving me an apologetic look. "It's awful. We all agree on that. And that's why we have to work together to stop it. And we will. But those dogs are not Kieran's missing cats. She –"

"No, they aren't!" Olga yelled. "They're goddammed bred to suffer. In a way that's more obscene." Perhaps realizing she had been off on a rant, she wound down. "I'm just saying," she muttered.

I tried to think generous thoughts about Olga. Clearly she was a soul in pain. Unrelenting moral indignation tends to be exhausting. But the marathon of persuasion that Alison had spoken about earlier – changing people's hearts and minds about their treatment of animals – ought to include more than horrifying them, I thought.

Because the question was: does horror alone motivate us to change behavior? Horror makes our minds shut down. Horror makes us want to flee. How do you turn horror and indignation into an epiphany . . . . a moment in which some small part of someone's soul realizes that what they are thinking, or doing, or supporting with their buying dollars, is just not *right*? Ninth Life had done this, much to their credit, but it had taken years. I didn't envy Alison and Ian trying to persuade Olga of the merits of the long game.

Ian handed the women glass of wine each and he and I exchanged rueful glances. Hey, at least Olga hadn't driven him to yelling yet.

Susan took a sip of wine and cleared her throat, motioning to the fliers that Olga had tossed onto the coffee table. "This is really excellent," she said, removing her glasses and smiling at Olga.

Olga eyed her in evident suspicion, clearly amazed. "You, um, think so?"

Susan nodded. "No one could look at this cat and not be outraged." She was silent for a moment then asked her: "What does seeing him make you want to do?"

"Kill someone," Olga said immediately.

"Okay," Susan said patiently, "but if you couldn't? What would be choice number two?"

"Get him the hell out of there," Olga said.

"Then let's figure out how to make that happen," Susan said.

Olga looked incredulous. "Could we? Get him out of there? How?"

Susan smiled. "Okay, listen. He exists somewhere, right? I mean, someone took this picture?"

Olga nodded. "One of our volunteers, Marcus, works in that lab. He's sick to death about what goes on there. Apparently they have too many animal welfare violations to count. Marcus took the photo."

"And does the cat have a name?"

Olga looked at Ellen. I could see that she was hardly daring to hope. "Maybe. Why? What do you have in mind?"

Susan held up Olga's flier. "I love this. I love the caption. No one could forget it. But this flier does only half the job."

"So what's the other half?" Ellen asked, intrigued. "What do we do?"

"We make a new flier. We put the cat's name on it. That will make people see him as he is — as someone's pet. Someone loved him enough to give him a name. Someone is missing him. Let's just call him

Rufus as a place-holder while we're strategizing. And when we re-design the flier we include what's referred to in the trade as a 'call to action.' We keep the caption, which is too powerful to omit, show them the cat's photo, just as you've done, Olga, call him by his name . . . and then we ask people to *do something*. To join with us to free Rufus. To get him out of there. To put an end to his suffering and put him where all cats ought to be – in a good home with people who'll love him."

Covering her face with her hands, Olga burst into tears.

I mentally high-fived Susan. She'd taken what was good about that horrifying flier and spun it differently. Hence the name of her business: Idea Magic. She was also a pretty damned good psychologist. I guessed Olga had gotten used to being criticized for her passion, which probably was responsible for her being so combative. Better a bruising offense than a steady defense, right? But Susan had made an end run and caught her by surprise.

"I get it," Ian said, excited. "Rufus becomes our poster boy for companion animals suffering in research labs."

"Exactly," Susan said. "And we paste Rufus's story – just as it is in this flier, all over the Internet. Facebook, Twitter. Even in print ads if you like. We start a Free Rufus campaign. It would serve, oh, at least four purposes. One, it would shame the lab director, who knows bloody well how many animal welfare violations his lab has. And he ought to be made to feel shame. Two, it would draw attention to this problem in a way that rhetoric alone couldn't. Three, it might start a dialogue in the media about companion animals being used in this way, which would help Ninth Life's long term campaign goal of getting legislation passed to prohibit their use in research. And four . . . it might just free Rufus. What do you think . . . Alison? Ian?"

I knew I should leave to get to my appointment, but I just couldn't. Not yet. Dammit, I was invested in what might happen to Rufus. In fact, *I* wanted to adopt him.

"I say we go for it," Alison told her.

"Yes," Ian agreed.

"Can you send me the photo jpg?" Susan asked Olga. "Here's my card. And try to find out the cat's name, okay?"

Olga beamed at her. "I will."

"I'll talk to my partner Brian about this," Susan said. "About designing a Free Rufus campaign. I'm excited."

"More wine?" Ian asked, holding up the wine bottle, clearly relieved that this hadn't turned into a donnybrook with Olga.

Regretfully, I realized that I did indeed have to leave. And I wondered: did the world get changed just like this? By two or three or five people sitting around in living rooms working on how to put right what was wrong? I recalled what Margaret Mead had to say about that: *"Never doubt that a small group of thoughtful, committed citizens can change the world; indeed, it's the only thing that ever has."* And I found myself envying this group their solidarity. When things got bad they had each other to lean on. Crap, I'd better go before I started really feeling maudlin.

"I think I need to go to my appointment," I said, huskily, getting to my feet.

"Kieran, just to let you know . . . you probably have five days," Ellen said, realizing belatedly why I was there. "Based on our experience with animal theft, that's my guess. And maybe not even that long. Bunchers don't keep animals around longer than they can help it. They're a liability. Keeping dozens of stolen pets penned up, some of them very upset and very noisy, just increases the chance that people living on the next piece of property, or the guy who comes to read the meter, will notice them and ask questions. So . . ." she trailed off, looking at me sympathetically.

"So I better not waste any time," I said, getting to my feet. "Olga, Ellen, nice to have met you. And you, too, Susan. Good luck with the Free Rufus campaign, you guys."

Ellen wrote something down on the back of one of the **IMAGINE** fliers and handed it to me. "Call us if you need to," she offered. "We'll help in any way we can." She looked over at Olga who nodded agreement. I took the flier, folded it, and stuck it in the back pocket of my jeans.

Alison walked with me to the front foyer, holding my jacket and the file folder she had put on the coffee table for me. "Sorry," she said, quirking her mouth in apology.

"For what?" I asked her, shrugging into my windbreaker.

"The lousy timeline. Five days or less. When were the pets stolen?"

"One batch Saturday night and one batch last night."

"I was thinking," she said. "When you find them, if you need us, you know, for transport or anything, please call. We have a van. And Ellen and Olga said they would help."

"Listen," I said. "I want to ask you something. About OTC."

"Sure. Ask away."

"Do they do that anymore? Open the cages? I mean literally."

She frowned. "Well, not recently. Cooler heads than Olga's are prevailing in that group, I think. Why do you ask? Do you think you might need some cage-opening?"

"Maybe."

"Well, Ellen did offer to help in any way she could, didn't she?"

"That she did."

"Call us if you need us," Alison reiterated. "We'll be in town most of the month. Got to go now." Then she turned and walked back into the house, closing the door behind her.

Checking my watch, I saw it was 4:43. Fooey. I had cut it pretty close. Praying for light traffic, I hurried to my car.

Chapter 7

Mara Riordan, the owner of the German shepherd, showed me into the living room of her home. She had obviously been crying – her eyelids were puffy and red. Ditto her nose. And her frizzy brown hair was worse than tousled – it was, frankly, a fright, standing up in tufts.

"I'm a mess," she apologized. "I haven't slept a wink in the two nights that Riley has been gone. But come in, please. Just about everyone missing a pet in the neighborhood is here. We're talking, trying to figure out what to do. I'm so glad you could come – I told the others you'd be here. Coffee and snacks are in the kitchen. Please help yourself. Then I want to introduce you."

I did a quick count. Mara's "just about everyone" amounted to twelve people, most middle-aged, some sitting on the sofa and armchairs, some perched on folding chairs, some at a table in the dining room, and others cross-legged on the floor. If grief had a color, the air would have seethed an ugly purple-grey like a day-old bruise. These people's hearts had been broken. Someone they loved very much had been wrenched away from them and they were in grief-stricken, heart-broken despair.

I made my way to the kitchen where there were plates of cookies, a cutting board with cheese, a basket of crackers and, as promised, coffee. I filled a mug with coffee to take back into the living room with me, ate a few pieces of cheese and two chocolate chip cookies, then became aware that someone was sitting very quietly at a small table in the corner. A kid, a girl of about seven, with aggressively curly red hair and freckles. She was coloring on a large white piece of paper, crayons spread out in front of her.

"Hi there," I said.

She looked up at me but said nothing.

"The cookies are good," I said. "Chocolate chip."

"I know," she said. "My mother made them. But I don't feel like eating."

I walked to the table where she was sitting. "Can I sit down?" I asked. "My name is Kieran."

She shrugged. "If you want to. My name is Livia."

I sat at the table opposite her. She was coloring a drawing she had made of a shaggy, perky-eared brown dog on a green lawn in a front of a white house.

"That's a nice picture, Livia," I said. "Is that your dog?"

She nodded. "It's Bandit. He's gone."

We sat in silence, Livia coloring, me sipping coffee. Somehow I felt it was more important right now to be here with Livia than to be with the group in the living room. I wanted to tell her something to cheer her up, but found I couldn't think of a thing.

"Are you the lady who's going to help us?" she asked.

I peered into my coffee cup, as if I might find an answer there. Well, was I going to help them? I already had an employer. But I needed to know if any of them had seen anything, anything at all out of the ordinary on Saturday night. Was I going to have to trade my assistance for their information?

"My brother Roger left Bandit outside," Livia said, drawing a very tall, dark brown fence around the yard. "He was supposed to walk him around the block and bring him in, but he didn't. He went to his room to talk to his friends on Facebook. My parents and I were shopping. When we got back Bandit wasn't there. He wasn't any-where. He was gone." Livia aggressively added some more pickets to the fence. "Roger's grounded for life," she said in fierce satisfaction. "My dad took away his iPad and his phone. Roger says he'll die. I hope he does."

Tears ran down Livia's cheeks, and she dashed them angrily away. I handed her one of the paper napkins I had taken along with the cookies. I am not good with crying kids.

"Did you ever have a dog who ran away?" she asked me, snif-fling into her napkin.

"Well, I never had a dog, but my cat ran away once."

She looked at me hopefully. "What happened? Did he come home?"

What happened? When I first moved to Victoria, I lived in an old house in a quiet neighborhood close to the University. Trey had just come to live with me, and I knew beans about cats, or about the fact that they would live a lot longer if they were kept indoors. I saw cats lounging on porches, cats in flowerboxes, cats sunning themselves on shed roofs, and thought nothing of just opening the door and let-ting Trey wander the neighborhood. And everything was fine until it wasn't. The evening he didn't come home, I didn't start to worry until dark. Then I walked up and down the street, shaking his kibble bag, calling for him. I told myself not to be too concerned, that he'd be home the next morning, waiting for me on the front porch.

But he wasn't, and that's when I went into panic mode. I called vets' offices, the shelter, my neighbors. I made up fliers, stapled them to telephone poles, tacked them on bulletin boards at the library, the bakery, the convenience store, gave them to local kids on their way home from school. Then I combed the neighborhood, looking under every bush and parked car, knocking on every door, talking to anyone who would listen. I was unable to go to work. My life became search-ing for and worrying about Trey. God, why had I ever let him out? He had used up eight of his nine lives in that damned psychology lab . . . he deserved far better than to perish at the teeth of a pissed-off dog, or under the wheels of a car. Where could he be? He was a people-wary cat, so I was pretty sure he hadn't just mindlessly followed someone home, or allowed himself to be seduced by cat treats.

Finally, I drove the neighborhood repeatedly, looking for his body. I would rather have found him dead than to have to go through the rest of my life remembering him missing. Missing is purgatory. Missing is fearful imaginings. Dead is final. Dead is the end of fearful imaginings. Your heart can move on from dead. However, I didn't find his body, which left me still in guilt-ridden, tearful, terrified purgatory.

Then, the third night he was missing, I had a thought. What if he hadn't wandered away? What if he was trapped somewhere, simply unable to come home? I became convinced that this might well be the case. So I made up new fliers and put them in my neighbors' mailboxes, under their doormats, beneath their cars' wipers. The flier had Trey's photo on it and asked people to please look inside their garden sheds, travel trailers, basements, back porches, or any hidden place on their property, just in case a grey cat had gotten in when they weren't looking. I also offered a reward: fifty bucks, which doesn't seem much now, but seemed pretty hefty to me then.

And, improbably, it worked. A ten-year-old boy called to say that he and his father had been winterizing their RV on the weekend, and he remembered that there had been a grey cat hanging around. When he saw my flier (and the reward) he went out to take a look, and, sure enough, there was the same grey cat, locked in the RV, looking mournfully out the back window. He looked an awful lot like the cat whose photo was on the flier, the kid said. Could I come and check? Oh, and bring the fifty bucks, just in case? I was there with my cat carrier within five minutes, and sure enough, it was indeed Trey, scared and hungry, but otherwise unscathed. We went home, I fed him two tins of tuna (he threw up the second one) and I didn't stop hugging him for hours. Since then he has been microchipped, worn a collar with his name and my phone number on it (just in case he dashes past the UPS delivery person when I open the front door), and hasn't set a whisker outside.

"Kieran?" Livia asked again. "Did you find your cat?"

"I did, sweetie," I told her. "I had to look hard for him, though."

"Will you look for Bandit?" she asked, after a moment.

Oh for crap's sake. I would rather have thumbscrews applied to my extremities than disappoint crying children. But, as I had reminded myself just a few minutes earlier, I already had an employer. Did

I want to add the dozen or so in the next room? No, I didn't. But, I knew missing. Knew it intimately. I could still feel it, all these years later. I knew exactly what they were feeling. And if not me, then who? What was I to do for these people if I chose not to help them: urge them to pray to St. Jude, the patron saint of lost causes?

So I caved. "Sure, Livia," I heard myself say. "I will. I'll look for Bandit."

ᑲᑐ

All heads turned to me when I walked back into the living room.

"People, this is Kieran Yeats," Mara said. "She's the investigator I told you about. I'll just let her talk now."

I cleared my throat. "Hi. Thanks, Mara. Yes, I am an investigator. I work on animal cases. I'm working for Norma Carruthers. Her cats were stolen last night. I —"

"Miz Yeats," a white-haired guy with a young face and dark-rimmed glasses interrupted me. He looked a lot like Anderson Cooper. "What the hell's going on?" He shook his head angrily. "I'm Al Holland. Call me Dutch. My two old beagles were taken either out of my yard or off the sidewalk late Saturday night. They always went out for a few minutes just before the eleven o'clock news. Just for a pee. Sometimes they visit Stevensons' flowerbed four houses down. They've done that for years. But for God's sake, can't our pets be safe in our own neighborhood? I get it that I maybe shouldn't have been so trusting. But Norma's cats? They're always inside. And didn't she have a cat sitter?"

"She did," a woman called from behind the couch. "I met her once at Norma's a while ago. A nice young girl."

"Hmmf," a prissy-sounding woman with a sharp nose, seated on the couch beside Dutch, looked at me accusingly. "Well? Are you looking at her?"

"Looking at her?" I asked.

"You know, for the job."

For the job? This broad had evidently been reading too many ninety-nine cent Kindle potboilers. "I've already eliminated her as a suspect," I told the woman, eager to get her off Jen's trail. "I know her personally. She didn't have anything to do with this."

Dutch ran one hand over his hair and when he looked up at me I saw there were tears in his eyes. "Sorry," he said, "I'm just –"

"We all are, Dutch," Mara told him soothingly. "We're frustrated, sad, and madder than hell. Let's let Kieran talk some more," she said to her neighbors.

· I put my hands in my pockets and continued. "I've already met with Detective MacLeish of the Oak Bay Police Department. And I met with a couple of animal welfare groups today also. The consensus seems to be that one person or group of people was responsible for all the animal thefts in this neighborhood. " I paused to consult the better angels of my nature who told me, yeah, I was doing the right thing. Then I said: "I'm willing to work for you folks too, if you want me to."

"We've already talked about it," Dutch told me. "We do want you to work for us. But I have to ask you . . . do you have any ideas about why they were taken? Who the hell would want my old beagles? I mean they're purebred, but they're fixed. So you sure can't breed them. And who would take Lorna's old calico cat? Or Bernie's Schnauzer? Are they being, what, held for ransom? None of us has been phoned by anyone asking for money and the fliers have been up for two days. Like I said, I don't get it."

I had just opened my mouth to attempt a seriously watered-down version of what OTC and Ninth Life had told me when a woman called out stridently from a chair behind the sofa: "Is this going to turn out to be like the animal thefts that happened just north of here? I remember that. Dozens of pets were missing. The RCMP just . . . gave up. No leads, they said. Maybe coyotes, they said."

"Well, that was up-island," someone interjected. "This is civilization. Is Oak Bay going to send someone out to investigate?" she asked hopefully.

"Duh, no," someone else said derisively. "That's why Kieran's here."

I cleared my throat. Time for the dirty rotten truth. "Probably the police won't send anyone out. Pet theft is, unfortunately, not one of the law's priorities. And to complicate things, according to Detective MacLeish, the Oak Bay department is just . . . too swamped with fentanyl cases."

A chorus of exclamations ensued. "Fentanyl? But we're taxpayers! Isn't this what we pay the police for? To investigate crimes?"

Oh jeez. Did I have to become an apologist for the cops? "I really can't tell you for certain what the police will or won't do," I said. "I suggest that any of you who want to, go down and file reports. At least then the thefts will be on the record." I gave people my steeliest confidence-building look. "But why don't we assume they'll be too busy and try to solve this ourselves."

"Do you think we – you – can do that?" Dutch asked, evidently wanting to believe.

"Do you even have any leads?" the skeptical, potboiler-reading woman demanded to know.

I looked at her sternly and mentally crossed my fingers. "Yes, I do have a few leads and yes, I do think I can solve this. But I'm going to need your help."

Dutch nodded as if he had made up his mind about something. Maybe me. "Okay," he said. "What can we do?"

"Well, first you can tell me if anyone saw anything out of the ordinary Saturday night late, or early Sunday or Monday mornings."

A grey-haired woman at the dining room table spoke up. "I'm Evelyn," she said. "About one in the morning Saturday night, well, Sunday really, I was in the kitchen – I've been having trouble sleeping and I was up making cocoa – and I saw a light-colored van on my side of the street, well, cruising, I guess the kids would say."

"Cruising?" I asked.

Evelyn frowned. "Yes. Driving slowly. As if it were looking for something. The streetlight isn't terribly bright right there and I didn't think much about it. I thought the van was just looking for an address."

"Okay, I said. "Where was your pet then?"

"Well, the thing is, I really don't know. Baxter, my cat, is," she hesitated, looking embarrassed, "not fixed. I just can't keep him inside. He goes off on . . . adventures, you know, *cherchez la femme*. He's usually gone three or four days. But he always comes back. I don't know if I should even be here. He might not be missing at all. Not in the way other people's pets are missing."

"You should be here," Mara told her firmly. "Right now he's missing. Period. And you have some good information. So don't beat yourself up about not having him fixed." She smiled at Evelyn. "And when he's back with you, I'll bet you have him fixed right away."

"I will," Evelyn said. "I've been putting it off. I know it's the right thing to do. And I can't stand the thought that he might not be roaming, but have been stolen instead. I just want him back!"

"Thanks, Evelyn," I said. "You didn't happen to see the van's license plate, did you? Or anything that might help identify it? Did it have any dents? Decals? Bumper stickers? A trailer hitch?"

"No. I'm sorry. I didn't notice any of that."

Well, it was too much to hope. "Anyone else see anything?"

"Yeah, I saw something," a stocky man in a red plaid shirt said. "I'm Marv. Maybe the same van, I'm not sure. The wife and I were just coming home. Maybe one-thirty. I saw a van parked in the driveway of the house belonging to Jim Mortenson – it's at the end of the cul de sac. I think the van was brownish, although it could have been like Evelyn says, a light color. Tan maybe. I didn't take too much notice of it. The house is for sale and I figured it belonged to a relative or someone who was there watering the plants or taking care of the inside and staying the night."

I sighed. This was the problem with interviewing witnesses together. They polluted each other's memories. Evelyn's van was light colored. Marv's was brownish . . . or maybe it was tan. "Anyone else see anything?"

Headshakes.

"Okay, here's something else for you to think about. And you're probably going to have to talk this over together. I'd like it written down. I want to know who comes around your homes. And who's been there recently. The lawn guy, the paperboy, the grocery delivery person, the dog walker, the poop scooper . . . anyone who might know you have pets and know your habits. I'd like their contact numbers also. And vehicle descriptions if you can recall them."

Nods.

"Next," I said, "This is for the cat owners: have you checked with people in about a five or six block radius? Asked them to open their toolsheds and garages? Their RVs? Their out-of-commission cars?"

Some nods, some headshaking.

"You need to do that. Okay, let's move on. By the way, does someone have a pencil and paper? Anyone bring their laptop or tablet? Someone who can write down information and send it to me? Who wants to be secretary?"

"I have my laptop," a freckle-faced man with red hair called from the dining room. I bet he was Livia's father. "I'm Finn. I'll be secretary," he said wryly. "I've been writing down what you said anyhow. Fire away."

"I need a list of all the missing animals," I told the group. "Names, descriptions, your names, phone numbers. I'd also like photos of the animals. Give them or send them to Finn. He can email them to me. Finn, I'll give you my email address in a minute.

"And here's another job. You can divide this one up. I want you to take your photos of the missing animals and visit every shelter, every humane society, every SPCA, every rescue group on the island . . . and I want you to do it by the end of business tomorrow."

A clamor broke out. Hell, let them be upset. I needed to know where the animals *weren't*. I didn't believe for a minute that the animals had been turned in to a shelter as strays. But I needed to know that. And I needed to know it tomorrow. If OTC was right, we had little time to lose.

"Quiet!" Dutch yelled. "We can do it. So you have to take time off work. So what? We can Google to find shelter addresses." He looked at me. "What else?"

"While some of you are driving around to shelters, I want someone or a couple of someones to be scouring the classifieds for people who may have found animals or who may be selling animals. Look in Craigslist and Kijiji also. If you turn up anything promising, I need you to just make a note of the ad, what it says, and the number. Do not call anyone yourselves, okay? Do not. Let me do the calling."

"We understand," Finn said to me. Then, to the group: "Let's get started. Come give me your information."

I looked around. The people at the dining room table were already talking earnestly to Finn. The others had coalesced into two groups and were looking up information on their phones. Good. And the mood seemed to have changed from angry despair to energized determination. A spasm of guilt seized me: how could I give these good people false hope? And was it false? Crap. At least I was giving them something to do, something to keep their minds off their losses. Wasn't that good for something? And there was one more thing I had to do. I put two fingers in my mouth and whistled. Heads turned back to me.

"I'm not going to be able to take your phone calls individually," I said. "Sorry. There are just too many of you. And I might be in situations tomorrow or the next day where I couldn't answer my phone anyhow. So I'd like you to report anything you find in the next couple of days, or anything you remember, to one person, and then I'd like that one person to call me. I need a liaison. Who will it be?"

"I'll do it," Dutch said, when no one was rushing to volunteer. He looked around. "Is that okay with everyone?" When no one spole, he nodded to me. "So I guess I'm it. Your liaison." He pulled his phone out of the pocket of a brown leather jacket lying over the back of the couch behind him. I gave him my number. "I'm not going to work until this is all settled," he said. "My partner can take care of the business. We're architects, but there's nothing pressing." He put his phone away and frowned thoughtfully, looking back over his shoulder at people talking. "Oh, I should ask you something. I'm embarrassed that no one else thought of it."

"Let me guess . . . it's about money. You're wondering how exorbitant my rates really are."

"Yeah," he said, "something like that. Of course you don't work for nothing, but, well, how much do you charge?"

"Five hundred dollars a day. I ask for a thousand up front. But don't worry about that right now. When I thought there was just one case, Norma was paying me. Now that I have, oh, over a dozen clients, maybe one of you can go discuss things with her. Split my fee."

"Yeah, that makes sense," he said. "I can do that tomorrow."

I looked at my watch. Time to go. "I have another appointment," I told Dutch, standing up. Actually, I was so tired I could have stretched out right there on the carpet and drifted off. Later, I told myself. There'll be time for that later. "You folks have a lot to talk about. I'll see myself out."

Chapter 8

Driving out of Mara's street onto Beach Drive, I felt scattered, beleaguered, and more than a little overwhelmed. I turned off the coast road at a little overlook and just shut the car off and sat there for a few minutes, fiddling with my phone. My gaze traveled across the rock-strewn cove below me to the horizon, where dark clouds hung low over the ocean like the bloom of artillery flak.

Well, what about it? Did I think I could sort this mess out, find the missing pets, do what the RCMP hadn't been able to do up-island? Really? What should I have told people? That, hell, I would try my damndest, but left myself enough wiggle room so that if I failed, I could remind everyone that I hadn't put my hand on my heart and sworn? I recalled what Yoda had famously told Luke: *There is no try. There is only do or not do.* Oh yeah? When it was just the Bengals I had to find, somehow things hadn't seemed quite so daunting.

෨෨

On my way home I made a stop at one of my favorite low-brow eateries: Old British Fish and Chips. I ordered four pieces of halibut, hold the *poutine,* please. How *poutine* had gained the status of near-national craze was quite beyond me. A dish comprised of French fries and cheese curds smothered in gravy, it had originated in Quebec and spread like a culinary plague across the country. Now it was on the menus of far too many dining establishments that ought to have known better. In my opinion, it was just, well, slimy, and in terms of a disgusting eating experience was eclipsed only by squid tentacles. Taking the halibut pieces, I escaped to my car. What had happened to our national pride anyhow? *Poutine* indeed.

As I pulled into my driveway, I noticed a note on my front door. Now what? I ripped it off in a fit of pique, folded it, and stuck it in a pocket of my jeans. Later. Even if it were an invitation to tea with the Queen, it would have to wait. I fumbled with my suddenly too-heavy keys, unlocked the door, closed it firmly behind me, then leaned against it. Gathering what little strength I had left, I tossed my jacket in the general direction of the coat tree, dropped the file Alison had given me on the little table in the hall, and dragged myself into the kitchen. Trey was waiting by his empty food dish.

"Yang," Trey commented sadly.

"Don't start with me, fat boy," I admonished him. "I haven't forgotten your early-morning faithlessness."

He sighed heavily, and I decided to let him off the hook. "Hey, I brought halibut," I told him, brandishing the bag. "Your favorite." I found two clean dishes in the cupboard and began cutting the fish into small pieces. Sniffing the air, he discerned that it was indeed halibut, moaned a little, then collapsed on my feet in a feigned fainting fit. "You are such a drama queen," I told him. "In case you're wondering at my sudden generosity, it's because you're here, safe, and not Rufus." Jesus yes, thank the powers that be that Trey had made it alive out of his laboratory hell. His two cage-mates, alas, hadn't, hence his name. I divided the fish into two bowls, put one on his place mat, and carried the other into my enclosed back porch.

"Fish, your crabbiness," I called to Vlad. A chuckle emanated from the rafters, and I left the dish on a shelf. When I came back into the kitchen, Trey was on the counter, attacking the batter I had scraped off the halibut. "Nope," I told him, putting him down firmly on the floor. "Think of your hips." Determining that *my* two pieces of fish were safe in the microwave, I left him licking the last bits of halibut from his food bowl.

My bed had never looked so appealing, I thought as I hung my clothes in the closet. A crinkling from my one of the pockets of my jeans reminded me about the note I had ripped off my front door and I groaned. Unfolding it, I read:

> *Can I see you for a few minutes? Maybe tomorrow morning?*
> *Helen.*

Crap, I thought. Helen was Helen Mikita, my upstairs tenant. She'd been a gem. Paid her rent promptly, didn't play loud music, worked from home, travelled a fair amount, and liked the cats. She even fixed her own toilet when it went rogue from time to time and started flushing itself. Something about the flapper valve. I hoped she didn't want to move out – where else would I find a tenant who understood plumbing? Yes, I'd talk to her tomorrow morning. Donning my comfy old sweats, I resisted the siren song of my bed. Just a few more things to do. Taking a seat in the uncomfortable rocking chair in the corner of my bedroom, I called Mac, hoping I could stay awake long enough to take in the information he had alluded to this morning.

"Hey, Mac. You said you had something to tell me?"

"Aye, that I do. I want to give you a woman's name and phone number. Miranda Blake. I've known her for years. She's a good egg, a retired RCMP constable, part of the team that investigated, or rather didn't investigate, the animal thefts up-island. She had a couple of good leads, but her superiors just didn't want to pursue them. Claiming that coyotes took the animals was a convenient way of closing the case," he said. "Anyhow, I thought you might want to talk to her. The leads she turned up might be useful to you."

"You said she was retired. What's she doing now?"

"Well," he said, "she was so outraged by the animal thefts, and the RCMP's stonewalling, that she threw in the towel on law enforcement completely. Took early retirement and started an animal sanctuary. It's up past the ferry docks. I called her and told her about your case. She'll be happy to talk to you."

"Thanks, Mac, I'll give her a call," I told him.

Getting up from the rocker was incredibly difficult, but I made my way to the kitchen where I scarfed down *my* pieces of halibut along with a heel of French bread I found in the fridge, and a hunk of cheddar whose green fuzz was easily scraped off. I really *did* need to get out to buy groceries. Oh well, maybe tomorrow. After pouring some kibble into the cats' dishes, I headed back to the bedroom. On the way I started a bath running – my favorite place for thinking. Hot water encourages right brain activity, I've found. I've never been much good at the left brained yellow lined tablet sort of thought process.

One last thing to do before the bath. Miranda Blake answered on the third ring, an enthusiastic chorus of dog barking in the background.

"I'm glad you called," she said, after I introduced myself. "Mac talked to me about your case. I may be able to help. I turned up a several people two years ago who I thought really ought to be closely looked at. That didn't happen during our investigation, but nevertheless, they might be individuals for you to talk to. I'll have to look in my old case notes. Can you come up here? I'll text directions to your phone."

"Okay," I said. "How about tomorrow? Sometime in the morning."

"Yeah, anytime. I'll be here," she said cheerfully.

And then there was just me and the bath. At last. It was almost eight o'clock. Ai yi. I had been up for nearly seventeen hours. I groaned, dropping my sweats on the bathroom floor and slipping into the hot water. Trey came and stationed himself anxiously beside the tub as he often does when I take a bath. He clearly regards immersing oneself in water to be another indication of human insanity.

"I'll be okay," I told him. "You wouldn't like to go get me a glass of Method and Madness, would you? Two fingers?"

"Mrap," he declined, curling up on my sweatpants.

"I thought not. Well, I'm trying to cut back anyhow. So let's summarize what the heck we know. Twenty-six animals have disappeared. Teleported to god-knows-where awaiting a one-way trip to hell. Wild At Heart was locked up tight as a tick last night so it's hard to imagine how those animals were removed. As for the others, they seem to have been snatched off the sidewalk or out of yards." I soaked a washcloth in hot water and slid down farther in the tub, draping the cloth over my face. It felt good. "Two people saw a tan van, or it might have been light brown, or even beige, or maybe just plain dirty. I've asked for an accounting of all the missing pets, plus anything anyone in the neighborhood might remember. Also a printout of Wild At Heart's alarm system records. There's something goofy going on there."

I looked out from under the facecloth at Trey. "You're pretty quiet," I told him. "Usually you have a lot to say at the beginning of a case. You're not still mad at me for yelling at Jen, are you?"

"Nerf," he said faintly, kneading his paws anxiously on my sweats.

"Oh, I get it," I told him, enlightenment dawning. "You've been counting cans again, haven't you?"

He had the good grace to look guilty. Trey regularly slid open the pocket door to the pantry where I kept the canned goods. I joked that his neurotic nature led him to count tins of cat food, but sometimes I wondered if he didn't actually do it. After all, his worst episodes of clinginess and paper-shredding occurred when the tin total dwindled to fewer than six. This display of concern for my well-being in the tub might be really more about him than about me.

"Tomorrow," I told him. "For sure. A mountain of cans will appear. Manna from heaven. Now, let's get back to discussing the job at hand. There'll be lots to do tomorrow: much to-ing and fro-ing. And you won't like the way I smell when I come home from seeing Miranda and all those animals. I'll probably be away all day. What are your plans?"

Snoring answered me. A peek over the edge of the tub showed me that promises of cat food had allayed Trey's anxiety sufficiently to let him doze off. Poor guy.

I toweled dry, slid my sweats out from under his snoring bulk, then gently scooped him up, and carried him to bed.

TUESDAY

Chapter 9

WAKING UP BEFORE the alarm feels like stopping the bomb's countdown a second before zero: a reprieve. I lay there for a moment stretching a little, returning gradually from the faraway country of sleep. But something had awakened me, I thought, as I reached to disable my clock radio's alarm, which I'd set for six. Or perhaps nothing had awakened me – maybe it was simply that my internal rhythms were in synch with the sun and the moon and the ever-expanding universe. Nah. Most likely I just needed coffee. I swung my legs over the side of the bed, slid my feet into my slippers, and realized as I reached for my phone on my bedside table that yes, indeed, something probably had awakened me: ten minutes ago I had received a text from Dutch, the contact person for the Oak Bay neighbors' group.

"Call me," it said. "I have news."

He answered my phone call promptly. "It's about Patty, Marv's wife. Remember Marv? The guy who thought he saw a brown van parked at the end of the cul-de-sac?"

I sat up straight and absently patted Trey who had emerged from under the covers. "Yeah, of course. I remember."

"Well, she called me about half an hour ago. She's pretty sure she saw a logo on the back of the van."

"She did? I'm all ears. Go on."

"Okay, she says the logo has, well, wings in it. She's very definite about the wings but can't say anything more, you know, like size or color. The memory only surfaced last night as they drove back to their house after the meeting with you, she said. Is that the way these things happen? That memories just . . . come back to you?"

"Sometimes they do," I told him. "Witnesses remember details of events at the oddest times. Often when you stop thinking hard about something, the file drawer opens all on its own. The hippocampus is a strange place."

"I wish she remembered more about the logo," he said. "I asked her if she thought she could draw it, but she said she didn't think so."

"Huh, wings," I said, my mind providing pictures of the few car logos I knew.

"Is this helpful, Kieran?"

"Helpful? You bet it is. If it pans out, it may just take us a giant step towards the animal thieves. Is Patty at home today in case I need to talk to her?"

"Yes," he said. "I made sure to ask her that."

"Okay, I'll get to work on this."

I carried my laptop into the kitchen and put it on the counter as I poured coffee, thinking over this piece of information. A logo with wings. Great information, but the downside of it was that there must be about a thousand automobile logos. How would I find the one that had wings among so many possibilities? Google could help, but how would I frame the question? I'd think about that in a minute. First, landlord business.

"Helen, it's Kieran," I said as my tenant answered my phone call. "I got your note too late last night to call you. And I know it's a little early, but I'm trying to get myself organized for the day. If you want to come on down we can have coffee and you can tell me what's on your mind. You'll have to put up with me in my sweats, however."

"No problem," Helen said cheerfully. "Be right there."

I realized belatedly that I was about to be proven a rotten hostess. I didn't have bagels or croissants or a yummy banana bread or anything besides coffee to offer Helen. How could we have a proper palaver if carbohydrates weren't involved?

"Breakfast!" I called to the cats as I topped up their kibble bowls, getting one chore out of the way. "Sorry, no mouth-watering Fancy Feast Turkey and Giblets. Just boring old dry food. A proper feast tonight." When neither Vlad nor Trey appeared, I guessed they were staging a hunger strike intended to guilt me into rushing out to buy canned food. Well, it wouldn't work.

Helen let herself in through the door in my laundry room that connected her upstairs suite with my part of the house.

"In the kitchen!" I called to her.

"I'll just follow the wonderful smell of coffee," she said.

"Go ahead and pour yourself some," I told her. "It's fresh. There's powdered white stuff in a container on the counter, right beside the sugar bowl. Packets of Truvia are there, too."

"Just black coffee, thanks," she said, taking a seat opposite me at the table. A tall, slender woman with curly, prematurely silver hair, a twenty-year-old's complexion, bright blue eyes, and laugh lines around her mouth, Helen was an advertisement for healthy living. A part-time lecturer in the psychology department at U Vic, Dr. Helen Mikita taught, researched and wrote about issues in anthrozoology – the emerging field of animal-human relations. She was in the middle of writing her latest book and I was full of admiration for her work ethic. There were undoubtedly battalions of writers who lazed around the house in their pajamas, waiting for inspiration to fall on them like Newton's apple, but not Helen. An early-morning run (she was a marathoner), a trip to U Vic for her twice-weekly classes, then back to her office upstairs. Today she was up and dressed in faded jeans and a comfy-looking blue chamois shirt, ready for another day while I, lazy sluggard by comparison, was still in my sweats.

Helen wrinkled her brow, clearly troubled by something, and my stomach sank a little in apprehension. She had been the most desirable of the applicants for my upstairs suite six months ago, and I hoped she didn't want to literally move on.

"It's the flapper valve again," she told me after a few moments of silence. "I'm worried about it because it's no longer amenable to reason. The toilet just . . . flushes itself," she said ruefully.

I laughed, a great sense of relief coming over me. "Well, fooey, why don't we just take care of things once and for all? We can give the damned toilet burial at sea. In fact, I probably should have done that the first time it malfunctioned instead of letting you deal with it. Why don't I just call a plumber?"

"Okay," she said, demonstrating a fair amount of relief herself. "My previous landlord, well . . . "

"Let me guess: was a cheapskate who let you take care of things?"

She laughed. "You could say that."

"Well, I'm not a cheapskate, but I plead guilty to letting you deal with the flapper valve. I was beguiled by your household repair abilities. But no more. Promise to tell me right away when things go wrong in future?"

"Okay, I will. "

"How's your book coming along?" I asked her. "Last time we talked, you told me you were writing a chapter on, um, kitten casserole? Did I remember that correctly?"

She threw back her head and laughed. "You remembered it exactly. It's the topic of one of my lectures, too. It sure makes the undergrads pay attention. No one sleeps through the kitten casserole lecture."

"At the risk of sounding like a dope, what in heck is the lecture all about anyhow? I'm intrigued."

"Aha," she said. "Kitten casserole has gotten to you, too. So imagine this: I invite you to dinner. You sit down and I bring to the table a delicious-smelling casserole. I dish it up and as you start eating, I tell you it's made from kittens. What's your reaction?"

"Disgust. Revulsion. Anger."

"Good," she said. "Now what if I told you that I was just fooling you and the casserole was made from chicken."

"Hmm. That would be okay, I guess. We eat chicken all the time. No one eats kittens."

"Oh? Why not?"

"Well, it's because we love kittens, don't we? Who would make a casserole from something beloved?"

"And we hate chickens?"

"Nooooo, we don't *hate* them . . . but it's okay to eat them."

"Oh? Why is that?"

I thought I saw where this was going. "I was going to say that it's the idea of meat, but that's not it. After all, meat is meat. And whether to eat it or not is a whole separate issue. But our reluctance to eat kittens is due to something else, isn't it? Good animals and bad animals? Good kittens and bad chickens?"

"So an animal would have to be made 'bad' in our mind in order for us to kill and eat it?" she asked.

I thought about this. "No, it's surely not that simple. Because chickens aren't bad. Lots of people keep chickens as pets. I read about a woman who has a sanctuary for rescued chickens in North Carolina. They have names. They have personalities. They come when they're called. Definitely good animals. But what about rats . . . aren't they bad? I mean didn't they carry plague-infested fleas and bring the Black Death when they scuttled off ships in Mediterranean harbors?"

Helen grinned. "Okay, what about Jaak Panskepp the neuroscientist? His rats weren't 'bad'. He learned that rats like to be tickled and giggle when you do so. His rats were adorable. Arguably 'good' animals. So not all rats are bad, are they?"

I was silent for a moment, trying to think of a 'bad' animal. I couldn't.

"It's a complicated subject, isn't it?" Helen said. "Our relationship with animals, I mean. Some are pets and some are dinner. It's a matter of perception, really. How we perceive something, like a kitten or a chicken or a rat, determines how we think or feel about it. And our thoughts and feelings determine how we'll act.

"Consider kittens and chickens. One reason we have such different perceptions of them is because we see them differently. Apart from the example you gave about the chicken sanctuary, most people have little contact with chickens. They only see their parts in the meat section of the grocery store or in an order of chicken nuggets. But our relationship with kittens is different. We give them names. We protect and cherish them. We shop for toys for them. We make sure to buy them the best food. We watch them grow into much-loved members of our families. We post videos of them online. We write goofy poetry to them. We love kittens and eat chickens not because they are fundamentally different – as you pointed out, meat is meat - but because our view of them, our perception of them, is different.

"In my class, we go on from the kitten casserole discussion to an examination of the moral cowardice involved in refusing to know anything about the living animal from which our chicken nugget is derived – the inhumane conditions under which it lived and its brutal death. That's when the discussion becomes pretty serious. Is it moral cowardice? Or is it an empathy deficit in which we rationalize it's okay for a creature to live and die in torment because it's 'only an animal', it's not like us, and after all, we have to eat?"

"Loaded questions," I said. "How do the undergrads react to them?"

"You know, I'm always amazed at how thoughtful most of my students are," she said. "Most of them have never contemplated how chickens become nuggets and is it morally defensible to eat them. I try to be gentle," she said with an impish smile.

"You must be a vegan," I said. "How did you come to make that choice?"

"Well, I didn't make a choice," she said. "Not a rational one, anyhow. I had, well, a road-to-Damascus moment. I was driving home to Toronto from the Shakespeare Festival in Stratford, Ontario, many years ago. A truck loaded with chickens bound for slaughter pulled up beside my car. Traffic stopped for some reason and I looked over at the cages stacked six or seven high, crammed full of chickens who couldn't turn around or even move. The chickens must have been terrified. I felt . . .very disturbed. I had no idea chickens were treated this way. And then a chicken turned its head around – that was all it could move – and looked at me. Time seemed to stop. I felt skewered, judged . . . and found wanting. And I got it." She shrugged. "I felt angry and ashamed that we were treating animals this way. It was disgraceful. Still is. Anyhow, the traffic started and I pulled ahead of the truck but I never forgot that chicken. I became a vegan the next day, although we called it vegetarianism back then."

"Wow," I said, feeling humbled.

"What about you?" Helen asked.

"No road-to-Damascus moments for me, alas. But I've given plenty of thought to veganism. It just makes moral sense. So I've been edging my way into it. I don't eat cows or pigs anymore. I buy cruelty-free cosmetics. I don't wear leather. Turkeys and chickens will be next to go. Then fish."

"You'll get there," she said. "Not everyone has an epiphany on the road to Damascus. Or even Toronto. Say, come to a lecture sometime," she invited. "We discuss plenty of interesting things. Today it's kitten casseroles. Friday it's our inner yahoo."

"Thanks," I said. "I will."

She looked at her watch. "It's past time to get ready for class. Enough philosophizing for one day. Thanks for the coffee, Kieran."

"I'm always up for philosophizing," I said, "but yes, both of us have things to do. I'll call the plumber."

❧

As I suspected, there were about a thousand automobile logos. Google, that ever-willing hound, fetched me precisely 1,284. For crap's sake. How long was this going to take? How could I cut down this list of Bentleys, Corvettes, Aston Martins, Mercedes, Chryslers, to a manageable number?

When I stopped panicking about it, however, the job didn't take nearly as long as I feared. I simply reviewed the huge array of vehicle logos that Google had found for me, made a list of the winged or wing-like logos, and went to each auto manufacturer's website. A quick search told me whether or not they made vans. Simple. So when I was done, and the coffeepot was empty, I had cut my list of 1,284 possibilities down to five: Chrysler, which made two van models – the Town and Country, and the Pacifica, whose logos were the same definite wing shape; the Mazda MPV, whose logo was a fanciful wing; the Toyota Sienna and the Honda Odyssey whose logos were only vaguely winglike, but which I decided to include because who knows what Patty had really seen at one in the morning. I double-checked on the websites and all five vans were manufactured in a light brown. Then I printed out the logos, nice and big, printed out side, front and back views of the vans themselves, put everything in a folder and got into the shower, feeling absurdly pleased with myself.

As I was finding matching socks, I called Patty, then, Evelyn with the wandering feline Lothario, telling them both I had some van images I wanted to show them. Last, I checked my email, hoping for something from Edgar. No joy there, but Finn had sent me a file with photos of the missing animals as well as their owners' names, addresses, and phone numbers. I looked at it briefly, then grabbed my folder of logos and hurried out the door.

Chapter 10

M ARV AND PATTY'S house, just six down from Wild at Heart, was another gracious two-story home with a stone and stucco exterior, a flagstone walk, a large yard, and about a dozen oak trees shading the property. Patty, earnest, bespectacled and sixty-something, met me at the front door. As she led me into the dining room, we passed an empty dog bed with a rawhide bone in it, and I winced.

"Daisy's bed," she said sadly. "I try not to cry whenever I pass it. But I'm not going to put it away." She looked at me confidently. "I'm certain you're going to find her, and all the other pets."

No pressure, Kieran. Bring 'em home. Make everyone happy again. "I'm sure going to do my best," I assured her.

"You said you had something for us to look at? Let's sit here at the table. Marv, come join us," she called into the kitchen. "And bring Kieran some coffee."

The three of us sat at the dining room table and I carefully laid out the five vehicle logos I had printed from the internet.

"Hey, this is like a police lineup," Marv commented, as he took a seat next to Patty.

"Don't rush," I told them. "And don't try to remember exactly what you saw. Just look at these and tell me if one stands out."

"I don't think I could tell you," Marv said, shaking his head. "I just recall seeing the van and wondering if it was Jim Mortenson's son come to take care of the property. Patty, you thought you saw the logo. So you say."

Patty studied the logos for a moment, then pointed to one. "That's it," she said firmly, pointing to the Chrysler logo, which was definitely a pair of wings. "I'm sure. What is it?"

"Well, it's the Chrysler logo. It's a little complicated because they make two vans . . . or rather made two vans. The Town and Country isn't manufactured any longer, and the Pacifica is brand new. So there are probably both models out there on the highway." I put the logos away and replaced them with the front, back, and side views of the Town and Country and the Pacifica. "Anything look familiar?"

Marv shook his head. "Sorry. No."

Patty shook her head also. "I can't say. I really only saw the back. And even that just briefly. How will you find which one of these is the right one?"

I finished my coffee and put the sheets of paper back into my folder. "Evelyn thinks she saw the van drive by late Saturday night. Actually early Sunday morning. I'll show these to her. I'm hoping she'll be able to help. I'm on my way there now. Thanks a million, you guys."

❧

Evelyn was waiting for me. Lord, I hoped no more coffee would be offered. I was already about jumping out of my skin. At the dining room table, I laid out the printouts of the side, front, and back views of the two Chrysler vans – the Town and Country and the Pacifica. Evelyn did not hesitate.

"That one," she said, immediately pointing to the Town and Country van. "Definitely. It's boxier than the other one, you see. I remember that. The boxy-looking front end. What is it?"

"A Chrysler Town and Country van."

Evelyn nodded slowly. "Okay. And you think that may be . . ."

I finished her sentence for her. "It may be the van the animal thieves used. May be. I have a few more inquiries to make, but I'm hopeful we're onto something."

She looked worried. "Okay . . . but even if it is the right van, how will you find who was driving it?"

I winked at her with a lot more confidence that I felt. "I have an ingenious friend who can find out."

Before I left Evelyn's driveway, I put in a call to that ingenious friend. "Edgar!" I said irritably when I was prompted to leave a message. "Is everyone at Poe Enterprises knee-deep in battling cyber-shenanigans? I don't even rate a human being to whom I can express my ire? What happened to the phone anwerer? Hmmf. This is just like the bad old days. Anyhow, I didn't get the information about the alarm system at Wild At Heart. I need it. Pronto. And I have another job for you that's just as urgent. I need to know the registered owners of all Chrysler Town and Country vans, color light brown, or beige, or bronze, or whatever the manufacturer's name for it is. All registered owners on the island. All of them. Email me a file. You have my credit card number. Charge me. But do it now, please."

I ended the call more than a little ticked off with Edgar. Oh, he always came through, but time was trickling away. If Patty and Evelyn were right, we were one giant step closer to the animal thieves. I needed Edgar to get me closer still.

☙

At my friend Lawrence's photo shop on Oak Bay Avenue, someone I didn't recognize was just changing the "Closed" sign to "Open." Good. I found a parking space right in front and went in, the door tinkling shut behind me. A small, slender young guy with curly dark hair, melting brown eyes, and the longest eyelashes I had ever seen on a male, greeted me. He was neatly dressed in jeans and a white button down shirt. I was impressed. Whoever he was, I thought he was four or five notches up from Doris, Lawrence's glum former employee, who always wore black, dyed her hair in a seasonally festive sequence of colors, and sported multiple disturbing tattoos. She did sell a lot of cameras, Lawrence told me, so maybe I was just being an old fogey about professional appearance.

"Hi," I said cheerfully. "Is Lawrence around? I'm a friend of his. Kieran Yeats."

"I'm Samir," the young guy said, showing a marvelously white smile. So much better for business than the dour Doris. "Lawrence's in the back. I'll get him."

While Samir was fetching Lawrence, I looked around. A lot had changed in a short time. True, there were still plenty of cameras and photographic accessories on display, but a door had been cut through the back wall into what I had thought was a storage room, but seemed now to be a large, well-lighted space, busy with the sounds of machinery.

"Kieran!" my friend Lawrence said, emerging from the large well-lighted space in back. Sandy brown hair, blue eyes, wire-rim glasses, impeccably pressed khakis and a navy pullover, Lawrence looked every bit the prosperous, conservative young businessman. Only I knew that beneath that conservative exterior beat the heart of a romantic, a soul longing for adventure. Poor guy, his adventures with me over the years had resulted in fits of terror, a broken arm, a wrecked car, and serious spiritual angst. But that seemingly hadn't served to dampen his enthusiasm. He advanced towards me with open arms and enveloped me in a bear hug. "Er, sorry," he apologized after a moment. "It's just that I'm so darned glad to see you."

"Down, boy," I told him, disentangling myself but happy that he had missed me. "I'm glad to see you, too. What's up in back?"

"I bought the shop next door," he said, hugely pleased with himself. "It has a huge warehouse space. Samir and his sister Aliya persuaded me to go into, well, the T-shirt business."

"T-shirts?"

"I know, it sounds a bit wacky, but we're making tons of money. We have several big customers – U Vic, some high schools, several nonprofit groups. Samir is a great salesman."

"And Aliya is a whiz with computers," a young female voice called from behind Lawrence.

"True," Lawrence said, laughing. "Aliya, this is my friend Kieran."

A young woman with the same curly dark hair and amazing eyelashes as Samir's – she had to be Samir's twin – dressed like him in jeans and a white button down shirt, held out her hand, after wiping it on a rag she held. "I may be a little grimy," she said. "Sorry. I was adjusting the ink nozzles for a T-shirt run."

I shook her hand. "T-shirts," I said. "Who knew there was money in them?"

Aliya nodded her head earnestly. "The big orders bring in the big money, but our DIY digital printing service is especially popular with individuals. People upload their favorite photos to our website, pick a T-shirt style and color, and presto! We print the shirt, and ship it faster than anyone else in town. And for less money than the competition, too."

"I'll leave you two to hold the fort," Lawrence told Aliya and Samir with mock sternness. "C'mon into my office, Kieran. I don't know what I did before those two came along!"

As Lawrence showed me into his office, I was struck by several beautiful nature photos that adorned his walls: Canada geese in a cattail pond, a great grey heron launching herself off the surface of a misty lake and, one last photo so touchingly beautiful that I let out an "Oh!" of delight: a tiny grey vole sleeping in the throat of a purple iris.

"Oh, Lawrence, these are gorgeous! Who took them? I can't stop looking at the vole!"

"She has that effect on people," he said modestly. "In fact, she's the star of our most successful T-shirt. Everyone loves the vole in the iris. Putting nature photos on shirts was Aliya's idea, but," he cleared his throat diffidently, "I, um, I took the pictures. Now that I have some help, I can indulge my passion for photography. I opened this shop just to make money, but making money kind of hijacked my avocation. I'm awfully glad I can get back to it."

"How did you locate those young people?" I asked Lawrence when he had closed the door to his office and motioned me to a chair. "Isn't it a truism that good employees are impossible to find?"

"Would you believe they just came in one day and sold themselves? Doris resigned, and, well, I wasn't looking forward to running an ad in the paper and interviewing prospective employees. I put a sign in the window and the next day Aliya and Samir just . . . walked in. Their family is from Lebanon. The two of them have degrees in humanities from the American University of Beirut. They cheerfully admitted when I interviewed them that they had no idea what they wanted to do with their lives, but they had good local work references at various jobs. They came as a package," he said, laughing. "Samir actually *likes* customer service, and Aliya enjoys the computer end of things. She started our website and writes our blog." He shook his head. "Their work ethic is amazing. Of course, one day they'll go off and start their own business . . ." He trailed off.

"Or maybe not," I told him, sensing his anticipatory sadness. "Maybe they'll like it here so much they'll, oh, want to buy into your business. It could be Baines and, what's their last name?"

"Hammam."

"Okay, Fox and Hammam."

"Maybe so," he said, brightening. "Say, what are you up to?"

"I thought I might enlist your help," I told him. "But if you're too busy – "

"Nope," he said, grinning. "If you need me for a case, I'm always available. What are you working on now?"

I described the case of the missing animals and he whistled. "How awful for Norma and the pet owners. How can I help? Do you need me to take photos?"

"I'm not sure," I said. "Want to come along with me to Wild At Heart? Bring your camera just in case. In any event, I'd like to borrow your brain. There's something screwy about the alarm system and you might notice something I missed. I'm waiting for a report from the alarm company, but in the meantime, I sure wouldn't mind another pair of eyes looking at what I've already seen. It's as though I'm missing something important. The cats didn't just de-materialize. I need to talk to Norma, the cattery owner, and I'd appreciate it if you were looking at the doors and windows while I was talking."

"Sure thing," he said eagerly. "I'll just go tell Aliya I'll be out for a bit. She's the older of the twins by about five minutes. So she claims she's the brains of the duo." He grinned. "Or at least the boss. Samir's gracious enough not to disagree. And their little brothers who come in to help with T-shirt packing and shipping don't dare disagree either."

"Sounds like Aliya has those guys well in hand."

Lawrence nodded. "She's quite something," he said in evident admiration. "I'll just go talk to her for a minute. I see you're parked out front. I'll meet you there."

∽

As we headed off down Oak Bay Avenue, Lawrence cleared his throat nervously. "Can I ask you a favor?" he said, his tone apprehensive.

"You bet. Shoot."

"Can we not go to Old British Fish and Chips for breakfast? I don't think my stomach could stand the Rock Cod Special this early in the day."

I laughed. "Sure thing, junior. How about that bagel shop on Broad? I can have the lox and cream cheese on an onion bagel and you can have . . . something plain."

"Thank you," he said fervently. "I guess I've just developed a wimpy stomach."

"No problem," I told him. "Mine's not what it used to be, either. I'll hover while you go in and get the food. And make my coffee decaf, please. I'm so well-caffeinated I could leap the Parliament Buildings. So let's go fortify ourselves. Norma Carruthers has had a tremendous loss. I don't know what to expect: finger-pointing at Jen, weeping and wailing, or just plain rage. Something emotional, though. Oh, and when we're done, I need to go up north to see a woman Mac recommended. I'll tell you about I while we're driving."

Chapter 11

A SMALL WOMAN with aggressively bushy brown hair, Norma Carruthers met us at the front door of Wild At Heart in a state of barely controlled fury. I introduced Lawrence, explained why he was with me, and she indicated with a wave of her hand that he could go ahead and do what he needed to do. Giving me one arched-eyebrow look, Lawrence wisely left us for the kitchen.

"I'm mad as hell about all this," Norma said unnecessarily as we stood in the front hall.

I nodded. "I understand. I'd feel that way too if I were in your place."

"Eleven of my cats are . . . somewhere," she said, her lips tightening. "I'd like to just murder whoever's responsible. One of the litters is barely three months old. And the kitten Jen was working with is quite small. He needs to be here. Come on through to the cattery," she said. "I'm cleaning, so you'll have to excuse the mess."

We went through the screen door and she closed it carefully behind her. The two Oriental carpets I had seen earlier were rolled against one wall and a bucket, a sponge mop, and a tote with an array of cleaning supplies stood in the middle of the floor. "Let's sit on the couch," she said. "Actually, I don't know what the hell I'm doing. I'm only cleaning because I need to keep busy. It's not like anything needs to be cleaned." She smiled grimly at me and held out a hand. "Jesus, I haven't even introduced myself. Norma Carruthers."

"Kieran Yeats," I said, shaking her hand.

"Jen speaks of you often. Please tell me you have some leads."

"I do," I told her. "But I'm just at the beginning of this. I've met with the neighborhood pet owners, and now I need to ask you some questions."

"Sure," she said. "Ask me anything. Oh, would you like some coffee? There's some in the kitchen. Or I could make tea."

"No, nothing, thanks," I told her. Her offer was thoughtful, but definitely no more coffee.

"I was rude," she said. "Just now, at the door. I'm usually not like this." She looked across the room to the bank of stainless steel cages, two of which were now occupied by gorgeous bronze-colored cats with back rosettes. Somehow their presence made the emptiness of the other cages more pronounced. "Thank God I still have these two," she said. "I'm trying not to catastrophize, but I have to prepare for the worst. I still have Take A Walk On The Wild Side. He's the big male," she explained. "But the smaller cat, Wild Honey, well, she's technically a kitten still. She's seven months old." Norma gave a rueful laugh. "Honey just won Best Kitten at the cat show, but she's Take A Walk's daughter. So it's not as though I could start over with the two of them."

"Well, let's assume you won't have to," I told her. "I'd like to go over a few things."

"Okay."

"Who knew you were going to be away? Anyone you might have told about the cat show and your absence."

She frowned. "I don't usually tell anyone. Apart from my regular cat-sitter, that is. This time I hired Jen, though, as you know. Well, the people at the kennel knew, too," she said hastily.

"The kennel?"

"Yes. I took Bear, my dog, to the kennel so Jen didn't have to deal with him. He's a sweetheart, but I wanted her to just concentrate on the cats."

"Is he still there?"

"At the kennel? No. I picked him up this morning. I think he's in the dining room, under the table. Either that or he's in the kitchen bothering Lawrence. He's in mourning." She opened the screen door from the cattery into the rest of the house and called: "Bear?" The most enormous dog I've ever seen ambled from the dining room past her into the cattery, a dog the size of, well, a black bear. She closed the door carefully after him and patted him absently. "He's a Newfie," she explained. "He weighs in at about a hundred pounds – just a baby still. The cats love him. He's big and warm and furry and gentle. They'll be missing him." She wiped her eyes angrily. "I am not going to cry over this."

Bear came and regarded me with soft brown eyes, sighed, and lay down at my feet. He didn't seem to require patting from me, so I didn't embarrass myself by attempting it. I'm not a dog person.

"He would have been useless even if he had been here during the break-in," she said. "Bear loves everyone. He might have just licked the thieves to death."

"So no one knew you'd be away?" I asked "Apart from people at the kennel."

"I don't think so. Maybe one or two of the neighbors saw me go out early in the morning with the two cats. It was very early, though. Well before six. I had to catch the float plane flight to Vancouver."

"Did you see anyone?"

"You mean, on the street?"

"Yeah."

Norma thought for a moment. "No. Well, there was the newspaper delivery person."

I raised my eyebrows. "Really. Who is he? A kid? An adult?"

"It's a she. A woman in her sixties. Janet, I think her name is. She delivers the paper by car."

"Hmm. What does she drive?"

"A beat-up old thing that needs a tune-up. I hear it coughing every morning."

"Color?"

"Well, I don't know. Why do you ask?"

"A couple of your neighbors saw a light brown van on the street late Saturday night."

"Oh. So you think . . ."

"Maybe," I said. "Probably."

She looked off into a corner of the room, obviously thinking. "I don't think I know anyone who drives anything like that."

It had been too much to hope for. "So, who else comes around regularly? Lawn mowers, window washers . . . "

"Let's see. The lawn gets cut every week or so in the summer. Josh, a neighborhood high school kid works for several of us. He hasn't been around yet this year, but when he does come, he has an old red truck. Windows? Well, I get the upstairs windows done maybe once a year. I use Clear Outlook. I have for years, but they haven't been here in awhile."

"Do you use a cat food or litter delivery service?"

She shook her head. "No. I buy the food from my vet and just schlep it home."

I thought some more. "What about inside. Do you have a cleaning person?"

"Yes. A young woman named Stephanie."

"Would she have known you were going away to the cat show?"

Norma frowned. "I don't think I mentioned it to her. But I suppose I might have. I'm just not sure."

"Hmm. What does she drive?"

"Something black with a crumpled front fender."

"Does anyone else come in regularly?"

She laughed. "It's not as if I have a staff. But I know what you mean. No."

Norma looked over at the cat cages where the bigger of the two cats, presumably Take A Walk, came up to the bars of the cage and chirped sadly at her. "Sorry, fella," she told him. I hoped she wouldn't start crying. But she seemed tougher than that.

"So . . . other people who have been in here recently?"

"I had a computer tech come in to work on my computer. I just couldn't deal with taking it to the shop. He was a little strange, come to think of it. But then he's a tekkie."

"When was that?"

"Oh, maybe a month ago. I didn't notice what he drove. But he came from that computer place on Oak Bay Avenue. Presumably he's okay."

I wasn't so sure about that, but let it pass.

"How about adopters? Have you turned anyone down in the past little while? Anyone local?"

She nodded. "Sure. Not everyone is cut out to own a Bengal."

"How did these people take being refused?"

"Some understood. Some didn't. Just because people have the money to afford a Bengal doesn't mean they should have one. I'm pretty fussy. But I know what you're getting at. No one was furiously angry with me but a few acted a bit miffed."

"Can you let me have the names of the people we've talked about?" I asked her. "The newspaper deliverer. The lawn guy. The window washers. The computer tech. The cat sitter. The cleaning person. Spurned adopters. And anyone else who might have known that you have these cats and could have figured out that you sometimes go away? Phone numbers too, if you have them. You can text them to me."

Lawrence knocked at the screen door.

"C'mon in, Lawrence," Norma told him. "The other door on the alarm is over here," she motioned him to the sliding door to the sunroom. "Go out onto the deck if you need to," she told him.

As Lawrence did so, I asked Norma: "Who has keys to your house?"

"Well, I have one, Jen has one, and my regular cat-sitter has the other one. I know what you're probably thinking, but I can't see that Emily, my cat sitter, could be involved. I've known her for years."

"What about relatives?"

"Oh, I forgot. Heather, my daughter has one. She lives up near Butchart Gardens. She and her husband have a little farm up there."

"What kind of farm?"

Norma grinned. "It's kind of kooky, but . . . it's a mushroom farm."

"A mushroom farm? Really? There's money in that?"

"Well, things were rough at first, but they're doing okay now. They raise quite a few different kinds of mushrooms. Porcini and so on. Restaurants buy from them."

"And do you two get along okay?"

Her eyes darted away from mine in evident embarrassment. "As well as mothers and daughters usually get along, I suppose," she said.

Oho, I thought.

She was quiet for a moment, then asked me: "Kieran, the pet thefts from my neighbors. And my cats' disappearance. I don't quite get it. Is this all about money?"

"Ultimately, yes."

"But no one is going to get, oh, fifteen hundred dollars or so for Dutch's beagles or Evelyn's wandering tabby tomcat, are they?"

"No," I told her. What I wasn't going to tell her, though, was the rest of what Ian and Olga had told me. Bunchers got paid well enough for their work. True, they didn't get paid what a Bengal kitten would have brought, but well paid, still. And they did it over and over. Evidently it was a living. But I was not going to say a word about bunchers to Norma. It was too horrible a prospect for any animal owner to have to contemplate.

"There's something you're not telling me, isn't there?"

Lawrence had come in from the deck and cleared his throat, thoughtfully rescuing me from Norma's further speculations. "We'd better go," I told her. "We have some other people to talk to."

"Oh, I have something for you," she said. "Dutch came by earlier. We're all splitting your fee. So I have a check."

She handed me the check and we all walked together to the front door.

"About Jen," Norma said. "I'm mad as hell about this, and I'm scared that I'll never see my cats again. But it's not Jen I'm mad at. I hope she doesn't think that. I don't hold her responsible."

"Have you told her that?" I asked.

"Probably not clearly enough. I don't know quite how to talk to her about it, though. She feels bad, I feel bad . . ."

"Well, maybe let things rest for a day or so. Jen's a tough kid. Don't worry too much about her. You have enough to worry about. Oh, one last thing . . . . insurance. The Bengals were insured, weren't they?"

"Sure," Norma said. "For their replacement value," she said, sounding bitter. "They couldn't be insured for their future earnings potential, though. Unfortunately, they're not considered as valuable as Kentucky Derby Winners."

"Right," I told her. Then I couldn't think of any more questions to ask. "Okay. I'll be in touch. Thanks, Norma."

As Lawrence and I walked to my car, my phone buzzed. At last. I took a quick look. Edgar had sent me an email. One file. But only one file.

"Crap," I said.

"Problems?" Lawrence asked.

"No. This is the alarm system report. I expected two files from Edgar, but this is only one. I'd like to study it, but I don't have time right now."

"Why don't you send it to my office e-mail?" he said. "I can get Aliya to print it out and we can look at it when we get back. I'll call her to expect it if you like."

"Okay. That would be helpful. By the way, did you find anything amiss when you looked around the house? A broken lock? A jimmied wondow? A mangled door casing?"

He shook his head. "Nope. Nothing that would help us. Just cupboards, windows firmly closed and locked."

"Thanks for looking, junior. Say, are you sure you want to come along up north with me?"

"Sure I'm sure," he said. "There's nothing pressing that Aliya and Samir can't handle."

"No voles to photograph today?" I teased him.

"Nope. No voles. So I'm all yours. Besides, how often do you get to meet a former Royal Canadian Mounted Police constable who now runs an animal sanctuary?"

"How often indeed?" I asked him, as we slipped into our familiar, easy back and forth. I realized how much I'd missed Lawrence and mentally forgave him the bear hug.

"Say," Lawrence said as I pulled away from the cattery, "I don't want to sound like a clod, but have you ever, well, eaten a porcini? I understand some of them are as big as dinner plates. I mean, restaurants make burgers out of them."

I shuddered. "Have I ever eaten one? Not bloody likely. Are they on the menu at Old British Fish and Chips? Or McDonald's?"

"Nope."

"I rest my case."

He was quiet for a long moment and I suspected that he was mulling over more than mushrooms "What's up, junior?"

"All those people that Norma mentioned, well, that sure sounds like a long list of suspects."

"No kidding," I said despondently. "I also have a file waiting in email for me from Finn, one of the pet owners, that probably contains dozens more names. All the service people the pet owners could recall."

"Wow."

"Yeah. When I put the two files together, I'll probably have, oh, four hundred potential suspects."

"Really? That many?" Lawrence said in alarm.

"No, probably not quite that many. I'm just indulging in a little dark humor. It's a cunning ploy to cover up burgeoning terror. The thing is, I really don't have a few hours to sit quietly and cull the list down to a reasonable number. I'm scared to death that while I'm futzing around examining lists of suspects, the animals may be moved. Right now, though, they ought to be someplace close by. On the island, anyhow. But if I wait too long . . ."

"I see," Lawrence said. "Brother."

"Well, let's get out of the pessimism pit," I told him, feigning cheer I did not feel. "After all, as Sherlock Homes was fond of telling Watson, once you eliminate the impossible, whatever remains, no matter how improbable, must be the truth. All I have to do is eliminate the impossible. Right?"

"I see," Lawrence said. "Rule out the people who couldn't possibly have stolen the animals."

"You got it."

But despite the Holmesian homily I had just shared with Lawrence, a yammering voice of panic whispered: *Hurry, hurry.*

Chapter 12

I MISSED THE turnoff from the highway to Miranda's sanctuary on the first pass. On the second pass, however, I turned in at a wooden sign that read 41266.

"That's odd," Lawrence said, putting away his phone. He'd finally had to call the sanctuary for directions while I was driving.

"That there's no sign for the sanctuary?"

"Yeah. How will people find it?"

"Maybe that's the point," I told him.

"Oh," he said thoughtfully. "You mean they don't want people to find it? That's certainly . . . strange."

"It is a little strange," I agreed. "But they must have their reasons."

♥

When Miranda Blake had decided to chuck the RCMP for the animal rescue business, she had evidently done it in a big way. As Lawrence and I had discovered, her shelter wasn't advertised. But the road from the highway was well-kept and led through a forest of tall evergreens to an asphalt parking lot and a sprawling old-fashioned ranch-style house surrounded on either side by yards and yards of chain link fence. Inside the fence I could see numerous small cottage-like structures, painted bright primary colors, and redwood bark paths which meandered from one cottage to another. Oak trees with spreading branches, just leafing out, shaded the premises. I figured the sanctuary occupied a couple of acres and wondered how she had been able to afford such a large spread. Early retirement from the RCMP wouldn't have funded this. Well, maybe she'd had an angel.

I parked beside four other cars in the parking lot and Lawrence and I walked up to the front door of the house where a wooden sign in a flowerbed asked us to PLEASE RING BELL AND WAIT. A green wrought iron bench had been provided for those of us who needed to wait, and I rang once, joining Lawrence on the bench.

"Nice," he said. "Peaceful. I bet the animals like it here."

In a few minutes a middle-aged woman with a friendly smile, her longish grey hair tied back with a hank of purple yarn, opened the door to the house. "C'mon in," she said. "You must be Kieran. I'm Connie. Miranda said to expect you. She'll be just a few minutes."

We went into what was plainly a reception area and sat where Connie indicated we should, on two chairs in front of a big battered grey metal desk. On the desk were a tower computer, a large monitor, a printer, and a landline phone. A single bookcase with veterinary medicine tomes, a copy of a fat book titled Animal Law, and a few piled-up phone directories stood against the back wall, sharing space with an ancient tan metal filing cabinet. I was impressed with how bare-bones the place looked – evidently no money had been wasted out here. The phone rang and Connie said: "Excuse me," and answered it. Maybe another hapless wanderer calling from the highway.

"Well, hi there, cutie," a low, seductive voice called out from behind me.

I half turned in my chair, intending to give the owner of the voice a tongue-lashing when it began trilling: *"Earth angel, earth angel, will you be mine?"*

I laughed out loud. The singer was a small, nondescript-looking grey bird, perched on the top of a very large cage. Somehow I had missed him when Lawrence and I walked into the waiting area. I was open-mouthed in my admiration as he continued warbling that old doo wop song, never missing an oooo or an ohhh, getting all those corny forever and evermore rhymes just right as he confessed that he was a fool in love. I laughed again, delighted. Heck, I'm always a sucker for anyone who calls me their darling dear.

"Gosh," Lawrence said, "a singing bird. I've never seen one – just heard about them. Is it a cockatiel?" he asked Connie.

"Oh fuck off," the bird told him thoughtfully. "Just . . . fuck off."

"Jimmy, stop that," Connie called out. "No, he's a parrot," she told Lawrence. "An African Grey Parrot. They're very smart. But Jimmy is incorrigible. He swears like a sailor. We could probably get him adopted pretty quickly otherwise, if someone wanted to listen to his endless playlist, that is. But given his penchant for the f-bomb, it will take a pretty understanding person to adopt him."

Jimmy screamed, executed a few pirouettes on top of his cage, bobbed his head, and launched into another doo wop ditty.

"There's a mooooon out tonight," he began. Alas, I recognized this old chestnut, too. Jimmy did an equally good job with it, especially the whoa-oh-oh-ohs and the strollin'/stolen rhymes. Masterful lyric writing imprints itself on my brain every time.

Then, inexplicably, he fell silent.

"What's the matter?" I asked him, getting up to go over to his cage. "Cat got your tongue?"

He turned his back and muttered.

"Do you have many animals like Jimmy?" Lawrence asked.

"If you mean with behavioral issues, well, yes we do," Connie told him. "One of the reasons Miranda founded this sanctuary is to provide a place for animals the traditional shelters can't handle or don't have room for. We don't take in animals from the public, you see. Jimmy came in with a bunch of cats from a hoarding situation the police discovered. Not only does he curse and sing doo wop endlessly, but he's been plucking feathers from his chest. We do have a bird vet coming to see him. He was probably pretty stressed by all those cats, so we're giving him his own space here, and lots of time. He'll come around."

"Hey, guy," I said, touched by his plight and amazed by his faithful rendition of those old fifties songs, "want to sing some more?"

He turned around to look at me and I saw what Connie meant. His chest looked moth-eaten, half-naked, pink where he had torn his feathers out. He whistled once, warbled feebly about having a girl in his arms, then fell silent and turned his back on me again.

"He's a conflicted soul," Connie said. "He doesn't know whether to curse or sing love songs. And I think he's ashamed of his mostly naked chest. Poor thing."

"Living with thirty-four cats in a single-wide trailer might make anyone a bit addled," a new voice said.

A tall, sturdy-looking woman dressed in jeans and a cream-colored fisherman-knit pullover entered the reception area from the hall, handing Connie a file folder. "I'm Miranda," she said with a smile, looking me over appraisingly with pale blue fighter-pilot eyes. I sensed that behind that ready smile, she was as tough as nails. "You must be Kieran." She tucked a stray wing of dark hair behind one ear, then extended a hand and we shook.

"I am," I told her. "This is Lawrence Fox, my associate."

"C'mon back to my office," she said. "It's just down the hall on the right. I'm currently sharing it with a very scared feral from the thirty-four hoarded cats in the single-wide we rescued last week. Oh, and a dog."

"Fuck off," Jimmy called cheerfully to us as we left.

"We love you, too, Jimmy," Miranda called to him, closing the hall door to the reception area behind us.

"Please excuse Jimmy," she said, motioning us into her office. I was impressed that it was as Spartan as the reception area, containing only a desk, a couple of chairs, and a cat tree in front of a window.

"We've only had four or five rescue parrots, but they've all been problems," she explained. "I think I feel sorrier for them than I do for almost any other animal who ends up here. It's obscene to capture them in the first place and try to make pets of them," she said hotly. "It rarely works out for the parrots. When things go badly for them, they end up being passed along to family members or given to pet stores for resale or . . . they end up in places like our sanctuary. If they're lucky."

"Why don't they make good pets?" Lawrence asked. "I've seen TV shows about parrots and they seem pretty friendly to their owners."

"Oh, they may tell you in English that they love you as they share your dinner at night," Miranda said, "but they don't. You may love a bird, but it will never love you back. It can't. They're so unlike companion animals." Miranda shook her head. "Dogs and cats are generally grateful for food and affection, and often make us believe that they love us, but a parrot may well never even *like* you. And it may get mad at you for something like taking a trip or going away to college and stay mad at you for the rest of its life. And that might be a very long life. So I urge people to think three or four times before they adopt a parrot.

"I must sound like a parrot grinch," she said. "I'm not. I just try to be realistic with people. I tell potential parrot adopters that living with a parrot is not like living with a feathered child. It's more like living with an alien. Parrots aren't . . . mean . . . they're just odd. Some people would call what they possess savagery. I wouldn't. I just think of it as wildness. Their hearts will be forever wild. If you understand this and choose to share your home with one, we'll consider adopting to you. Otherwise, no."

A fearful hissing erupted from the cat tree and I realized I had overlooked the cat who was sitting on the middle shelf. She was a small anger with legs, a fluffy orange cat, who spat warningly at us, then hopped up to the top shelf where she disappeared into a cubbyhole. Undoubtedly we had disturbed her serenity.

"Another problem child," Miranda said. "We're calling her Felicity because we hope she'll become happier. Positive thinking," she chuckled. "Oops," she apologized, taking a seat behind her desk, "almost squished you." She bent over, addressing the space under her desk. "Good boy. Max is my underdesk dog," she explained. "He may or may not come out to see you. He's, well, he's in mourning." She settled back in her desk chair and regarded us curiously.

"Do you miss the RCMP?" I asked Miranda. "All this," I gestured around me, "seems like a big change."

She smiled ruefully. "Sometimes I miss it," she said. "Mostly I miss the camaraderie. Oh and I miss the red serge uniforms we wore for formal occasions, too. They connected me to the Mounties' proud history. Do you miss the Crown Counsel's office?"

"Oh, well," I equivocated, then decided to tell her the truth. "Not a bit. I didn't find much camaraderie there. Maybe that made it easier to quit."

She nodded. "What happened? Anything in particular?"

"Yeah," I told her, outlining the Owen Mallory case.

"Ouch," she said. "You won the battle but lost the war."

"Something like that. No more hoping for justice with a capital J for me. I bailed on the law in a fit of futility. Decided I'd rather advocate for living animals."

She grimaced. "I know what you mean. My squad and I were investigating animal thefts up-island when we stumbled upon a fentanyl import and distribution ring. That took precedence. The animal thefts, which were heartbreaking, as I'm sure you know, were simply put on the back burner. Eventually my superiors closed the case. Coyotes, they decided, not only to put a period at the end of the sentence, but also to save face. We were all put on the fentanyl investigation, but I couldn't get the pet owners out of my mind. Their grief." She seemed to come back from some distant place in her memory.

"We all have our own ideas about how to make the world a better place, don't we?" she said. "Some of us are called to serve the poor, some to protect children, some to prevent or cure disease, some to protect the environment, some to serve justice." She gestured to include me in this last point. "I guess I was one of the latter, too. But when I listened to my heart, I knew what I wanted to do. I'd always wanted to work with animals – even thought about becoming a vet at one time – but my own vet talked me out of it. He said every vet starts out as a vivisectionist, and I knew I couldn't do that. So when I got thoroughly disgusted about being called off the animal theft investigation, I decided to put my efforts where my heart was. As I'm sure Connie told you, here we help the lame, the halt and the blind, so to speak. Animals who other shelters have given up on . . . or don't even try to help." She laughed. "It's no less frustrating, but I sure do enjoy seeing broken animals made whole again.

"Mac told me a little about your investigation," Miranda said. "Multiple thefts from an upscale Oak Bay neighborhood, right?"

"Right. I'm still scratching my head over how the thieves defeated the alarm system at the location from which the Bengal cats were taken, but I'll solve that in good time. I have the report from the alarm company for the day and night of the theft, and I'll go over it with Lawrence in a bit. I met with Ninth Life and Open The Cages yesterday and they pretty much convinced me that bunchers were responsible."

Miranda's nostrils flared and she narrowed her eyes in anger. "Bunchers. How I detest them. They're some of the worst people I know. They're lazy, opportunistic cowards. Stealing someone's beloved pet is as bad as stealing their child, in my opinion. And worst of all, they break the bond of trust, and the duty of care that we owe to animals. I'm old-fashioned: I believe the so-called 'dominion' over animals that God gave us is a solemn responsibility. It's not ownership or carte blanche to do with them whatever we choose. Anyhow, don't get me started," she said, shaking her head.

"So, when Mac told me about your case, I thought right away of three guys we came in contact with several years ago." She opened a desk drawer and took out a sheet of paper, handing it to me. "Here are their names. I haven't kept track of them, so you'll have to run them down. But there are several online investigation services that are quite reliable. They use publicly available information and have it located in one easy place for you. All you need is a credit card," she said. "When you don't have access to law enforcement's resources, they're the next best thing."

I nodded. "I use one of those services. It's proven very helpful. And when I need information that's not publicly available, well, I know a hacker."

She smiled. "Hackers have their uses."

I looked at the paper she had handed me. "Two of these people have the same last name: Thomas and Connor Malvern."

"Yeah, father and son. A family bunching business," she said sarcastically. "Connor is the son. The elder Malvern, Thomas, was the brains of the business and the son was a weak, opportunistic follower. But the other guy – Peter Borchardt – he was a real piece of work. To be honest, he scared me. He was a friend of Connor's and was known to local authorities as someone involved in dog fighting. As for Thomas, he'd be getting a little long in the tooth now, though. And he wasn't particularly healthy even when we knew him. Diabetes and heart disease."

I carefully folded the paper she'd given me. "Thanks, Miranda. My only question about these guys is how they intersect with my suspect list."

"I hear you. I believe they will, though. This sounds like something the Malverns would be involved with, and they probably didn't just toss a dart at a map of Victoria. One of them, or Borchardt, has a connection with someone on your suspect list."

A whining sound came from under Miranda's desk. She moved her chair aside and a black-faced dog who resembled a small German Shepherd emerged.

"Hey, Max," she said to him. "Come out to visit?"

He walked around the desk and put his nose to Lawrence's sneakers.

"This is good," she said in evident surprise. "Lawrence is the first person he's been interested in since he came here."

Lawrence blushed and held his hand out to Max. "Hi, boy," he said tentatively and Max sniffed his fingers.

"Max is a sniffer dog," Miranda said. "He's a Belgian Malinois. They have maybe the most sensitive noses of any dogs. He got a snootful of fentanyl in a raid carried out on a drug house and almost perished from the overdose. His handler, Duncan, was shot and died that day in front of him, so Max was doubly traumatized. The RCMP called me and we took him in. We've had him for about six months. As I said earlier, he's been traumatized. Even animals can get PTSD. And he's in mourning. He misses Duncan."

Max evidently liked Lawrence's scent because he put his front paws on Lawrence's knee and looked up into his face. Lawrence bent over and Max very gently licked his cheek. Then he pawed at Lawrence's leg.

"He wants you to get down on the floor with him," Miranda said in amazement. "Just kneel beside him."

Lawrence gave me once surprised look and knelt on the floor. He patted Max's head and the dog moved closer to him, nudging his arm, which Lawrence closed protectively around him.

"Is this okay?" Lawrence asked.

"It's very much okay," Miranda told him. "I think Max is quite taken with you." She looked over at me and made a motion with her eyes, directing me to look at something on the wall. I did. It was a copy of the famous poem by Oregon poet William Stafford called "Choosing A Dog". I read the first few lines:

"It's love," they say. You touch the right one and
a whole half of the universe wakes up, a new half.

A shivery feeling came over me and I realized I was in the presence of something wonderful. That new half of the universe that Stafford writes about might just be unfolding for Lawrence.

After a long moment, Lawrence looked up at Miranda. "Could I . . . who would I talk to about, well, about adopting him?"

"Me," Miranda said.

"What would I have to do?" Lawrence asked her.

"Think about it for awhile, then come back and talk to me. Max knows a lot of commands, and I'd want to teach them to you. There's paperwork to fill out, too. And you'd have to get ready for him. He needs . . . stuff. A bed, dishes, food."

"Okay," Lawrence said, clearly dazed. "I've never owned a dog, or any animal. But something happened when I put my arm around Max. And his story . . . it really got to me. He lost his best friend." He rose to his feet, clearly reluctant to go. "I'll call you," he told Miranda. "For sure." He looked back down at Max. "Does he shake hands?" he asked her.

"He does," Miranda said. "Just tell him what you want him to do."

"Max," Lawrence said, holding out a hand. "Shake." Max put his paw in Lawrence's hand and they shook. "I'm coming back," Lawrence told him. Max lay down with his head on his paws, his eyes on Lawrence. "Don't worry."

"He knows," Miranda told Lawrence. "He knows."

Miranda walked us to the front door of the sanctuary.

"Good luck," she said. "Call me if you think I can help some more with your case, or if you just want to talk about it. Nice to have met you, Lawrence."

"Uh huh," Lawrence replied in a daze. I had to hold the door so it didn't spring back and hit him.

When we were in my car, driving from the sanctuary back out onto the highway, Lawrence asked me: "Did I make a total fool of myself back there?"

"No, junior," I told him. "You were poleaxed by oxytocin. The attachment hormone. It's a chemical thing. You couldn't help it. You were putty in Max's paws."

He looked dreamily out the window.

"Or," I told him softly, "we could just say you fell in love."

Chapter 13

"HI BOSS, HI Kieran," Aliya said, greeting us as Lawrence and I walked back into Henderson's. We went into Lawrence's office and Aliya followed us, leaning on the doorframe. "Kieran, I printed out the file Lawrence sent me – the one from the alarm company," she said, handing me a sheet of paper.

I looked at it. "Shit," I said, then apologized to Aliya. "Sorry. My language is awful."

"No problem," she said. "I have three brothers."

"Not what you were expecting?" Lawrence asked.

"Not at all," I said. I handed the report to Lawrence.

"Huh," he said. "According to this, Norma's alarm system was armed at 11:44 Sunday night and disarmed at 3:16 Monday morning. Oh, then armed again at 3:18. That's good, right? It confirms what Jen said. She armed it before she went to bed, disarmed it when she let herself out, then armed it again as she was leaving to go to your house."

I briefly thought about tearing my hair out in handfuls. "So we know how the cat thieves *didn't* get in and out, right? They didn't use the front door or the sliding door in the cattery . . . or any of the downstairs windows because they're all on the alarm system."

"Right," he said.

"Can I ask a question?" Aliya said diffidently. "I don't want to butt in."

I looked over at her in surprise. "Sure, ask away."

"It seems to me that one obvious question is –" she broke off uncertainly.

"Go ahead, sweetie," I told her. "I'm baffled. Any question is welcome."

"It's a simple question. Is there a door that *isn't* on the alarm system?"

Aliya looked at me, I looked at Lawrence, and Lawrence looked off into the middle distance, as if reviewing what he had seen at Norma's this morning.

"Well, the front door is on the alarm system," I said. "And so is the sliding door leading from the cattery into the sunroom. I don't believe there is another door, let alone one that isn't on the alarm system. Did you see one, Lawrence? You looked around in the kitchen and dining room."

"Nope."

I thought for a moment. Was there a door that neither Lawrence nor I had noticed? Fooey. There seemed to be no help for it. "We have to go back,'" I told Lawrence, pulling out my phone to call Norma.

"I agree," he said solemnly. "We missed something."

❧

"It's no problem," Norma said as I sheepishly explained what we needed. She walked us toward the kitchen. "There is another door. I didn't mention it because it's not usable. Not anymore. When I had the house remodeled and the alarm system put in, the contractor didn't take the door out, he just . . . disabled it. It's permanently locked. It was a whole lot less money to do that than to take it out and re-construct the wall. It's right through here."

"It's in the kitchen?" Lawrence asked in amazement. "How did I miss it?"

"Well, it's not *in* the kitchen," Norma said. "You'd have had to open the door to the storeroom to find it."

Just to the right of the kitchen counter was a door all right, but it looked like a pantry door to me. I could see why it had fooled Lawrence. It was a trifle too narrow for an outside door, and was painted the same daffodil yellow as the pantry on the adjacent wall.

"This door leads to the storeroom," Norma explained, opening it, and flipping on a light. "I use the storeroom for paper towels, garbage bags, toilet paper, cleaning supplies, Christmas decorations, suitcases, things like that. It used to be a mudroom, I think, before I bought the house. Anyhow, the door that doesn't open is through here. On the back wall of the storeroom. Ta da," she said with a flourish of one hand. "The door used to lead out onto the deck, but as you can see, it doesn't lead anywhere anymore."

"I never guessed," Lawrence said. "Door Number Three."

The storeroom was about eight by eight, hardly more than a mudroom as Norma suggested. Shelving units lined two walls, laden with packages of paper goods, unidentified items in cardboard boxes, suitcases, plastic bins, a couple of huge bags of dog kibble. "Can we go in? " I asked Norma. "I'd like to take a close-up look at the door."

"Oh sure," she said. "You two go ahead. I'll stay here. It's close quarters in there."

Inside the storeroom, Lawrence and I took a couple of steps toward the door – indeed a couple of steps was about all anyone could take – and I examined it carefully. It was a perfectly ordinary, sturdy, brown wooden exterior door with an old lock and a doggie door installed in its bottom third.

"The key to this door?" I called to Norma, who was standing behind us.

"Oh, lost long ago," she said. "When I had the sunroom put on the deck, and the alarm system added, I had all the doors re-keyed. Except this one, of course. The contractor locked it and I guess the key was thrown away. It hasn't been opened since. As you can see, the door doesn't even have a handset. It's just a relic now."

Okay, so there was another door, as Aliya had suggested, but it was a door no one could use. No one except . . . as I was putting my thoughts together, Bear gave a couple of joyous *arf arfs* from the back yard, then rushed in through the doggie door, barreling into Lawrence, almost knocking him off his feet. The plastic flap on the doggie door went *thwack thwack*, Lawrence grabbed me to keep his balance, and we did a crazy polka among the paper goods.

"Ooof, sorry Kieran," Lawrence said, letting me go and stumbling into a tall shelving unit, from which a twelve-pack of toilet paper fell on his head. "Brother," he muttered, putting the toilet paper back in place. He reached to straighten the shelving unit, dislodging a large, thin, slick-finished piece of wood that had been wedged behind it. The doggie door's security panel. Trey had once had a cat door with a security panel just like this, but a lot smaller.

"Bad dog, Bear," Norma said as Bear cavorted in the kitchen. "He's just an exuberant boy," she said to us apologetically.

Bad dog indeed, I thought to myself. That hound is a million dollar liability. But I was more interested in examining the doggie door. An opening about two feet tall and just a little narrower, with a clear plastic flap. And a security panel which could be put in place at night, or whenever Bear was at the kennel. Aha. A metaphorical light went on in my head.

"Did you put the security panel in Bear's doggie door the day you took off for the cat show?" I asked Norma, straightening up.

She shook her head. "No. I left for the cat show on Sunday. I put the panel in when I came back from taking Bear to the kennel the day before – Saturday afternoon. I always do that right after I get home so I don't forget." She frowned. "The odd thing was, though, that it wasn't in when I came back on Tuesday. So maybe I didn't put it in like I thought I did."

"Hmm, are you sure it wasn't in?" I asked her.

"Oh, that I'm sure of," she replied looking indignant. "One of those big bags of dog food on the shelf behind you had been ripped open. Raccoons. I said to myself: 'Norma, you're losing it. You left the panel out!' but I've never done that before." She looked at me entreatingly. "I'm sorry. Maybe I didn't put the panel in on Saturday. I just can't remember. My mind has been occupied with worrying about the cats. Is it important?"

"Probably not," I said reassuringly. "Don't worry about it. Just a detail. I'm a little OCD about details. We've taken up enough of your time. C'mon Lawrence."

Bear and Norma walked us to the front door. "Did you learn what you needed to about the storeroom door?" she asked.

"Thanks," I said. "I did."

"Call if you have more questions," she said.

❧

As we pulled out of Norma's driveway, Lawrence turned to me. "Well, I have questions," he said. "What difference does it make whether Norma put the security panel in the doggie door or not? I mean the storeroom door doesn't open. So why do we care about the doggie door? Or the panel?"

I laughed. "Remember the Beatles' song "She Came In Through The Bathroom Window'?"

"Yeah, I do," he said a little impatiently, "but the downstairs bathroom window is on the alarm system, so no one . . . omigosh, you don't literally mean the bathroom window, do you?"

"Nope." I said.

"You mean someone came in . . . *through the doggie door?* Is that even possible?"

"Sure," I said. "If you're small. Aliya could have gotten in. Or Samir."

"Huh." He was quiet, thinking this over. Then he said: "And we know the panel wasn't in because raccoons were able to come in and raid the dog food. So . . . Norma must have forgotten and left it out. Right?"

"I don't think so," I said. "Putting the panel is something she says she always does as soon as she comes home from taking Bear to the kennel. It's pretty much automatic. No, I think she put it in all right, but someone took it out. So they could . . ." I paused, waiting for him to make the connection.

"Come in through the bathroom window, like the song says. Well, really through the doggie door. Wow." We sat in silence for a moment, then he said: "That was pretty ingenious. Well-planned, too. Any idea who it might have been?"

Who indeed? Answer that one, Kieran, I thought, and you'll have the identity of the cat burglars. Or burglar. For that matter, why was I assuming they were they? One person could easily have pulled off this heist. One small person.

A miserable cold rain began as I turned out onto Oak Bay Avenue and I started the car's wipers. Thunder rumbled somewhere off the tip of the island, and I noticed that most of the light had leaked out of the afternoon. The sky was now opalescent, blotted with dark clouds scudding in from the south. We'd probably have a dandy storm tonight. Ah, spring.

"Let me drop you back at your shop," I told Lawrence. "I need to go talk to someone and ask some questions I really don't want to ask."

"Questions about . . ."

I sighed. "If I were a detective in a potboiler, oh, Sam Spade, or Hercule Poirot, I might say, as corny as it sounds, that this was an inside job."

"An inside job? Do you mean literally? But . . . no one was inside the cattery Sunday night."

"You're wrong," I told him. "Someone was inside."

"What? Who?"

"Jen."

"No!" he said. "It can't be. I know that kid. She can't be involved."

"Oh hell, Lawrence," I said. "Maybe neither of us knows Jen as well as we think we do. Maybe she was mad at Norma for some reason. Maybe she took the security panel out of the doggie door and let the thief or thieves in for reasons we can't even imagine. Maybe money. That's always a good reason."

"I don't believe that," Lawrence said loyally. "Do you? Really?"

"I don't know what to believe. I do know it's time to talk to Jen again, though."

Chapter 14

I'D BELIEVED EVERY word Jen had told me about Sunday night at Wild At Heart. Maybe I shouldn't have. Or maybe she hadn't told me everything. Admittedly, I have a blind spot where Jen is concerned. She's the daughter of my best friend, Zaira Lau, a veterinarian who everyone calls Zee, or Dr. Zee. I'm Jen's godmother, although what kind of religious guidance I could offer the kid if something happened to Zee often flummoxed me. After all, I'd already shared with Jen my God-is-an-alien theory. I just hoped she didn't repeat it.

So, did I see a thirteen-year-old girl who I loved as the mastermind of the theft of the Bengals from Wild At Heart? Well, no. Okay, if she wasn't a criminal mastermind, then, did I see her as an accomplice? Someone who had removed the doggie door panel and shoved it behind the shelving unit knowing that doing so would provide the thief with a way into the cattery? Oh brother. I didn't want to think that. But if not Jen, then who? I knew I needed to see her again, to revisit her story. I hoped I could do it without communicating the doubt I now felt. Doubt is a miserable thing. It's the camel's nose under the tent flap of trust. I hated what I was feeling . . . but the only way to stop feeling it was to talk to Jen again.

My phone buzzed and I looked at it briefly. Email from Edgar. At last: the report on who owned brown Town and Country vans. I'd have to look at it later, though.

The rain had stopped, but the late afternoon sky still looked grey and fretful, as if it might weep at any moment. I filed away thoughts of weeping and shut off my car's wipers, turning off the highway at a spot I knew well: a gravel road identified by a sign that said Z LAU DVM.

I'd known Zee, and Jen, for a long time. I had no idea who Jen's father might be or have been, or even if he was a Lau, and Zee had never enlightened me. As long as I had known her there had only been Zee and Jen, a mother and daughter of plainly Asian descent. Some days I believed Zee's ancestry was Chinese, some days Vietnamese or Cambodian, but that was another piece of herself that she did not want to share. I sensed a mystery there, but I'd never pried. Zee was my friend, Jen's mother, Trey's vet. Whoever else she was was her own affair.

And although she maintained a vet clinic here north of the city, and treated the ill and injured who were brought to her, what she really loved was the challenge of animal misbehavior. Or what distressed owners called animal misbehavior. Zee maintained that the problem usually lay with owners' thick-headedness. Among her memorable clients were a boa constrictor who hugged her owner's boyfriends too enthusiastically on sleepovers; a Scottie who was driven to shrieking fits whenever anyone stepped on the third board of the staircase; and a Siamese cat who waited for the mail and shredded her owner's brokerage statements. Of course Zee treated run-of-the-mill cases of feline sofa-shredding and canine leg-humping, but I suspected she lived for the covetous boas and off-the-beam Scotties. I was hoping that the book she was writing would feature more such lurid tales.

The gravel road to Zee's ten acres wound in and out among the gnarled trees of an old nut orchard . . . almonds or hazelnuts, I could never remember which . . . and eventually opened up onto a large meadow. I knew that in only weeks the expanse would be vivid with wildflowers and noisy with birds. Now, however, it resembled the meadow which Keats' knight-at-arms bemoaned in the poem about the faithless faerie lover: withered sedge and silent birdsong. Ah well, to everything there is a season, right?

Zee's practice and home comprised a two-story cedar-shingled house and an adjacent barn. A fenced pasture near the barn accommodated equine clients, and I saw Zee in the pasture: a small figure in a black turtleneck and tan cargo pants, walking a white horse with brown spots on its rump. She saw me drive up and called to someone in the barn. A red-headed girl with braids hurried into the pasture, a young woman named Ginny, I recalled, a veterinary student with a particular interest in horses. Good luck with that. I had been up on a horse exactly once, at age fourteen, and my canter ended badly when the horse spooked at god-knows-what and decided the wisest thing to do was to hurl me into the ditch and gallop home to the barn. I landed in the weeds with a wrenched shoulder, had to walk miles back to the riding stables, and never set foot in a stirrup again.

Zee waved, handing the horse's reins to Ginny.

"Go ahead into the house, Kieran," she called. "You can start water boiling for tea. I need to talk to Ginny for a moment."

In Zee's kitchen I filled a blue iron kettle, put it on the stove to boil, and found two mugs and some Oolong teabags in a cupboard. Unless Zee had some yummy carbohydrate treat, that would be it for teatime. I took a seat at the scrubbed pine table, wondering where Jen was. In times past, she would have noticed my car drive up and come to join us. Hmm.

"I imagine this is not completely a social visit," Zee called from the front hall, exchanging her muddy outdoor shoes for a pair of soft moccasins.

"Not completely, I agreed.

"The cats," Zee said, going to the sink and washing her hands. "Jen told me the story."

"And the dogs," I added. "Neighborhood pets."

"How many animals are missing?" she asked, preparing tea.

"Twenty-six animals belonging to twelve owners." Somehow, saying the numbers aloud made things infinitely worse. When it had been just "the animals" or "the cats and dogs" it was bad enough. But each one of these animals had a name, and place in someone's heart. I'd been trying not to think about that.

"I can see you have taken each owner's sadness upon yourself," Zee said, handing me a mug of tea. "They are like weights. They lie heavily on you."

"Yeah, well," I equivocated, clearing my throat, "it's not me I'm here about. It's Jen."

Zee took a seat at the table and looked at me over the rim of her mug. "Are you sure about that?"

I dodged Zee's efforts at inviting me to talk. "I'm sure. How is Jen taking all this?"

Zee shrugged. "Not well. She believes the theft of the cats was due to some negligence on her part. She is doing penance cleaning out the horse stalls."

"Ugh."

Zee looked at me appraisingly. "You want to talk to Jen to remove some doubt that you have in your mind. It is like a pebble in your shoe. Walking freely is not possible until you remove it."

I sighed. "Yeah, it's a little like that. But . . ."

"But?"

"But I don't know how to talk to her about this. She'll think I suspect her."

"Do you?"

"Maybe. Of something. Not of taking the cats herself, or even being the mastermind of the pet thefts. But maybe she inadvertently . . . helped somehow. Enabled the theft." I shook my head.

"I think you can discover that," Zee said. "That is what you do, correct? You talk to people, you discover things. Sometimes they are separate, discrete facts. Like unconnected dots. But you always connect them."

I snorted. "Flatterer."

Zee raised an eyebrow. "Does anything else worry you about talking to Jen?"

I blew out a big breath. "Yeah. I don't want to have to tell her the possible, no probable, fate of the animals."

"Which is?"

I looked over my shoulder to make certain that Jen was not within earshot. I was pretty sure she was in the barn, but the last thing I wanted was for her to overhear what I was about to say. "That they were probably taken by bunchers and are now crowded together in some shitty, inadequate caging awaiting a trip to an educational institution or a pharmaceutical company's lab."

"Ah," Zee said sadly. "I thought as much when Jen told me about the thefts. I can see why you would want to protect her from such a horror."

"So if she asks me, I might have to flat out lie to her. But at the same time, I want to be sure that *she* is telling *me* the truth. What hypocrisy."

Zee shook her head. "There is nothing intrinsically noble about truth-telling, Kieran. Sometimes the young need protection from it."

"That's what I thought," I told her. "I just wanted to be certain you agreed."

"I do," Zee said. "I'll make some more tea and thaw some cookies that Jen made recently. Why don't you go out to the barn, then persuade her to come in once you've finished talking? I think the words will come once you begin."

❧

I found Jen in the back of the barn in one of the empty horse stalls, a red wheelbarrow full of horse manure beside her.

"Hey, kiddo," I called softly. "This looks like more work than Hercules had to do at the Augean stables."

"Ha," she said, leaning on her shovel and looking at me with reddened eyes. Either she hadn't been sleeping much, or had been crying, or both. She was wearing an old denim jacket with holes in the elbows, and a stained pair of jeans. Her boots were caked with mud and clumps of whatever smelly stuff she was shoveling. She hadn't bothered to gel her hair and it flopped limply over her forehead. Something was very wrong when a thirteen-year-old girl neglected her coiffure. "You haven't found them, have you?" she asked me hopelessly, peeling off her work gloves and stuffing them in a back pocket.

"Nope," I said. "But I'm closer. Come and talk to me?" I sat on a bale of straw and patted a place beside me.

She stood her shovel against the wheelbarrow and sat down heavily.

"I dream about them at night," she said at length. "Especially Wild Thing, the kitten I was working with." She pulled some pieces of straw out of the bale we were sitting on and shredded them between her fingers. "I got very attached to him. In fact, I was going to ask Norma if I could adopt him. He wasn't doing well with his siblings. He's a lot smaller than they are and I think they frighten him. His mother didn't seem to want him either. When he was tiny, she would move him over to one side of the cage, like she was discarding him. I had to bottle feed him. If he'd been a barn cat, I don't think he'd be alive now. Mother cats sometimes do those things," she informed me wisely. "They have their reasons." She threw the pieces of straw on the stable floor. "Adopting him would have meant a lot of money, but well, I have my savings. And my job. Or I *had* my job. I doubt if Norma's going to want to hire me again."

"Adopting Wild Thing, that seems like a reasonable expenditure," I told her.

She looked sidelong at me. "Yeah? But we have to find him, don't we? Not just him. Them. All of them."

"Yeah, we do," I said, accepting the offer of assistance implicit in 'we', "and that's why I'm here. I've been trying to figure some things out and I think you can help me."

"Me? How?" she asked.

"There's something that doesn't add up about the theft from Wild At Heart," I said.

She turned her head and looked at me. I saw misery in her eyes and despair, along with a smidgen of hope. I took a deep breath, planning to get her talking and keep her talking. "Tell me what it was like to work for Norma. Who came around when you were there?"

"Well, I usually went there on Saturdays," Jen said thoughtfully. "Sometimes after school, but usually on Saturdays."

"Okay." I mentally consulted the list of people Norma had given me. "What about Norma's daughter, Heather. Did you ever meet her?"

"Yeah, maybe two or three times. She was bringing mushrooms to a restaurant in Victoria and stopped by."

"What did you think of her? Did you like her? Did she like the cats?"

"Well, I didn't much like her because she and Norma argued. I don't think she *disliked* the cats, but she didn't gush over them or anything."

"What did they argue about? Could you hear?"

"Yeah, I heard. Most of it, I guess. They argued at the kitchen table. Sometimes over tea. I was just around the corner in the cattery. It was, well, embarrassing." Jen shook her head. "Isn't this gossiping, Kieran?"

"No, sweetie. It's not. This is an investigation. You're just answering questions. "

"Okay", Jen said. "As long as it's not gossip. Heather didn't like the fact that Norma spent so much money on her cat breeding business."

Interesting. "What made you think that?"

"She said so. She said once to Norma that she didn't know why she was doing this – breeding cats that looked wild, renovating her house for more space for the cattery, spending tons of money flying off to cat shows. She said one or two ordinary cats were enough for anyone and that Norma was obsessed. A crazy cat lady."

I laughed. "I don't think crazy cat ladies breed exotic cats. I think crazy cat ladies have thirty-four cats in a single-wide trailer and are probably hoarders, but I get it. Heather didn't approve of her mother's devotion to her cats and to Wild At Heart."

"No she didn't," Jen said. "She told Norma that she should spend her retirement money going on trips or cruises. Enjoying herself. But it's really none of Heather's business, is it? I mean, it's Norma's life. Look at what Heather and her husband do – raise mushrooms That's kind of weird. Weirder than breeding Bengals."

"It's weird all right," I agreed. So things were not exactly harmonious between Norma and her daughter. Well, her eyes had told me that when we were talking earlier, so I wasn't surprised about the confirmation. Did I think Heather had something to do with the Bengals' theft? Well, no. I was glad Jen had told me about the friction between Norma and Heather, though. Probably the most Heather was guilty of was her particular event in the usual mother-daughter relationship Olympics.

"Anything else about Heather?" I asked Jen.

"Well, yeah, one thing." Jen looked over at me, frowning. "She asked Norma how her conscience would let her breed cats, you know, bring more kittens into the world when the shelters were full of cats literally dying for homes. Like the Bengals were the reason cats were put to sleep in shelters. That really bothered me, Kieran."

"Wow," I said. "She pulled out all the stops, didn't she? That was a low blow."

Jen nodded miserably. "But is it true?"

"Well, it's true that shelters are very crowded. But times have changed. Most shelters are no-kill, meaning that animals are kept until they find homes. Heather's implying that the breeding of a few exotic cats is the reason for shelters being overcrowded is just plain wrong. I'm sorry she said that and upset you."

I could see the relief in Jen's eyes.

"Look, kiddo, if all the cat breeders in the country went out of business tomorrow, the situation in shelters would remain the same. People who want to own exotic cats are just . . . different from people who want to adopt from shelters. If someone couldn't own, say a Toyger, they probably wouldn't go to a shelter for a tabby. People who want exotic cats want, well, living room leopards." I shook my head, angry at Heather for putting this idea in Jen's head, for inducing guilt in her. "Shelters are overcrowded because irresponsible cat owners don't get their cats spayed. Or neutered. It's easy to blame breeders, but they're not the problem. People's distractedness or laziness or ignorance is the problem."

Jen nodded. "I kinda thought so."

"Did you and Norma ever talk about this?" I asked her.

"No," Jen said. "And I don't think it bothered her." She made a rueful face. "It just bothered me because I didn't know if it was true or not. I wouldn't want to think that I . . . was helping to do something wrong."

"You weren't," I said firmly, wanting to strangle Norma's daughter. "And Heather was a butt-head to have brought the subject up. I think she was just pulling out all the stops to get her mother to slow down and enjoy being retired."

"Okay," Jen said.

"Who else did you run into at the cattery?" I asked.

Jen frowned in thought. "I met Norma's regular pet sitter a couple of times. Emily. I like her. She's bubbly. And she really liked the cats a lot, of course. She came a couple times to drop off catnip toys. She makes them. They're cool."

"Did you ever see what make of cars Heather and Emily drove?"

"Cars? Oh, I get it. Something the cats could have been loaded into." She shook her head. "Heather had a red van with the name of the mushroom farm on the sides. When I went to let Emily in, she was driving something blue and small. Maybe a Toyota. I don't know much about cars, but I don't think she could have fit all those cat carriers inside it. Well, maybe she could have, if she squished them all together on the back seat." She looked at me appraisingly. "I think I see what you're doing."

"Oh?"

Jen nodded wisely. "Trying to eliminate suspects. Right?"

"Right." I said. Thinking guiltily of suspects, I decided abruptly to tell Jen what I had figured out about how the theft had happened. Well, part of it, anyhow. Not the inside job part. She was a smart kid – I wanted her to come to that conclusion herself. When I told her about the doggie door and the security panel, her eyes flew open wide.

"Wow. They got in and out through the doggie door? So you think that maybe Norma forgot to put the panel in?"

"Maybe," I said. "But she's pretty definite about the fact that she put it in on Saturday after she came home from taking Bear to the kennel."

Jen nodded, clearly thinking.

Dammit, I had to ask the question. "Did you notice that the panel wasn't in the doggie door when you went into the storeroom on Sunday?"

Jen shook her head. "I didn't go into the storeroom on Sunday. I mostly don't. There isn't anything I need in there – it's house-cleaning stuff, I think. Norma keeps the cats' food and litter in that closet in the cattery. I can see why you're stumped, though," she continued, turning to look at me.

"You can?" I asked. My stomach clenched. Okay, here it came. Was this the moment when I would know if she was guilty? Of something?

She nodded. "I can see why you're asking about who came around Norma's and what I thought about them. Because one of them has to be well, the person who planned the theft, right? And maybe that same person took the panel out of the doggie door and carried the cats away."

Her dark eyes were clear and guileless. What I saw in them was puzzled concern . . . definitely for the missing cats, and possibly for me, the hapless investigator.

Jen nodded again and turned away from me. But I had seen what I needed to see – she was not guilty of anything. She had not been part of this crime. We sat in silence together, the white horse with brown spots stirring in his stall, whickering once. Outside the late afternoon had grown brighter and rays of sun shone through spaces between the barnwood planks like the probing of magician's swords. I decided to talk to Jen about the theft again.

"Jen, help me think about who could have planned the theft. I think you're right when you said the same person probably took the cats. I think so, too. But that someone knew when Norma was going to be away at the cat show. They also knew Emily didn't sleep over. What they didn't know was that you were going to be there. You were very lucky. Anyhow, do you have any ideas about who might have known Norma's plans?" Had Jen inadvertently passed the information about Norma's absence to someone she shouldn't have?

"Well, it wasn't like it was a secret," Jen said matter-of-factly. "Norma had all her appointments written on that dry erase calendar above her desk."

I remembered the calendar. "Yeah, I saw it. The question is: who else saw it?"

"Heather or Emily could have seen it," Jen said, then shook her head. "Emily for sure. I don't think Heather even went into the cattery the times I saw her, though."

"Norma said she had a computer tech come out to work on her laptop recently. Apparently he asked lots of questions about the cats."

"Yeah," Jen said. "I drove up on my bike when he was still there. He came in a little white car from that computer repair place on Oak Bay Avenue. There was a sign on his car. They were working on the laptop at the dining room table, though. He wasn't in the cattery."

"Okay."

"But," Jen said, turning to look at me, "Stephanie would have seen it."

"Who?"

"Stephanie. Norma's cleaning lady. She came on Saturdays. She cleaned the whole house. The cattery, too."

"Oh? Tell me about Stephanie, sweetie."

"Well, I liked her at first. But not after a while."

"No? Why not?"

"You kind of know when someone's pretending to be . . . someone they aren't, right?"

"And Stephanie pretended to be someone she wasn't? How so?"

Jen sighed. "She really didn't like Norma's cats. But she let on that she did. Of course they were all in their cages when she came to clean the house, but she never, you know, talked to them, or went over to the cages to pet any of them."

"So she wasn't a cat lover. Is that all you didn't like about her?"

"I guess," Jen said, biting her lower lip and looking down at her boots. "No, there's something else, too."

"Uh huh?"

"She asked me how much it would cost to adopt one of Norma's kittens. I thought this was pretty strange considering she didn't really like them, so I tried not to give her an answer. I told her Norma charged different prices for show cats and pet cats so it would depend upon the kitten. Which is true. But it wasn't the whole truth. Was that wrong?" she asked, looking up at me. "I know how much Norma charges but I just didn't want her to have one of Norma's kittens."

"No, I don't think that was wrong. After all, she could have looked on Norma's website. But did Stephanie ask you again about prices?"

"No. She just left it. I ended up telling her she needed to ask Norma about adopting. But I don't think that Norma would have seen her as a good adopter."

"Why not?"

"Well, I'm sorry about how this may sound, but could she really afford one? It's not just the adoption fee, it's the vet bills, and the food, and all the other cat expenses. I've heard Norma talking on the phone about all this to potential adopters. And if Stephanie was working, the kitten would be alone a lot. Norma wouldn't want that. Worse than that . . ."

"Worse than that?"

"Oh, I'll just say it. She never seemed very . . . sharp, you know? When I talked to her, she just seemed out of it. Like in a daze. Cleaning Norma's place seemed like it was hard work for her. And speaking of work, she was late more often than she was on time."

"That was okay with Norma? Stephanie's being late?"

"I don't know," Jen said. "I never said anything to Norma about her coming late when I was there. Or that I didn't like her."

We sat in silence for a minute and then Jen asked: "Do you think Stephanie was involved?"

"I don't know, Jen," I said honestly. "I'm still trying to figure things out. Maybe, though. Was she at Norma's last Saturday?"

Jen nodded. "Yeah. I brought my stuff in the afternoon just after she left. Norma mentioned she's been there. Norma and I had dinner together then she went to bed early. She was gone when I got up on Sunday morning."

"Hmm," I said. "Well, there's no harm in wondering about Stephanie's involvement. Heck, someone was responsible. Someone who knew Norma's plans. Listen, your mom wanted me to ask you to come on into the house when you're done here. Apparently we're having some cookies you baked a while ago."

"Don't tell anyone I bake, okay?" Jen whispered.

I laughed out loud. "Certainly not. I won't ruin your rep, kiddo. But who would I tell? Trey? He'd want you to bake him some salmon fritters." I ruffled her hair. "Finish up here. See you in the kitchen."

❧

As I walked from the barn across the yard and into the house, I realized that I'd removed the metaphorical pebble from my shoe. Not having it there sure as hell felt good. I was glad for many reasons that I had decided to talk to Jen again, but perhaps the most important outcome of our talk had been that I learned three very important pieces of information. One, that Jen, who was an excellent judge of character, hadn't liked Stephanie; two, that Stephanie hadn't particularly liked the Bengals, but was sure interested in how much she would have to pay for one; and three, that Stephanie had been at work at Wild At Heart on Saturday.

"Jen said she'd come in for tea in a bit," I told Zee. "She wants to finish shoveling horse manure first."

Zee looked up from the report she was reading at the kitchen table. "How are you feeling now after talking with her?" she asked me.

"Better as far as Jen is concerned. Much better. Of course she didn't have anything to do with this. But otherwise . . . I feel as though my brain is a ball of yarn bristling with ends. I don't know which one to pull first. And I'm scared to death I'll waste time pulling the wrong ones. It's making me panic. I need a magic decoder ring or a sorting hat." I looked at my watch. "Actually, I need to go home and fret," I told Zee. "I'll have to sample Jen's cookies another time. Will you make my apologies to her?"

Chapter 15

A T HOME I fed the cats another dinner of halibut minus batter, producing a near-swoon from Trey.

"You guys are the fortunate beneficiaries of my distractedness," I told the cats, dividing the fish into two bowls and placing one on the kitchen floor and one in the pantry on Vlad's shelf. "Maybe I'll get to the supermarket tomorrow. And maybe not. So let's all give thanks to Old British Fish and Chips."

I ate my own dinner – a piece of halibut, a small container of cole slaw (I'm sure there was something green in it), and a piece of garlic bread – at the kitchen table, then tossed the plastic utensils and styrofoam containers into the trash. For a few moments I just sat there, waiting for a pot of coffee to drip, gathering my wits. Then, with a sigh, I got up and fetched my laptop, a lined yellow tablet and some pens, the hard copies I'd printed out of files I had received from Finn, Norma, and Edgar, and arranged everything on the table in front of me. Then I settled back with Finn's four-page long list of contacts drawn up by the people from whom pets had been stolen. I experienced only one confidence-withering stab of panic as I looked at the list, and the two additional lists, equally long, waiting for me. Was I not smart, confident and persistent? Hmmf. Taking a few sips of what I was certain would not be my last cup of coffee, I began to look for names in common. It was going to be a long night.

∾

Midnight. Trey had long since deserted me and one leg had gone to sleep. Abandoning my lists, I got up, stretched, and decided to take a few laps around the living room.

The list Finn had e-mailed me contained seventy-six names; Norma's list contained twelve; Edgar's list of van owners was an appalling 127; and Miranda's suspect list *mirabile dictu*, was only three. I wrote them all down and just started eliminating people.

Janet the newspaper carrier delivered to eight people, but she was sixty-something. I considered her unlikely. Sure, she might have provided information to someone, but I just didn't think so. Five individuals had their lawns cut and flowerbeds weeded by a kid named Jason, but he was seventeen and, as I had learned from Norma, he drove a red pickup and lived with his parents in the neighborhood. Three of the people who had had pets stolen used Emily the petsitter, but my gut, as well as Jen's description of her, told me no. A buncher who made cat toys? Nah. Two people had used the same roofing company; two had used the Oak Bay computer repair shop; and two people had had redwood bark delivered by the same plant nursery. Equally unlikely, I thought. These were all small, local businesses with websites and, I was sure, an extensive list of references. I couldn't see any of them running an animal theft business on the side.

However, four people had used a cleaning lady whose name was Stephanie. Only Norma's list identified her as Stephanie Walters. However, I noticed that several other entries in Finn's list did not contain last names either. Jason the lawn guy, Janet the paper deliverer. Maybe their employers couldn't produce them in the rush to send information to Finn. Probably no big deal.

My mind circled back to Stephanie the cleaning lady. Was she worth looking into? I decided yes. Especially since what Jen had told me about her seemed well, off. I snorted. Who else did I have? All those names and one suspect? Well, that didn't matter if it was the right suspect.

I lay on the couch in the dark and thought. What about Miranda's suspects: Thomas Malvern, his son Connor, and their buddy Peter Blanchard? They had nothing in common with the pet owners, or with Norma. They were not on any of the lists. And they had nothing in common with Stephanie as far as I knew. Yet there must be an intersection. If the guys Miranda had given me were indeed the bunchers, how had they decided to pick this unlikely, affluent Oak Bay neighborhood?

I walked back to the kitchen and looked at Edgar's list of Town and Country van owners – all six dismaying pages of it. Hell, there was nothing for it but to begin reading. So I began: Arnott, Bechtel, Cunard, Dodson, Edgerton. Time passed. No names jumped out at me. No names matched the names on Finn's, Norma's or Miranda's lists. I was rapidly becoming gritty of eye and short of temper. Maybe I needed coffee . . . or just one shot of Method and Madness. Maybe I should stop here and take this up tomorrow. Or maybe I could look at just a few more names. Macintosh, Nelson, Owens, Parker. No Malvern. Oh, hell, might as well continue on to the z's. So I did. Aggravatingly, as I read past the w's, no Walters. And no matches to the other lists. Well, what had I expected? I smothered a twinge of disappointment as well as a yammering *what now?* that bubbled up from somewhere in my id. Lists and databases. They're great when they contain what you need, but when they fail you, what then?

Before I had a chance to think more about how the hell to proceed, my phone warbled. It was Dutch. Wow, it was close to midnight and he was still on the job?

"Kieran," he said as I answered, "Sorry to call so late. But I wanted to report in. And I just learned something that might be helpful."

"No problem," I told him.

"I'm a night owl. What's up?"

"I have bad news and possibly relevant news."

"Let's have the bad news first."

"Well, I heard from the people who drove around to private shelters, pet stores, county and city animal facilities, you know, every possibility they could think of. They took photos of the animals with them. Nothing."

"Okay, so now we know the animals weren't taken out of spite and dumped at a shelter or a pet store." Of course, they could have been stolen out of spite and dumped in the woods, but I really didn't think so. "What's the possibly relevant news?"

"One of the pet owners, a woman named Fiona – she lost two Siamese cats – has been monitoring the newspapers and online For Sale sites, including Kijiji. She turned up an interesting ad."

"You're killing me with suspense, Dutch. What did it say?"

"Bengal kittens for sale. Of course it could mean nothing. It could be another breeder advertising kittens."

"Jesus. Did she call the number? Please tell me she didn't."

"No. She didn't. I think I made it clear to everyone that they were to leave the investigating to you. We don't want to scare anyone off."

"Good work. Give me the number."

He did and I jotted it down at the top of the list of van owners that Edgar had sent me.

"Was there a website?" I asked. "If it's a legitimate breeder advertising kittens, there ought to be a website."

"No, nothing like that. Just a number. No name, either."

"Did the ad mention prices?"

"Yes, kittens starting at $500."

"Bargain Bengals," I snorted. "Either this is a scam and they're really tabbies, or . . ."

"Or it could be someone with Norma's kittens trying to get rid of them at bargain prices."

"Yeah, it certainly could be. In any event, I'll have to wait to call the number tomorrow. I don't want to seem too eager. Thanks, Dutch."

"Say, if you need me to help in any way . . . my business has a van. For when you find the animals."

I smiled. That made a total of three offers I'd had for transport: one from Olga and Ellen, one from Miranda, and now this one from Dutch. Such confidence was daunting. Now if I could only live up to it. "I'll call you if I need you, Dutch. Thanks for the offer. And thank Fiona for me, please."

All right. What in hell was going on? Bengals for sale? Someone had finally twigged to the fact that the eleven Bengals which had been stolen to round out a buncher's quota would be worth considerably more if sold to individuals wanting exotic pets than to an animal dealer?

Hardly daring to hope, I grabbed my list of suspects, looking hurriedly down the list of contacts Norma had given me. There. There was the number I was searching for. Now, where in hell was the number Dutch had just given me? I knew I scrawled it down as we were talking, but where? I spent a few panicked seconds locating it, then hardly daring to hope, compared the two phone numbers. Holy shit. They were the same. Stephanie Walters was the Bengal kittens' advertiser.

There was one last thing I needed to do, one last "i" to dot.

I looked at my watch. Just after midnight. I hoped it wasn't too late."

"Hey, kiddo," I said when Jen answered her phone. "Sorry if I woke you."

"I wasn't really asleep" she said. "I haven't been sleeping well, since . . . you know."

"Yeah, I know. Say, I have an odd question to ask you. It's about Stephanie."

Stephanie," she said, clearly perplexed. "Okay."

"Tell me about her butt."

"Her . . . butt?"

"Yeah. Is it small? Smaller than mine? Smaller than yours?"

"Definitely smaller than yours. And smaller than mine, too. Remember I said she looked unhealthy? Well, she's like, really, really skinny, Kieran."

"Huh. Okay, kiddo. Go back to sleep."

"What? Is that all? You can't tell me why you want to know?"

I sighed. "That's all I can tell you now. Talk to you later."

I ended the call, feeling punch-drunk from mingled exhaustion and exhilaration.

"Got you!" I yelled in triumph. "Got you, Stephanie. I bet you fit through the doggie door just fine. After you pushed those squishy cat carriers full of Bengals out ahead of you."

I shut off the kitchen light, leaving everything where it was on the table. I'd get back to thinking about this tomorrow. Formulate a plan. Right now, however, I needed to sleep. Yawning, I undressed in the bedroom in the dark, tossed my clothes over the rocking chair, and slipped between my comfy flannel sheets. My feet found the warm, furry mound of Trey who grumbled a little but didn't stir.

"Good boy," I told him, stroking him with one foot, then fell into the embrace of sleep.

WEDNESDAY

Chapter 16

THE DAY DAWNED cold, grey, and drizzly – perfect spring weather in Victoria, I thought. Where were the crocuses or the rosebuds or the robins on the wing anyhow? I felt bleary and a trifle bloody-minded. A hot shower helped with bleary but did nothing to improve bloody-minded. Dammit all, it was Wednesday. The neighborhood pets had now been missing for three full days, the Bengals for two days and three nights, and my ire for the animal thieves was growing by the hour. I had had an idea overnight, but to carry it out I needed Lawrence's help. I figured seven wouldn't be too early to phone him – after all, weren't all entrepreneurial young lads awake, up, showered, and bushy-tailed by seven?

I threw on clean socks and underwear, plucked yesterday's turtleneck and cords from the rocking chair, laced up my sneakers, and declared myself ready for the day. When my watch told me it was 7:01 I called Lawrence.

"Kieran?" he croaked, sounding as though he were at the bottom of a well. "Is everything okay?"

"Everything is definitely not okay," I told him, filling him in on how Stephanie had been the one who came in through the bathroom window, so to speak and was even now hawking the Bengals for sale on Kajiji.

"Holy smoke," he said, gratifyingly impressed. "She's got some nerve. Did you call the number Dutch gave you?"

"No, junior. That's why I'm calling you. I have a plan and it involves you. Are you free this morning?"

"I can be," he said, sounding more focused. "Aliya and Samir can open the shop."

"Actually, I need Aliya too. I want you guys to do a little play acting: to pretend to be a couple eager to adopt two Bengal kittens. Do you think she'd be willing?"

"Probably," Lawrence said. "She's quite interested in this case, and I think she'd be thrilled to be involved. I can call her."

"I'd appreciate that. But first, I need you to call the number Dutch gave me and talk to Stephanie. I don't want my phone number recorded on her phone. I don't want her or her accomplices to hear my voice. I have plans for them."

"Gotcha," Lawrence said. "I'll call when we hang up. Want me to arrange a meeting to get the kittens?"

"Exactly. Ask her to meet you at McDonald's on Pandora," I said. "Why don't you set the meeting up for early this morning? Then call me back. I'll be here. I have some work to do on my computer."

"Will do," Lawrence said. "I'll get back to you as soon as I can."

I started a pot of coffee and turned on my laptop: time to do a little investigating courtesy of my online people-finding service. I typed Stephanie Walters' name and city into the search program, hit GO, then drummed my fingers impatiently on the table as the service's search engine scanned the hundreds of public records from which their reports were generated. Sitting still suddenly became intolerable, and I got up to make sure the cats' kibble and water bowls were filled for the day. I poured coffee, found some stale peanut butter cookies in the cupboard, then sat down to see what my cybersleuthing service had turned up.

Stephanie Walters was twenty-four, unmarried, and lived in Saanich, although the address given was a P.O. Box. Hmm. Well, I could track down her physical address later. However, the report did include a phone number – the cell phone number she had given her employers, and the number Dutch had given me last night. I shook my head. It would have been so easy to have bought a burner phone for her Kajiji advertisement. Then no one could have matched Stephanie the cleaning lady and Stephanie the Bengal thief. Including me. Ah well. I guessed she figured she hadn't needed two phone numbers. Either she was inordinately careless or inordinately stupid. I voted for the latter.

Before I could think more about this, my phone warbled. Lawrence.

"Done," he said excitedly. "A woman answered and sounded pretty darned eager that my, um, girlfriend and I wanted to adopt two Bengal kittens. She did tell us to be sure to bring a thousand dollars in cash. Jeez, Kieran," he said, wounding worried, "are you going to get this back?"

"You betcha, junior," I told him grimly. "Every penny. How is Aliya feeling about this deception?"

"She sounded fine about it," he said. "In fact, she sounded pleased that you wanted to involve her. She wondered if we needed to bring a cat carrier along."

"Yeah. I'll bring Trey's. When are the prospective adopters due at McDonald's?"

"Nine."

"Okay. Why don't I meet you two at your shop, in say, half an hour. And junior?"

"Yeah?"

"Good work. See you there."

I parked on Oak Bay Avenue in front of Lawrence's shop, right behind his green Range Rover. Lawrence and Aliya hurried out and I met them on the sidewalk. I handed Lawrence a brown envelope and it hurt me to part with it: a thousand dollars in hundreds.

"The money," I said. He gulped and put it in an inside pocket of his leather jacket. "Don't hand it over until you have the kittens. And remember to tell her that you have an aunt who might be interested in two Bengal kittens also. Your whole family is crazy about Bengals." He nodded. "Here's what we'll do. I'm assuming she'll bring them in one of the carriers stolen from Wild At Heart. So you two will transfer them to Trey's carrier, then take off for Zee's. I want Zee to check them out before I call Norma and hand them over. I've already called her, so she'll be expecting them. Then I'm going to follow Stephanie. At least that's my plan."

"Sounds good," Lawrence said, then got behind the wheel of the Range Rover.

Aliya walked with me to my car and I gave her Trey's orange cat carrier. She stowed it on the back seat of the Range Rover, then hesitated on the sidewalk.

"Are you really okay about this?" I asked her.

"I am asking you to lie and dissemble, after all. Lawrence can go by himself if you'd rather not."

"No, I'm okay with it," she said as we stood there in the drizzle.

"I know what we're doing is right."

"Good," I told her, "because I have something else I need you to do. Apart from being charming and eager, besotted with Bengals, and Lawrence's girlfriend, that is."

She laughed. "Okay, what else?"

I handed her a small round black plastic device about the size of a quarter. "Take this," I said. "I've never tried it out but it's supposed to be a great tracking device for pets. It has a GPS locator in it." She looked at it and nodded, comprehension dawning.

"I get it. You want me to plant this somewhere on the woman who shows up with the kittens. Like in a pocket. Or in her car. Once we actually have the kittens, that is."

"Right, I said. "Drop it someplace inconspicuous."

"How does it work?"

"I have its app on my phone. I can track it in real time if I'm not too far away. If I lose her, it'll give me a fix on its last known location."

"You're going after her, aren't you?"

"You betcha."

"Where will you be while we're in the restaurant?"

"In the parking lot. Lawrence knows to call me after you get the kittens. Just to tell me you've been successful. Okay?"

"Okay," she said, brown eyes wide.

"Then what?"

"Then you two take them to my friend Zee's and I follow Stephanie."

If she had been Lawrence I would have administered a sisterly good-luck punch to the shoulder. Instead I tried a reassuring smile and said: "Let's go get those Bengals."

☙

Things went pretty much to hell in the McDonald's parking lot. As that canny Scot Robbie Burns said in his poem about the mouse: the best laid schemes o' mice an' men gang aft agley. Yes indeed. Agley was about right.

Anyhow, I arrived at McDonald's just before nine and parked in a space near the entrance from which I had a good view of the door. Lawrence's Range Rover was already in the lot, and a small, dirty black Honda with a dented front fender was parked two down from him. Stephanie's Honda. Just as Jen had described it to me. I assumed the Bengals were in the black Honda (I took a photo of the car's license plate) so the gang was all there. Afterwards, I wondered why I didn't just pop the lock on Stephanie's car door, stash the kittens, carrier and all, in my car, wait for Lawrence, Aliya, and Stephanie to come out of the restaurant, grab Stephanie, retrieve my thousand dollars, drive her to some secluded forest clearing, and bludgeon the truth out of her. But I didn't. I was still on board with Plan A, which called for stealth and finesse. I suppose it was hubris, the tragic flaw so beloved of Greek dramatists, that did me in. I had thought up an ingenious scheme and of course things would unfold according to my script. Right? Right.

About ten minutes after I arrived at McDonald's, Lawrence, Aliya, and a small, pale, cadaverously skinny woman in her twenties, dressed in black jeans and a faded denim jacket, dark hair tied up in a ponytail, came out of the restaurant. I was surprised. Why hadn't they stayed for breakfast? I was hoping Lawrence and Aliya could get Stephanie talking, not only to introduce the idea of the Bengal-loving aunt, but to try to suss out how many more of Norma's Bengals she might have for sale. Evidently that wasn't going to happen. Puzzled, I watched as Stephanie hurried over to the Honda, fetched a black soft-sided cat carrier out of the back seat, and carried it over to Lawrence's Range Rover. There were a few moments of fumbling awkwardness as Aliya peered into the cat carrier, then took it in her arms. Lawrence exchanged a few words with Stephanie and handed her the brown envelope containing my cash. Then several things happened at once. Aliya put the cat carrier in the back of the Range Rover, looked around the parking lot, saw my car, and came running toward me. Evidently alarmed, Stephanie gave me and my car one appraising look, got into the Honda, backed out, then laid rubber out of the parking lot. Lawrence had to jump out of the way to avoid being hit.

"Shit!" I yelled, seeing Stephanie drive away.

"Kieran!" Aliya said, seizing the Karmann Ghia's door handle. "The kittens!"

A horrid feeling of dread seized me as I hurried with Aliya back to the Range Rover.

"In the back," Aliya said.

I kneeled down to look in the carrier and the smell assailed me first. Diarrhea. "What the hell?" I asked. The kittens were wrapped in towels and what I could see of their fur looked wet and disheveled. Climbing onto the back seat, I carefully unzipped the carrier. But no eager, playful kittens leaped out to greet me. I put my hand on one of the kittens and he raised his head, mouth open, panting, struggling to breathe. He opened his golden eyes and mewed at me faintly, then closed his eyes and resumed panting. His fur, and the towel he was wrapped in were cold and wet. Where in hell had these kittens been? Out in the rain?

"Lawrence, Aliya!" I yelled. "Get in the car." They did. These kittens ought to go to a vet's. Right now. Shit. I realized I had no idea which vet Norma used. Oh, to hell with it.

"Call Zee," I told Lawrence. "Tell her the kittens are sick and we're coming in with them. And drive."

He pulled out of the parking lot, phone to his ear, and as we turned from Pandora onto the highway, he said, a note of panic in his voice: "She's not answering. I just get her voice mail."

"What? Then call Jen. Jesus, I hope she can handle this."

"I hope so, too," he said grimly.

"Kieran!" Aliya said. "The tracker! I couldn't drop it anywhere on her. I'm so sorry. How will you find her?"

"Don't worry about it," I told her. "I'll find her. We have bigger problems than the tracker, though. I want you to take one of these guys."

I opened the carrier and took out one smelly kitten, wrapped like a burrito in his wet towel. Unwrapping him, I dropped the soiled towel on the floor of the Range Rover.

"I hope you're not squeamish," I told Aliya. "This little guy's back end is covered with . . . well, you know. You can smell it."

"I'm not squeamish," Aliya said calmly. She reached between the seats and took the smelly, limp, damp kitten from me.

"Unzip your jacket," I said, improvising furiously. "Put him under your sweater, next to your skin. He needs to get warm. Then hold him."

She nodded and tucked the kitten under her sweater. I did the same, tucking the other little guy under my turtleneck and half zipping my jacket around him, cursing Stephanie. The little spotted cat shivered against my skin.

"I reached her," Lawrence said. "Jen. She said Zee had to go out on a client call but that she knows what to do."

"Thanks, junior."

"Kieran, this one keeps gasping." Aliya said urgently. "Is there something more I can do?"

"Just hold him close and keep him warm," I told her. "And if you're so inclined, a little praying wouldn't hurt either."

Chapter 17

I was proud of Jen. Projecting an image of unruffled calm, she met us at Zee's front door, accompanied by a kid of about her own age – a handsome young guy with cafe au lait skin, medium brown dreadlocks, and startling pale green eyes. His well-worn black sweatshirt bore an image of Bob Marley with the words ONE LOVE underneath it. A friend of Jen's, I guessed.

"I'm Donovan," he said in a lilting Jamaican accent. "Let me take one of the kittens from you."

"Wildfire," Jen said, taking a careful look at the kitten Aliya handed to Donovan, who hustled away down the hall, murmuring a little to the Bengal in his arms. "I'm guessing URI," she told us. "Upper respiratory infection. Maybe not, though. Zee will know when she gets here. Donovan's taking him to Zee's ICU. I set it up. We've had to do this sort of thing before," she reassured me.

She held out her hands for my kitten, looked at him closely, then announced in a small, disappointed voice: "Wildest Dreams." I realized that she must have been hoping one of the Bengals was Wild Thing, and my heart contracted a little for her. She gave me a tight-lipped look at odds with the calm she was projecting and I realized that she was considerably more worried than she was letting on. Of course she was – she was thirteen and a huge responsibility had landed in her lap. Cradling Wildest Dreams against her, she paused a bit in the hall.

"Coming, Kieran?" she asked and I realized she wanted me with her.

"Sure, sweetie," I said, wondering what use I could be back there. But maybe my job was moral support.

Realizing that Lawrence and Aliya were still hovering uncertainly behind us in the kitchen, I took what I hoped would be forgivable liberties with Zee's hospitality. "Why don't you two make breakfast for, oh, six?" I suggested. "Coffee, eggs, toast. I think the ICU's going to be a bit crowded. Lawrence, you probably know where everything is."

Lawrence nodded. "Will do," he said. He'd accompanied me to Zee's several times over the years and knew his way around.

"Is this a vet hospital?" Aliya whispered to me as I prepared to follow Jen down the hall.

"Yes and no. It's my friend's house. Zee Lau. She's a vet and an animal behaviorist. Jen's her . . . Lawrence can explain it all to you," I told her. "Do you mind helping him with breakfast?"

Aliya looked around the kitchen uncertainly. "Well, I'm a lousy cook . . ."

"No problem," Lawrence told her breezily, taking off his leather jacket and draping it over a kitchen chair. "I'm a totally amazing chef. You can be sous-chef. Just follow my lead and we'll have a great breakfast ready for everyone by the time they're finished."

I caught up with Jen as she backed through the swinging doors of a room at the end of the hall. "I started getting the room warmed up as soon as Lawrence called me," she said, her voice quavering a little. "I got Zee on the phone. She told me what to do until she gets here. Omigod, Kieran, what happened to them?"

"I don't know, sweetie. They sure look like they've been out in the rain, though."

Jen put Wildest Dreams on the stainless steel examination table, beside Wildfire, who Donovan had just finished drying off. Both kittens lay limp and still.

"Jen?" Donovan asked, worried. "Are they even breathing?"

Jen grabbed a stethoscope from a cart against the wall, putting it to each kitten's chest in turn. "They're breathing," she said in relief. "They sound bubbly, though."

"I put plastic over the big cage back there, just the way you told me," Donovan said, vigorously toweling Wildest Dream's fur. "Should I put them inside now?"

Jen bit her lip. "We need to start subcutaneous fluids." She looked at me. "I'm not sure what to do first."

I remembered my experience several years ago when I had had to administer sub-q fluids to Trey. The process went so much more smoothly if the fluid was warm, Zee had suggested. The cats didn't mind the ordeal as much. "I think it's better to warm the bags of fluid, right?" I suggested. "And you'll need to find needles and tubing. That'll take a few minutes. So maybe oxygen first?"

Jen nodded. "Right. Of course. Donovan, there are bags of fluid in the cupboard over there. Will you take two out to the kitchen and warm them up? Run a bowl full of hot water, and just put the bags in it for, oh, fifteen minutes or so."

Donovan left with two bags of Lactated Ringer's and Jen said to me, sounding desperate: "I'm not thinking straight. My brain feels scrambled. I'm just faking it until Zee gets here. I'm afraid they'll die, Kieran."

I squeezed her shoulder and said with a confidence I did not feel: "Nah, they won't. And you're doing just fine. You're doing what Zee told you to do. Let's put them in with the oxygen."

"Please be okay, guys," Jen begged as we placed the limp kittens inside the large cage behind us, then sealed up the plastic cover. Then there was nothing to do but wait.

"How did you find them?" Jen asked me. "And how come there's only two? What happened?"

"One of the neighborhood pet owners called me. Someone noticed a phone number advertising Bengal kittens for sale. He thought the ad might be about Norma's kittens. Lawrence and Aliya posed as adopters and we met the seller at McDonald's. Basically I bought the kittens."

Hope flared in Jen's eyes. "If it's only money, I could . . . "

"Buy the rest of the kittens?"

"Yeah," she said in a small voice.

"I don't think so. Not now. The seller delivered two half-dead kittens to us. No one who wants loving, healthy pets would want more of the same. Even the fictitious aunt who Lawrence invented."

"Okay, I get that. Maybe. But couldn't you just *ask?*" Jen's eyes pleaded with me.

I shook my head. "The seller just about ran Lawrence over on the way out of McDonald's." I debated for a moment about telling Jen the identity of the Bengal thief, then decided to keep her in the dark. Jen was sometimes a hot-headed kid, and I sure didn't want her calling Stephanie and going off on her. Or pleading for the rest of the Bengals. I needed to do things my way.

"They were in a tearing hurry to get their money and get away," I told Jen. "I don't think there'll be any more negotiating with them."

Jen looked down at her sneakers. "So how will you get the rest of the kittens back? And the adult Bengals? Wasn't the seller, like, your lead?"

"Yeah. But I'm not dead in the water." I winked at her. "I have another idea. Can I borrow your laptop?"

"Sure," Jen said, plainly mystified. "It's in my room. Should I go get it? Or you can use it in there. It's on my desk."

"I'll just go use it in your room. Better you wait here for Donovan and Zee. I'll be back in a few minutes."

On my way down the hall to Jen's room, I passed the kitchen where I smelled coffee and toast. Lawrence and Aliya were laughing a little as they rustled up breakfast. Good. They hadn't let the miserable awfulness of the situation bring them down.

In Jen's room, I opened her laptop, turned it on, and called up the website of a data retrieval service at which I had an account. The snoop service, would, for an exorbitant fee, locate physical addresses from cell phone numbers, thus proving again the sad but indisputable fact that there was no privacy on the Internet. The service was not entirely reliable as it often returned addresses that were several months out of date, but it had proven useful to me in the past. I hoped this was one of the times it would prove useful again. I put in my user name and password and, when prompted, Stephanie's cell phone number. After a wait of about fifteen seconds, it returned an address on Saanich Highway. I frowned. Really?

I closed out my account at the snoop service, and called up Google Earth, entering the address I had been given. Switching to street view, I got a picture of a road leading into the forest. Oh goody. For this I paid money? I decided to switch to satellite view and got something I did not expect: several acres in the forest, with clearings here and there hidden by fringes of evergreens. It looked as though there were half a dozen small structures in cleared areas, each well surrounded by trees. All I could see, however, were roofs and trees. Access to the individual structures seemed to be via a network of dodgy-looking dirt roads, all branching off from one main, slightly larger road, all leading down to the ocean. Hmm. Switching back to street view I virtually drove down the highway a bit, past the turnoff, and was rewarded by the image of a convenience store. "Yes!" I exclaimed. "Civilization!" There were cars in the small parking lot, so presumably the store was still in business. Zooming in on the store, I made out the sign above the front door: "Larsen's Market". Using Google again, I quickly found the address of Larsen's, borrowed a bright pink Post-It note from Jen's desk, and wrote down the address, tucking the scrap of paper into the back pocket of my jeans. Maybe the people who owned Larsen's knew something about this multi-structured enclave in the forest. Maybe I would get lucky. Maybe the rest of the Bengals and all the neighborhood pets would be there. Maybe the Delphic Oracle would speak to me, too. Something had to give, I thought grimly. Time was growing short. The last thing I did before turning off Jen's laptop was to erase my browsing history. Jen was an ingenious kid and I did not want her following my trail of cyber breadcrumbs.

Back in the ICU, Zee had arrived and the situation was well in hand.

"You did well," Zee was telling Jen, who was holding one bag of Lactated Ringer's solution above a spotted kitten while Donovan held the other. I could see fluid dripping slowly from the bag, down the plastic tubing, and into the large needle skewering the fur between each kitten's shoulders. "Both of you," she said to Donovan who gave her a brilliant smile. Encouragingly, the kitten Jen was tending lifted its head and gave a silent meow.

"You also, Kieran," Zee said, turning around as I entered the makeshift ICU and the doors whacked closed behind me.

I felt inordinately pleased. Zee did not bestow compliments lightly.

"How are they?" I asked.

"Their URI is not serious," she said. "I won't administer antibiotics, which might not be useful in any event. They are mostly chilled, wet, weak, frightened, and dehydrated from diarrhea. I made slides of fecal samples and examined them. They have Giardia from drinking contaminated water, I would guess. They have also been drinking milk – cow's milk. I found dried milk on their fur."

"Milk. Huh."

"Yes. Cats do not have the proper enzymes to break down the sugar in milk. It usually produces digestive distress."

"Right. I recall your telling me that once. Thanks to you, I never give Trey or Vlad milk."

"When they have been rehydrated and begin eating, I will start treatment for Giardia." She shook her head. "It is not life-threatening. They will recover. Although they do need baths." She wrinkled her nose. "We will just have to put up with bad smells until they are stronger."

"Lawrence and Aliya are making breakfast," I told Zee. "I hope they aren't disassembling your kitchen. I thought we could all use some food."

Zee nodded. "A wise decision. Let's go to my office, Kieran. I would like to speak with you." To Jen and Donovan she said: "Give each kitten 150 ccs of fluid. Then put them back in the oxygen tent."

In Zee's office, we sat in easy chairs looking out over the meadow beyond her house. The off and on rain was off for the time being, but a flotilla of clouds scudded across the horizon like ships with dark sails running before the wind.

"Will the kittens really be okay?" I had to ask.

"These two, yes. But if the others are exposed to similar conditions for much longer . . . especially the other three-month-olds, or any animals who are already ill or old . . . "

I ground my teeth in frustration, thinking not only about the remaining three-month-old Bengals but Dutch's elderly beagles as well. "I get it, Zee. I have a possible lead on the others. But my car is back in town. I'll have Lawrence drop me there." I felt guilty sitting in a cozy armchair while the stolen animals were shivering somewhere in the cold rain, so I got up and paced a little.

"Perhaps you should have breakfast first," Zee suggested. "I imagine you have not eaten. I also imagine you are about to rush off into the wilderness in search of the remaining animals."

"You imagine correctly," I said. "I'm mad as hell, Zee."

"I can see that," Zee said. "But do not let your being aggravated interfere with your good judgment."

"I don't know how much good judgment I have," I told her. "Or ever had. It's mad that usually gets me up and doing things. I had good judgment when I worked for the Crown Counsel's office. I was dispassionate. I was careful. What did it get me? Usually very little. Usually not results I wanted. Things are more straightforward now. I work for my clients. I get mad on their behalf. And I get results."

Zee was silent for a long moment. I hoped her silence didn't mean a Confucian homily was in the offing. I really wasn't in the mood. I looked out the window and thought a little.

"You know, Zee, a lot of this case doesn't make sense."

"I agree," she said.

"Who would endanger the health of animals they intend to sell? Would the eventual would-be purchasers at the labs even want the animals if they were ill? I doubt it. So why would the thieves go to all the trouble to steal animals only to fail to take decent care of their stolen property? Wouldn't they want to keep them healthy? Protect their assets?"

"A good question. But perhaps the not taking care was unplanned."

"What do you mean?"

"Perhaps something unforeseen happened."

"To?"

"To the thieves. From the condition of the two Bengal kittens you rescued, it seems that the animal thieves are not providing even basic care – food, clean water, shelter from the elements."

"Yet someone gave the kittens milk."

"Yes. Someone did."

"Who? The sorcerer's apprentice?"

"Perhaps. Someone well-meaning, it seems."

"Well-meaning but ill-informed. Shit. This makes it even more urgent that I get my butt out 'into the wilderness' as you put it, and find them."

Zee steepled her fingers, and looked at me inscrutably. I knew her well enough to know that she had something on her mind.

"Spill it," I said.

"Will you take someone with you? When you go out into the wilderness? After all, you have told me that there may be four adversaries."

I said nothing, mulling this over.

"Perhaps you can consider this over breakfast," Zee said. "I should go and reclaim my kitchen from the chefs." She got up from her armchair and gave me a meaningful look, a hand on the doorknob. "Shall we set a place for you at the table?"

"All right, all right," I said testily. "I just have to make a phone call first."

Zee closed the door quietly behind her.

Deciding not to overthink what I was about to do, I took out my cell phone. To my relief, the number I was calling rang only once before it was answered.

"Miranda?" I said. "Kieran Yeats. I have a proposition for you."

Chapter 18

MIRANDA WAS PROMPT. She pulled up the lane in a dark blue cargo van identified only by the words The Sanctuary painted in white on each side, and a phone number underneath. Hmm. I'd wondered what her animal refuge was called . . . now I knew. Nice and simple. She parked beside Lawrence's Range Rover and I went to meet her.

"Everyone's just finishing up breakfast," I said. "Come in for coffee?"

"Sure," she replied. "How are the kittens?"

"They seem to be doing okay," I told her as we walked to Zee's front door. "But it's pretty important to get the others in out of the weather. Wherever they are, they're not being taken care of."

"That doesn't sound like the Malverns," Miranda said. "They're absolutely not animal lovers, but they wouldn't want to take risks with their merchandise."

"Hmm. Did you come across a woman named Stephanie Walters in your investigation back a few years ago?" I asked her.

She shook her head. "I don't remember her. But that's not to say she wasn't involved, though. We just didn't pursue things."

"Before we go in, I want to tell you something," I said. "There's a girl in there, a young teenager, Jen. She's my goddaughter and, well, she doesn't know anything about what the bunchers had in mind for animals they stole. I just haven't had the heart to tell her. Visions of the Bengals in some lab would give her nightmares. She was staying at Wild At Heart the night the cats were stolen and although it's unrealistic, she blames herself for not hearing the thieves and coming downstairs to stop them."

"Good thing she didn't," Miranda said. "She could have been badly hurt. I won't say a word to Jen about bunchers, though. No need to insist on harsh truths. I'll follow your lead," she added. "No problem."

I shook raindrops off Miranda's navy squall jacket and hung it up on the hall tree just inside Zee's front door. We went on into the kitchen where Donovan was pouring seconds of coffee for everyone but himself and Jen. I found a chair for Miranda, seating her at the end of the big table beside Zee. Donovan brought her a mug and I introduced her as the director of The Sanctuary, omitting her RCMP background. I felt this was a little specious, but as I met Lawrence's eyes and he nodded in approval, I felt better.

"Hey, Lawrence," Miranda said warmly. "Max says hello."

"Hey, Miranda," Lawrence answered, a goofy smile on his face.

"How do you two know each other?" Jen asked curiously, finishing her orange juice.

"Oh, we were at Miranda's sanctuary the other day," I said. "I met a parrot who sings doo wop and Lawrence met a sniffer dog."

Jen looked from Lawrence to Miranda to me, sensing a story here. When no one said anything enlightening, she shrugged. "So, are you guys going to get the rest of the cats?" she asked me. "Did your idea turn out, Kieran? Do you know where they are?"

"Miranda and I are going to investigate that very thing," I told her.

"I don't suppose I can come along, can I," Jen said longingly. Zee gave me a sidelong glance.

I shook my head. "Nope. I need you here. When we get the rest of the Bengals, they may in rough shape. Zee, I'm assuming we can bring them here. I should have asked you first."

"Of course you can bring them here," Zee said. "Jen, why don't you and Donovan go into the back and set up as many cages as you think we will need. You know who roomed with whom at Wild At Heart."

Jen nodded, mollified, and she and Donovan left the kitchen. I was glad Zee had given her a job to do. I got up and closed the kitchen door firmly behind them.

"Miranda's told me we can take the Oak Bay pets to The Sanctuary when we find them," I said, deliberately not saying the word 'if'. "There'll be an assortment of dogs and cats. The Bengals, especially the remaining two kittens, are our first priority. I imagine they'll have all been out in the rain. So they'll come here."

"So you do have a lead, Kieran?" Lawrence asked.

"I do," I said. "Miranda and I are on our way there right now. It's back in the woods a little bit down the highway. I really can't make heads or tails of it from Google Earth. The roads look pretty iffy, especially since it's been raining so much. We'll just walk in, take a careful look, then decide how to proceed."

"You know," Lawrence said thoughtfully, "we could send in my drone."

Miranda looked at him in amazement. "You have a drone?"

Lawrence blushed. "Er, well, yes. We, that is Aliya and Samir and I, my employees, well, we use it for panoramic shots," he explained. "Video tours. I do a lot of real estate photography. We could let the drone take a look first, then make plans. It might be less risky than, well . . ."

". . . than blundering around in the woods alerting the thieves to the fact that we're coming," I supplied.

He adjusted his glasses. "Exactly. That's what I meant, of course."

I smiled at him. "A freakin' drone. You are a never-ending source of amazement." Now he really blushed.

"Just trying to be helpful."

"I'll take that help," I said. "But first I need to stop by my house back in Oak Bay. Someone needs to drop me at my car back at McDonald's."

"I can," Miranda said.

"And we'll need to go by the shop and get the drone," Lawrence said. "Is it on the charger, Aliya?"

Aliya nodded. "Yes. I can call Samir and have him pack it up. I suppose you want him to operate it?" she asked in a small voice.

"Good grief, no!" Lawrence said emphatically. "Remember that shoot in Uplands? The drone took a swim in the koi pond and I had to replace the camera. No, I was hoping you'd drive it. You've had a lot more practice with it than Samir has."

Aliya grinned. "Sure, boss. I'd be happy to."

Oy vey. All this cooperation was making me itchy. "We should go, then," I said to Miranda. I took the Post-It note with the address of Larsen's Market out of my back pocket and gave it to Lawrence. "We'll meet up there. See you soon."

ↄↄ

Back at home, Trey was on the couch, nestled in my grandma's mohair blanket. Miranda, who had come into the house with me, took a seat on the couch beside him.

"He's a survivor of a so-called benign learning experiment in the University's Psychology Department," I explained. "In fact, the only survivor of the asshole animal-keeper's two-week vacation."

"A bad story with a good ending," Miranda said, administering vigorous pats to Trey who rolled over and showed her his belly. "I like cats, although I don't get to spend as much time with mine as I'd like to. We have so many needy animals at the sanctuary."

"Was your cat a rescue?"

"Yeah, one of our first. Her name's Immelda." She laughed ruefully. "She adores my shoes."

"Excuse me for a jiffy," I said. "Speaking of shoes, I need to change mine for boots and do one other thing."

In the bedroom I kicked off my sneakers and found my hiking boots in the closet. When they were laced, I took a deep breath and got my .38 out of the shoebox where I kept it. I took a handful of shells out of the box as well, and sat on the bed with them in the palm of my hand. It had always struck me as odd how much they weighed. I guess it was their symbolic weight that troubled me – taking a life with them, as I had had to do once in the past, was indeed a weighty matter. Which brought me to the crux of my dithering, sitting here on the bed, juggling bullets in my hand. A couple of days ago, when Jen had come pounding on my door in the middle of the night, I had taken my unloaded .38 with me out to the front porch. I guess I thought that I could frighten away the nocturnal miscreants who were disturbing my sleep by just waving my gun at them. Actually, I had been stumblingly hung over and didn't recall what I had thought. Grabbing my .38 had surely been a reflex.

I don't like guns. When I left the Crown Counsel's office and started working for myself, or rather for the animals whose caretakers hired me to help them, I rapidly discovered that I needed a little help from my friends. Lawrence, Mac, Edgar . . . they all helped me in my solo enterprise. But I never considered that I would have to carry a gun. Until I met Boris Devlin.

People who believe animals are their property to do with as they please are often impervious to reason. I realized that my stellar skills at argument were of absolutely no use one day in a muddy pasture when Lawrence and I were gathering evidence to remove three badly emaciated horses from an abusive owner. We'd been hired by the horses' co-owner – Devlin's estranged wife – to get enough evidence to make a charge of animal cruelty stick and have the horses seized. It seemed a straightforward case, but I hadn't reckoned with how passionate and unhinged animal abusers can be. The horses had foundered in the mud and were simply too weak to get up. They needed to be removed immediately, I thought, if their lives were to be saved.

We'd been given permission by Devlin's wife to go into the pasture, so we certainly weren't trespassing, but Boris was having none of my explanations. He came bellowing across the pasture at us, armed with a two- by-four, but I wasn't in the mood to back down. I moved to stand between Lawrence and Devlin, told him to keep taking photographs, and yelled at Boris about how much trouble he was in. He ignored me and one of his board-waving lunges unfortunately connected with my forearm. I landed in the mud along with the horses and decided that the situation required more than my impassioned recitation of the criminal code. Lawrence phoned the cops, Boris was taken into custody, Mrs. Devlin came with her horse trailer and a few husky friends to remove the horses, and I went to the hospital. Mac came as my arm was being encased in plaster and volunteered to take me to the gun range to teach me to shoot. Reluctantly I agreed, and became, much to my surprise, a damned good shot. Looking back on that day in the horse pasture with the apoplectic Boris, I wondered if I would have been able to pull out my gun and use it to defend myself. I just wasn't sure. But each time doubt assailed me, I ran my fingers over the lump in my right forearm where the bone hadn't healed cleanly and remembered the expression on Devlin's face.

"Oh, crap," I muttered to myself in irritation. So I just loaded the damned gun. I took off my belt, threaded it through the belt loop on my holster, stuffed my gun in the holster, put the belt back on, and pulled my turtleneck down over the gun. It felt distinctly odd sitting in the small of my back, as it always did. Oh well. As some wag said, you inevitably get better results with a .38 and a reasonable request than you do with a reasonable request. Finding a more or less waterproof jacket in the hall closet, I put it on and walked back out to the living room to find a grey lump on Miranda's lap.

"Aha," I said. "You've fallen victim to cat creep. Trey is a stealth creeper – he senses a sympathetic soul, and before you know it, he's oozed like an amoeba from couch to lap, muttering about his woes as he gets comfy."

Miranda laughed. "No mutters yet. Just snores." She looked up at me with a measuring, blue-eyed gaze. "Ready?"

"Yup," I said, although I wasn't sure I was ready at all. "Let's do this."

☙

At Larsen's we pulled into the convenience store's small parking lot and found a place around the side, next to Lawrence's Range Rover. Actually Miranda's van and Lawrence's vehicle were the only vehicles here at this hour on a rainy Wednesday. Still, I thought it wise to leave the spaces directly in front for real customers. I wanted something from the Larsens – information – so maybe it was best not to antagonize them by hogging the parking spots.

"I'll go in," I told Miranda. "Maybe the Larsens know something about this enclave in the forest. Be back in a jiffy. You could hop in with Lawrence and Aliya . . . learn all about the drone."

Miranda nodded. "So . . . do you have a plan?"

I considered this. Did I? "Well, not exactly," I had to admit. "If we can get an idea of what's back there in the woods, I thought we'd just go on in, sneak around, try not to announce ourselves to anyone, find where the animals are being kept, if indeed they are being kept there, and, well, reclaim them."

Miranda raised an eyebrow.

"Yeah, I know, that's where my plan is a little weak," I admitted. "The reclaiming."

"Presumably the animal thieves may have something to say about that," she said. "The reclaiming part. Are you prepared to be, ah, firm and forceful?"

"Those are my middle names," I assured her.

She tucked a wing of dark hair behind one ear and gave me a feral grin. "Okay," she said. "I'll go admire Lawrence's drone while you're in Larsen's."

Inside the little market, I was met with the wonderful smell of brewing coffee. Oh, well, maybe not, I thought, as the door tinkled closed behind me. As I made my way between shelves of paper towels, bottled water, soap, and toiletries, a small display of cat food caught my eye. I plucked half a dozen cans of Fancy Feast off the shelf and carried them to the front counter where a middle-aged woman with frizzy brown hair and friendly dark eyes behind wire-rimmed glasses was recording something in a ledger. She looked up at me and smiled, closing the ledger, evidently happy enough for the distraction.

"Hungry cats?" she commented.

"Yeah," I said. "Cat food shopping has slipped my mind the last couple of days. I'm glad you stock what they like."

"Oh, we have a little bit of everything," she said. "We get a lot of camping and RV traffic in here from the highway. People on their way to or from the ferry docks. It's most of our business. You'd be surprised how many people take their cats in their RVs with them."

"Mine would absolutely rebel," I said, handing over a ten-dollar bill. "They're homebodies."

"Mine, too," she confessed, ringing up my purchases.

Having fortuitously established a cat-owning bond between us, I proceeded to what had really brought me into Larsen's and hoped I wouldn't sound too nosey.

"Do you know anything about the place next door in the forest? I drove by looking for a road to take me in there, but no luck. I'm looking for an acquaintance of mine. But maybe I got the location wrong." I decided to go for broke and offered my hand. "Kieran Yeats."

"Jan Larsen," she said, shaking my hand and putting my change on the counter. "No, you might have the right location. There are a few people living back there. They come in here occasionally. Mostly for beer. The road looks narrow and impassable, but cars do go in and out." Jan put the cans of cat food into a small bag and continued thoughtfully. "It's none of my business, but I wish the people who live back there would take better care of their little boy. I mean, I don't care how much beer they drink, or what they do, but – " she broke off, shaking her head. "It used to be a boarding kennel, you know."

Oho, I thought. Really? "A boarding kennel? As in animal boarding? Cats and dogs?"

"Exactly. It was quite a thriving place, oh, fifteen years ago. People would drop off their pets on their way to the ferry, then stop in here for coffee and doughnuts to take with them. But it's been closed for years. The land is still owned by the Malvern family, though. I used to see Thomas regularly. Not so much now. I don't think he's well. And now that his son has moved in with him, I don't see Thomas at all. Just the son, Connor. And that other man. And their woman friend." She paused, her lips tightening in disapproval. "If I were his dad, I'd kick Connor out, make him go get a job, sell off that land, and move into a nice retirement home. Thomas would get a good price for it – five acres of woodland with oceanfront." She sniffed. "You know, I really don't care what they're up to, although it can't be any kind of gainful employment."

I nodded my head encouragingly and she carried on.

"What really bothers me," she said, "is that they still haven't settled up their bill. It's three months overdue. I just won't extend them any more credit."

"It's rotten when people stiff you," I commiserated. "That's my beef with the young woman who lives with them," I said, taking liberties with the truth. "She owes me something. I've come to collect."

"Well, good luck collecting it," she said, a little color rising in her cheeks. Obviously the Malverns' unpaid bill was a great source of irritation to Jan.

I didn't blame her a bit. She was a small businessperson. I let her talk.

"The only one of them I allow to charge anything here nowadays is the little boy."

"Oh? The little boy?"

"Yes. I don't think they feed him enough. He's so skinny. I let him charge food."

I listened carefully. Jan was trying to communicate something other than her ire at the deadbeat Malverns.

"He's the only one of them with any . . . sense of right and wrong," she said bitterly. "He brings garbage bags full of beer cans to redeem for cash." She laughed, but it was a kind, bemused laugh. "Silly little boy. We aren't a recycling center. I told him that the first time he dragged a bag of cans up here but he looked so stricken that I told him I'd take them. All he wanted was a carton of milk and a sandwich, for heaven's sake. How could I say no? So I took his cans. Still do. My husband takes them into town for recycling eventually. I pretend to record his purchases and always reassure him that he still has money in his account."

"That's very kind of you," I said, a bit mystified at where this might be going. "Does the kid have a name?"

Jan frowned. "I think he said his name was Tribble. But surely I misheard. Isn't that the name of one of those aliens on the old *Star Trek* series?"

Now it was my turn to laugh. "It is. I think the episode was called 'The Trouble With Tribbles'."

"Maybe you'll look out for him when you go back there to get what you're looking for."

Aha. That's what was really eating Jan. Maybe even more than the Malverns' unpaid bill. "Um, are you worried about him, Jan?" I had to ask. "You know, there is Child Protective Services."

She shook her head. "I've thought about calling them from time to time," she said. "But I really don't know if I should do that. The stories you hear about foster homes. Maybe he's better off where he is. Although he could use a haircut and a bath. And some proper clothes. All that dirty oversized camo gear that he wears."

"I tell you what," I said, wanting to disentangle myself from Jan and her maternal angst about Tribble. She would have to do whatever she thought best. Child Protective Services was in the phone book. "If I see him, I'll let you know."

"Thank you," she said and I saw how important this was to her. Great. Missing cats and dogs, and now a starving kid named Tribble?

I took my cat food and hurried back out into the rain.

℞

Back at Lawrence's Range Rover, the drone had been unpacked and was poised ready for take-off or deployment or whatever on the back seat. Looking like an ungainly brown insect, it resembled a miniature helicopter with four rotors instead of one. A bulge under its belly was evidently the camera. Lawrence lifted it out gently and put it on the pavement in front of the Range Rover.

"Okay, Aliya," he said, getting back into the driver's seat. "We'll watch it on my tablet." He switched on the device and handed it to Aliya. "She can control it using arrows on the screen," he explained. "We'll be able to see where it's going in real time, although video is uploaded to the cloud so we can retrieve it later and edit if we want. We usually edit. For customers that is."

"Of course, the cloud," I agreed wisely, pretending to a tekkie familiarity I did not have. Miranda and I sat in the Range Rover's back seat and watched the image on the tablet as Aliya swiped the screen and the drone rose smoothly into the air. She was evidently very skilled with the controls because neither the image on the screen nor the drone wobbled a bit. I wondered what the hapless Samir had done to lose the drone in a koi pond. No telling. I looked from the screen to the drone itself, hovering in just in front of the Range Rover, and it rose to a height of about twenty feet, turned a corner, and disappeared into the forest. Then we watched the screen.

"It's a little foggy in there," Aliya said. "I thought I'd keep the drone at about this height."

For a while, all we could see was a narrow, muddy road and low-growing salal bushes, their leaves dripping with rain. A smaller road led off the main road to the left, and it looked to me like a pair of fresh tire tracks had scored a recent rut in the mud. "Let's look at that little road to the left," I suggested to Aliya and she turned the drone.

"There's a building or some kind of structure there," Miranda said excitedly. "Just ahead. Can you get us a view from above it, Aliya?"

The drone gained altitude and on the screen we saw a once-white single-wide trailer, dull and dirty now, moss growing on its roof, windows dull and opaque. A tin-roofed shed snuggled up to one side of the trailer and on the other side a vehicle was crookedly parked. I was hoping like hell to see Stephanie's black Honda but what I did see rendered me speechless. When I found my tongue, I yelled: "Holy shit! It's the brown van."

I hardly had time to blurt out my observation because a small figure in wet camo clothes, blond hair pasted to its head, emerged from the shed at the side of the trailer. He raised his head to look at the drone and I saw his eyes go wide in alarm. Reaching into the depths of his ludicrously too-big jacket, he pulled out a very business-like looking automatic pistol, coolly took aim at the drone, and . . . and then the image on the tablet's screen disappeared to black.

"Oh, no," Aliya wailed.

"Hey!" Lawrence shouted. "That kid just shot down my drone!"

Chapter 19

CROUCHING BEHIND A salal bush, Miranda and I peered down the narrow muddy lane that led to the long, single-wide trailer the drone's flight had shown us. Overhead, a canopy of evergreen branches obscured the sky, sheltering us somewhat from the rain that had been fitfully falling all day. There was a spooky hushed silence here in the forest clearing, as though something was holding its breath. We had left Lawrence and Aliya back in Larsen's parking lot with instructions to come when we phoned them. At the end of this road lay the Bengals, I fervently hoped. And maybe the Oak Bay pets, as well. I hoped, too, that Lawrence's Range Rover could navigate the ruts and puddles. He assured me it could.

The brown van with the wings logo was drawn up a little crookedly in a parking space beside the trailer, as if someone had left it there it in a hurry. Thankfully, the gun-toting drone-killer kid was nowhere in sight. For that matter, neither was the dead drone. I wondered where the kid had taken it. And why. An errant trail of rain snaked its way inside my collar, and I shivered.

"It doesn't look as though that van has moved in days," Miranda whispered. "The tire tracks are filled in with mud and rain."

"That timing would fit with the Oak Bay thefts," I whispered back. "The pets were taken off the streets Saturday night, the Bengals Sunday night. But there's no barking coming from the trailer. So the dogs are somewhere else. In that abandoned kennel setup Jan Larsen told me about, maybe. I'd give anything if the cats were here, though." I sighed. "I guess we'd better not kick down the door. After all, I may be way off base and this may well be where the caretaker lives. Or someone's mother-in-law hosting a Bible study group."

"Yeah, knocking might be best," Miranda said. "So . . . do you want to knock and I'll be backup or vice versa? This is your show. I'm just riding shotgun."

"Yeah. I'll knock," I said.

"Okay. Let's go."

I straightened up and squished through the mud to the trailer, expecting the kid with the gun – Miranda had told me it was an air pistol – to pop out and shoot me at any moment. Getting shot with an air pistol would be only marginally less painful than getting shot with a regular gun, I figured, so I was relieved when nothing happened. Three rudimentary wooden steps led up to the trailer's front door and I climbed them as quietly as I could. Always better to take the bad guys by surprise, right? Although exactly who I thought I was taking by surprise I wasn't sure. Stephanie? I doubted it. One of the Malverns? Peter Blanchard? I guessed that was why Miranda had her gun drawn. I decided to leave mine in my holster until I needed it. I mean, there was such a thing as an embarrassment of firepower. A small window in the trailer's front door was covered with a grotty-looking yellowed curtain that made me feel itchy, and I half expected it to be twitched aside in response to my knock. Nope. I knocked again, a little more forcefully, and to my surprise, the unlatched door creaked open about six inches. Crap. This wasn't good. Now what? My toes curled a little in my boots in apprehension.

What the hell . . . I decided to announce myself. "Hello?" I called. Nothing.

"Go in low," Miranda whispered in my ear.

"I'll be right behind you."

I pushed the door open a little more and scuttled to my left, into the dimness of the trailer's front room, hugging the wall. The smell was awful. A melange of ancient cigarette smoke, garbage, mold, old sweat and something else. No cat smells, though. Dammit, where were those Bengals? Evidently not here. I straightened up against the wall. To my left was a kitchen, from where the garbage smells were emanating. I could see a small sink and a window over it, mostly obscured by a curtain whose grungy mate hung over the window in the front door. Wonderful decorating skills. I felt Miranda come into the room beside me, and she pushed the door open wider with the toe of one boot, letting the light of the grey afternoon into the gloom of the trailer's front room.

In front of me, I saw a threadbare ancient recliner, upholstered in a very worn brown and orange plaid tweed. In it lay a skinny old man, grey lanky hair, stubbled jowls. He was clad in a soiled once-white undershirt and stained grey sweat pants. His hands were clasped in his lap, his head thrown back, toothless mouth open in a soundless cry. Whoever he was, he seemed very dead.

Miranda walked to the recliner and bent over, putting two fingers to the old man's neck. After a few moments, she shook her head.

"It's Thomas Malvern," she said to me, holstering her gun. "After I left the RCMP I had revenge dreams where I met him, his son, and Peter Blanchard again, but I never dreamed I'd meet him like this." Straightening up, she rubbed her hands on her jeans as if ridding them of something foul.

"Thomas Malvern," she pronounced after a long few moments, "you're dead and you deserve to be dead. You and your delinquent son and that other piece of work dedicated way too many years to animal theft. You were a buncher. The other two undoubtedly still are. You stole hundreds of cats and dogs from their homes and handed them over to buyers at labs or to guys who organized dogfights. All these innocent animals . . . you were responsible for wrenching them from good lives with people who loved them and delivering them to months of torture, followed by pain-filled deaths. All in the service of money."

She took a breath, then continued. "I wondered at the time why the cosmos didn't cry out in empathic anguish, why the hand of God didn't squash you, your son, and Blanchard like bugs. Well, the fact is that the cosmos doesn't give a rip about the pain you caused, does it?"

Miranda fell silent and I realized that she was in the middle of saying something that she needed to say to her old nemesis. I didn't interrupt her. "But sometimes, something goes right." She smiled, a wolfish smile that contained no mirth but a great deal of satisfaction. "Payback is a bitch, isn't it, Malvern?" she said quietly.

So we stood there, she with her hands in the pockets of her jeans, me silent beside her. I didn't have time to think of anything commiserative to say, because a small authoritative voice called firmly from the shadowy hall that led to the trailer's bedrooms: "Hands up."

We dutifully raised our hands and turned in the direction of the voice. I was pretty sure I knew who I would see: a skinny kid in an oversized camo jacket, wet blond hair in his eyes, a pistol pointing at our midsections. I was right.

"Hey, Tribble," I said. "We're friends. Jan Larsen says hello."

The kid looked at us down the muzzle of his gun. "It's Trouble," he said. "Jan doesn't hear so well. Have you come to take me away because I killed the old dog man?"

Jesus, I thought frantically. The kid's name was Trouble? Who would name a kid that? And did he really kill Malvern?

"Is the old dog man the guy in the chair over there?" Miranda asked the kid in a calm, quiet voice.

"Uh huh," the kid said.

"Did you kill him?"

"I might have," the kid said reasonably. "Sometimes I wished he would die, so my wish might have killed him. When you wish upon a star, makes no difference who you are, anything your heart desires will come to you," the kid said, quoting something from a Disney movie, I guessed. However, this cheery wishing upon a star for dreams to come true had gotten twisted in his brain. The kid was obviously frightened that his wish had power – that it had killed Malvern.

"Hmm," Miranda said, "Well, wishes don't kill people, Trouble. Sometimes people just die. I think that's what happened to the old dog man over there. He looks like he might have been sick for a long time."

When Trouble said nothing, Miranda continued: "Why did you want him dead? Was he bad to you?"

"No. He was bad to animals," the kid said in a sad, small voice. "Him and Stef and Con and Peter. They bring lots of dogs, and sometimes cats, to the cages near the big house. They put necklaces on the dogs so they don't bark. But they still cry." The kid's eyes filled with tears. "They cry until the man in the white van comes for them," he continued. "I don't like it when they cry. Once I asked if I could have one for a pet and we could take its necklace off, but Peter said no pets for Trouble."

"Shit. Shock collars," Miranda said to me in a low-voiced aside. "They put shock collars on the dogs. They can't bark but they can still whine. And the man in the white van . . . he must be the animal dealer."

"I can see why you wanted the old guy dead," Miranda told Trouble heatedly. "I would have wanted that too."

"I didn't always want him dead," the kid said, miserably. "Just when the dogs and cats came." He fell silent, and I realized that the stolen pets' arrivals and departures must have been truly painful for him. This was clearly one tender-hearted little guy. "Anyway," he said chillingly, "if you try to take me away I'll have to shoot you. Like I did with the flying robot. I have to stay here."

"Because . . ." Miranda let the question hang in the air.

"Because I have to guard the spots now."

The spots . . . the Bengals?

"Trouble, listen," I said. "We haven't come to take you away. We're here to help the animals that the old dog man and Stef and Con and Peter took. The dogs in cages at the big house. And the spots. The people who own the pets, they asked me to find them and bring them back. That's what I do. I help animals. My name is Kieran. And my friend Miranda is helping me."

The kid said nothing, but I could see that he was listening closely.

"Can you show us where the animals are?" I continued. "We'd like to find the spots first. Some of them are babies. The lady who owns them is very worried about them and would really like them back."

He looked from me to Miranda and back to me again. "The spots aren't there at the big house." he told us after a moment. "Stef has them. At her place."

"Okay," I said encouragingly. C'mon, kid, keep talking, I mentally urged him.

"A smaller place than this," he said. "Down a little road. They're in a cage together."

My upraised arms were getting tired, not to mention my brain. We had just been told a whole novel's worth of facts. "Trouble, can we put our hands down? What if we all sat on the couch over here and talked?" I asked him.

The gun wavered a little. I bet the kid's arms were getting tired, too. "Okay. You can put your hands down," he said.

We did.

He eyed the couch with evident distrust. "You can sit there. I'll stay here."

"Aren't you tired of holding that gun on us?" Miranda asked him as we took seats on the couch, a grimy relative of the recliner. We had to move piles of unopened mail and stacked-up newspapers to make room.

"Nope. I'm not tired," he lied. He shifted his weight a little. "How do I know you've really come to help the animals? I don't want the dogs and cats and the spots to die like the animals she –" he waved his gun disconcertingly at Miranda, "talked to the old dead dog man about. Peter and Con are very bad. Peter is so bad that I go out the window when I see him coming. And the white van always takes the animals away," he said hopelessly.

I could see desperation in his eyes. I hoped Miranda or I could figure out the right thing to say. This kid was the key to the swift discovery and rescue of the Bengals and the Oak Bay pets – if we could win his trust. But we needed to get him to talk to us and not bolt out the window as he said he did when Peter came around.

"Okay, listen, Trouble," I said. "The white van is not coming for the animals this time. We know that the old guy over there –" I pointed to Malvern, whose dead body was giving me the creeps, "and Stef, Con, and Peter stole pets a couple of days ago. Dogs and cats."

Trouble shook his head. "Nope. The old dog man stayed here. He was too sick to go. He was alseep when they went for the pets."

"Here's the thing, Trouble," I said, deciding to try to explain the Bengals' theft to him. "Stef helped Peter and Con steal the pets, right?"

"Uh huh," he said.

"But she figured out how to steal some other cats, too," I told him. "They're called Bengals. They're very rare. And expensive."

He frowned. "So they're the spots?"

"Yes. Cats with spots. She tried to sell two of them. For a lot of money."

He nodded. "I heard Stef and Con fighting about that. Con said keep them for the man in the white van like I promised. Con said if we screw him, he won't do business with us again. Stef said to hell with him, we can sell them ourselves and we can get lots of money and we won't need him."

The kid clearly had a great memory. "Well, Stef won that fight," I told him. "She advertised two of the spots for sale. But a friend of mine found out and told me. So I called Stef pretending to want to buy them," I said.

"I counted this morning and two were gone," he said. "Two of the babies. I was pretty mad at Stef. But you and your friends saved them?" Trouble asked, clearly wanting to believe.

"Yes. My friends and I tricked Stef."

Hope ignited in Trouble's eyes. "So they went back home? To the lady who wants them back? To someone who loves them, like she –" he gestured again with his gun to Miranda, "like she talked about to the old dead dog man?"

I sensed this was a kid who loved stories, who craved happy endings. "They will soon," I told him. "They're in a cat hospital right now, though. When we got them they were wet and cold. And sick. They'd been eating the wrong food."

"I know they're wet and cold," he said, his lower lip quivering. "The plastic blanket fell off the top of their cage. It's too tall to reach. I gave them some food, though, some milk. Stef didn't even *feed* them," he said indignantly. "Was milk wrong? Don't cats like milk?"

"Some cats like milk," I said, deciding to spare him the veterinary details. "The spots don't. And I think you did the best you could."

The kid lowered his gun, clearly thinking hard.

"Trouble, we are here to help," I told him again. "I promise you. We want to take the spots, and the other cats and the dogs back to their homes."

"To the people who love them," he repeated, clearly wanting to be sure about this part of the rescue story.

"Yes. To the people who love them," I assured him. "Will you help us? Show us where Stef has the spots? And then where the dogs and the other cats are?"

"Okay," he said finally, lowering his gun.

I blew out my breath. "Thank you, Trouble. First things first, though. You and I have to take a little walk. I'm afraid we're going to have to go out in the rain."

He shrugged. "Okay. How come, though? Can't we just go get the spots?"

Brother, it was tempting. "Miranda here used to be an, um, policeman. A Mountie. She has to do something first."

He looked Miranda over. "She was a Mountie? No way."

Miranda's mouth quirked in a smile. "No?" she asked him.

"No. Mounties wear red uniforms and have horses," he said with certainty.

"Well, yes, some of us do," she said. "Have horses that is. But we only wear red for, well, special occasions."

He wrinkled his brow.

"Like when the Queen visits," she said. "And besides, I don't do that job any more. I'm retired. We can't wear our uniforms when we retire."

"Okay." This seemed to satisfy him. "So what do you need to do here?" he asked her.

"Well, Mr. Malvern *is* dead," she told him.

"Uh huh."

He seemed unfazed by Malvern's open-mouthed, very dead presence. I wondered: had the kid had been so traumatized by animal cruelty and fear of Peter that the simple presence of a dead man was unremarkable?

"I have to call people to come and take him away," Miranda told him.

Trouble nodded. "Yeah. The meat wagon."

I burst out laughing. "The meat wagon?"

Trouble looked insulted. "Yeah. The meat wagon. I saw it on TV when the old dog man's TV worked. The police phone it when they find a dead body."

"You're absolutely right," Miranda said, hiding her grin. To me she added: "I'll call Mac if you take Trouble to the Range Rover. I'll let you know when it's all clear here."

"And then we can save the spots?" Trouble asked.

"You betcha," I told him. "Why don't you go put some shoes on, though. Oh, and can you bring the drone? We probably should take it back to its owner. We'll go wait in his car."

"The drone?" Trouble asked.

"The, um, thing you shot down."

"Oh, the flying robot. But won't he be mad that I killed it?"

"Nah," I said. "It can be fixed."

Trouble disappeared into the back of the trailer and I looked at Miranda in relief.

"Good work," she said. "I'll let you know when it's all wrapped up here." She looked over at Malvern's dead body with a certain amount of satisfaction. "One down, three to go. Good luck. Lawrence will fall into mourning about the drone, though. The flying robot indeed."

"Indeed," I said. "The kid's a great shot, isn't he? Call me?"

"You can count on it."

Chapter 20

"So here we are," I said conversationally to Trouble. It would take us half an hour of trudging through the drizzle and mud to get back to Larsen's parking lot, and I wanted to try and establish some kind of camaraderie between us. Ha. An aging investigator and an eight-year-old gunslinger. "The murmuring pines and the hemlocks. Bearded with moss," I said, waving a hand at the dripping evergreens.

"That's pretty," he said. "It's about trees, isn't it?"

"It sure is. It's from a poem. Do you know any poems?"

He thought for a minute. "In Flanders fields the poppies blow, between the crosses row on row. That's not about trees, though. It's a sad poem about war. I don't remember the rest. The old dog man knew all of it, though."

"It's a famous poem," I told him. "Written by a soldier just after a battle in a war long ago. He wrote it for his friend who was killed."

Trouble nodded. "That's what the old dog man said. He used to cry when he told it to me. He knew lots of poems about war. They all made him cry."

Jesus. A buncher with a heart. Maybe Thomas Malvern's soul hadn't been as shriveled as a raisin. Hard to believe.

"I'd like to be a soldier," Trouble said solemnly. "My father was a soldier. The old dog man told me that. I wouldn't mind going off to a war, like he did."

"Well, you certainly have a spiffy gun," I told him.

"Uh huh," he replied, falling silent on me. He hugged the drone to his chest and sneezed explosively. Great. Did the kid have a cold? Who knew how much worse it would get as the result of my dragging him out in the rain? Guilt nipped me.

I tried again. "Did the old dog man give you the gun?"

"Nope," he replied matter-of-factly.

I hoped I had hit on a topic of conversation that would keep him talking. Who the heck was this kid, how had he gotten such an odd name, and how had he come to be living with people who clearly terrified him? Was he a Malvern?

"I bought it myself," he said finally. "I used the old dog man's computer. And his plastic card."

"Wow, Trouble," I said in genuine admiration. "That was really smart." A thought went through my mind. "Do you still have the plastic card?"

"Uh huh. It's in my pocket."

With the gun, no doubt. Everything a young lad needed to navigate a naughty world. Still, I laughed out loud. "Good for you."

"I'm keeping it," he announced.

"I think you should," I told him.

We squished on. "How did you learn how to do that? Order something from the Internet?"

He shrugged. "It was easy. I helped the old dog man lots of times order things he needed. From the Amazon place. He couldn't see so well. Or remember things. I always had to type in the user name and the password."

I thought for a minute, then decided to press him. I really did want to know about his connection with the elder Malvern, and Con and Stef as he referred to them. And Peter, too. Why did they frighten him so much? "Why did you order the gun, Trouble?"

He gave me a sidelong look. "To shoot Peter. If I had to."

Aha. "Peter is a scary man, isn't he?" I remembered what Trouble had told me back at the trailer – that he went out the window when Peter came around.

"I guess," the kid said.

"I know the old dog man wasn't bad to you, but did the others hurt you, Trouble? Con and Peter and Stef?"

He looked over at me, his sopping hair hanging in his eyes. "Stef and Con some. But Peter . . ." I was silent and in a minute he continued on his own. "When I used to stay in the big house, back where they keep dogs in cages, one night Peter poured something on my arm, and lit it on fire with his lighter. It burned a lot. They laughed, Peter and Con. Stef too. I ran back to the old dog man's trailer and put my arm in the sink with cold water."

I was appalled. "Jesus, Trouble! Did the old guy help you?"

"No. He was sleeping. I took care of it," he said matter-of-factly. "The skin came off. It hurt for a long time. I didn't stay with Con after that. I stayed at the old dog man's trailer, in a room with boxes. And I ordered the gun."

"I would have done the same thing," I told him heatedly.

"Uh huh," he said. Then: "Kieran . . . I think we better hurry."

"Well, all right," I said. "It's hard to go faster through this mud, but we could put on a little speed."

"No, I don't mean that." He chewed his lip. "I know Miranda who used to be a Mountie is calling the cops, and the meat wagon has to come and take the old dog man away before we can go for the spots, but it's getting late."

I waited for the kid to explain.

"Con and Stef and Peter . . . they all take green pills. The old dog man used to take them too. The pills make them all sleep. But they wake up later in the afternoon. Then Con or Peter go to buy food and beer and come back and watch tv at the big house. Con's place. So . . ." he trailed off.

Green pills? I had only a sketchy idea what the kid was talking about. Drugs, maybe. But I got enough of what the kid was saying. "So we better get the spots before they discover the old guy is dead and the cops are all over the place."

"Yeah."

Crap. Discovering Thomas Malvern dead had put a new wrinkle into this. I certainly didn't want any of the other three coming down the road, discovering the police at Malvern's trailer, panicking, and moving the animals.

"Okay. My friend's car is parked in the back of Mrs. Larsen's store. When we get there, I'll call Miranda. Maybe there's a way to hurry this up."

"Will he be very mad?" Trouble said.

"Who?"

"Your friend who owns the flying robot. I don't want him to be really mad at me."

I understood Trouble's fear. Who knew what adults would be likely to do when they got ticked off at kids? If Peter Blanchard had burned Trouble's arm when he was in a good mood, who knew what Lawrence might do if he was mad? It made sense.

"No, Lawrence isn't like that," I reassured him. "We've been good friends for years. He doesn't get really mad. At anything. He'll be sorry his drone doesn't work, but like I told you back at the trailer, it can be fixed. You know," I told him, "one time a young guy who works for Lawrence was learning how to fly the drone and it fell in a pond. Lawrence didn't get mad. He just got the drone fixed. Most things can be fixed, Trouble."

And then we were at the Range Rover. Lawrence came out to meet us, looking up at the rain in fussy disgruntlement. He stood, peering down at Trouble, and I tried to imagine how the kid saw him – a slender, bespectacled, sandy-haired, *tall* adult. Right now, perhaps an intimidating adult. *C'mon, Lawrence*, I willed, *smile at the kid.*

"I'm sorry I shot it," Trouble said solemnly, handing him the drone.

To Lawrence's credit, he did summon up a smile. "Well, it's not the first time it's had an accident," he said, opening the hatch and stowing the drone inside. "It's all right." He came back around the side of the car.

"Trouble, this is Lawrence," I said. Aliya had hopped out of the passenger side of the Rover and I introduced her, too. "And my other friend, Aliya. Guys, this is Trouble. He's going to show us where the Bengals are."

"Great!" Aliya said enthusiastically.

Trouble looked Aliya over appraisingly. "Did you help Kieran trick Stef and get the little spots?" Trouble asked her.

"We sure did," Aliya told him, giving me one puzzled look, but gamely going along with things. "Lawrence and I both helped."

Trouble nodded, clearly having made up his mind that we were all on the side of the angels. Or at least of the Bengals.

"I have an idea," I said. "Aliya, why don't you take Trouble into Larsen's and buy him some hot chocolate? We all need to get out of the rain and Trouble could probably use something hot to drink. I think I saw donuts there, too."

The kid's eyes lit up and Aliya put her hand on his shoulder. "Let's go get that hot chocolate and some donuts," she said. "We can get to know each other. I work for Lawrence. My brother and I came here from Lebanon. Do you know where that is?" Trouble looked up at her appraisingly, and shook his head.

"C'mon," she said. "I'll tell you all about Lebanon." She held out a hand and Trouble took it. I had temporarily forgotten that Aliya had younger brothers. Trouble would be just fine with her.

Inside the Range Rover, Lawrence turned on the heater and I filled him in on everything that had happened at Thomas Malvern's trailer. Midway through my tale, a grey Saanich police car turned off the highway, accompanied by a coroner's van, and disappeared down the road that Trouble and I had just come from.

"I guess I don't need to call Miranda," I said. "With any luck, the police and the coroner will be done and out of there soon so we can go get Norma's cats. I think Trouble is worried that Connor or Stephanie or Peter will walk down to the trailer and see all the activity. I know that worries me. With any luck we can spirit the cats away before the three of them even wake up. The Oak Bay pets . . . well, we'll see."

"Okay," he said. "So we wait for the police and the coroner to come back this way, then, what, Miranda will call us?"

"That's the plan so far," I told him. "Then Trouble takes us to the Bengals. That will certainly save us time sloshing around in the rain. He wasn't very specific, but I gather Stephanie has stashed them in or near a small trailer off a narrow road not too far from Malvern's. Farther on is what Trouble calls 'the big house.' Although apparently

Connor, Stephanie, and Peter all live there now. I bet that's where the Oak Bay pets are."

"Complicated living arrangements," Lawrence commented tactfully.

"No kidding." looked at my watch. Almost two o'clock. *Come on, come on*, I fumed. How long did it take to load a dead man into a van and take him away, anyhow? Or maybe I was being an insensitive harpy. Whatever.

At that moment, Aliya pulled the Range Rover's passenger side door open.

"He's not here?" she asked in evident dismay. "I thought he might have come back here."

"Who?" I said, my heart sinking. But I was afraid I knew.

"Trouble!" she exclaimed. "He finished his hot chocolate, then went to use the rest room. But he didn't come out. Mrs. Larsen went to check. To see if he was ill."

"Let me guess. There's a bathroom window and it's open."

"How did you know?" she asked, clearly amazed.

"Never mind. I just do." What the hell? Had the kid betrayed us? Why? Weighed his odds and decided better the devil you know? Was he even now on his way to the big house to tell Stef, Con, and Peter what was going on and throw himself on their tender mercies?

"Okay," I said. "This is what we'll do."

Miranda suddenly appeared at Aliya's shoulder, rain running off her anorak's hood, a black garbage bag filled with bulky items in her arms. "What will we do?" she asked.

"Oh good, you're here," I said. "What's happening at Malvern's?"

"Oh, not much. The cops are about to leave. I told them a fairy tale about why I was there. The coroner's people were loading the body when I left. No need for me to stay any longer. I'll tell you all about it later. Where's the kid?"

I ground my teeth in frustration. "Gone. Bolted."

"Well, shit," she said, frowning, evidently nonplussed. "I don't get it. But you were about to elaborate on what we should do?"

"What the hell," I said. "Let's transfer four of your carriers from the van to the back of the Range Rover, Miranda. It's got a better chance of not getting stuck in the mud. Then to hell with exact directions. We'll do this without Trouble."

Chapter 21

As I helped Miranda transfer four medium-sized cat carriers from her van to the back of Lawrence's Range Rover, she brought me up to speed on what had happened back at Malvern's trailer.

"I had a chance to look around while I was waiting for the Saanich police," she said. "The place is a pit. I'm surprised anyone could have lived there. A couple of leaks in the ceilings of the bedrooms, wet, fusty carpets, black mold growing in the bathroom and the kitchen. Trouble must have lived in the small back bedroom – it's really a storage room with boxes stacked everywhere. He'd made a bed of blankets in an empty box. There's a pile of small size clothes that need washing – probably his – a flashlight, a box of cartridges for his air pistol, a book about a boy named Bomba who had adventures in the Amazon jungle, and some notebooks filled with printing and sketches. I found a big garbage bag and packed a few things: the book, the notebooks, the box of cartridges." She stowed the garbage bag carefully in the back of her van. "I also had a chance to poke around in the front room." Under Malvern's dead gaze? I shivered.

She continued: "In the bookcase, I found a fat file of Malvern's marked 'Important Papers' so I tossed that into the bag as well. I also helped myself to his laptop and his phone. I figured Trouble might as well have those things." She shook her head. "I know one of the Saanich police officers who came to the trailer – Lucy Singh. She told me that they'll be contacting the health department. The trailer will be condemned. Trouble won't be able to go back there. So I took the things I thought might be useful to him." She frowned. "But where is he?" she said in frustration.

"I'm trying to figure that out myself," I told her. "Peter Blanchard scared the crap out of him a while ago. He lit the kid's arm on fire. I think Trouble is a pretty skittish kid."

"For God's sake!" she exclaimed. "What a prince Blanchard is." She bared her teeth in a snarl. "When I knew him, he was up to his neck in dog fighting. He organized fights and organized the dog thefts, too. He was dirty long before he met the Malverns. But we could never make anything stick. And then, as you know, we got called off our big chance to nail the three of them. This fits right in with that kind of behavior. What a big, brave guy, abusing a little kid. Trouble might weigh fifty pounds soaking wet." She shook her head.

"Given that Trouble told us he used to bolt out the trailer window whenever he saw Peter, I don't think it's likely he'll go back to what he calls 'the big house'." I told her, "It just isn't safe for him there. I admit I had some unworthy thoughts about him a bit ago and wondered if he had changed his mind about us, but now I admit to being just perplexed."

"Hmm," Miranda said, "so he bolts when he's scared. I wonder what scared him while he was having hot chocolate at Larsen's?"

"I wonder, too," I said. "He's an odd little duck."

"Remember what he told us," Miranda said. "About the Bengals. He seemed pretty invested in their going back to people who loved them. So maybe he thought he could help us by getting to Stephanie's place first. Maybe he thought he could prevent her from taking more of the Bengals away."

The more I thought about it, the more likely this seemed. After all, he did say that he had to guard the spots.

"Here's the most interesting thing I found at Malvern's trailer, though," she said, reaching inside her anorak and bringing out a baggie. She held it out to me and I took it, not recognizing the grey-green pills inside it. I shook my head. "Greenies," she said. "Street fentanyl. These are more toxic than opioids or heroin. There must be over a hundred pills here. I found the baggie in the side pocket of the recliner. These maybe what killed Malvern. They're lethally potent and completely unpredictable."

"Jesus," I said, handing the bag back to her. "Malvern was an addict?"

"It seems so," she replied.

"Hmm," I said. "Maybe they all are. Maybe that's why Stephanie couldn't take care of the Bengals. Trouble did say that they took pills and went to sleep. Why didn't you leave the baggie for the cops to find?"

She grinned and stuffed the bag back into her jacket. "Standing in that squalid trailer, I had an idea. These pills might just deliver justice."

"I'm all ears," I said. "I'm always up for justice."

"Here's what I have in mind," she said."It's futile to think that Connor, Peter, and Stephanie will be prosecuted for animal theft or animal cruelty. Bunchers always have a way of wiggling out of charges against them. They keep false records . . . the animals were found roaming the streets, or surrendered voluntarily yadda yadda. Add to that the fact that crimes against animals, even if they do come to court, still have laughable penalties."

"Tell me about it," I said bitterly.

Miranda shot me a look of sympathy and continued. "So I thought if the law can't get these guys on animal cruelty charges, or theft, well, maybe possession of over a hundred bootleg fentanyl tablets – enough to constitute drug dealing charges – might interest the police."

"But the drugs were found in the old guy's trailer," I pointed out. "Not even I could have prosecuted the dead."

"I found them in Malvern's trailer, true enough," she said. "But what if the cops were to find them somewhere else?"

Now it was my turn to grin. "Such as the big house? After we've retrieved the Oak Bay pets, of course."

"Of course."

"You're a genius," I told her.

"I thought we'd be on the same page about this," Miranda said, closing the van door. "Right now, though, do you have any idea where we're going?"

༚

"Okay," I told Lawrence as we bounced through the ruts and potholes on our way to Malvern's trailer. "We're looking for a narrow road branching off this main road. It can't be too far. Trouble made the trip between the big trailer and Stephanie's trailer every day to feed the Bengals. And it has to be passable by car. Stephanie drove her Honda down it earlier today. Twice."

"What about here?" Aliya asked, pointing to a narrow trail leading off into the underbrush. Lawrence stopped the Range Rover while we looked at it.

"I don't think so," I said. "Not wide enough. And it's pretty overgrown – see all those salal bushes and wild rhodies? Maybe it's a deer trail. And I don't see ruts a car would have made in the dirt. Let's drive on."

"Look over there," Aliya said in a minute. "Off to the right. It's a slightly bigger road. A car could easily drive down it. And even though it's muddy, I can see the ruts that you're talking about, Kieran."

"I see them, too," I said. "Okay, Lawrence, let's turn in here. Slow and careful. We don't want to surprise anyone."

Driving slowly, low-hanging evergreen branches brushing the roof of the Range Rover, Lawrence pulled up behind a muddy black Honda Civic. Just ahead of it in a little clearing was a tiny grey travel trailer, square and boxy, looking like an oversized toaster.

"Wow," Lawrence said. "Bingo. Stephanie's car. Now what?" He turned to look at me.

"Now Miranda and I go have a chat with her," I said with far more confidence than I felt. "And with any luck we'll soon be loading nine Bengals into cat carriers and taking them back to Zee's."

"What will you do with Stephanie?" Aliya asked.

I didn't have a clue. Still, something would occur to me. It always did. Improvisation was yet another of my middle names.

"This will be interesting, to say the least," Miranda commented as we got out of the Range Rover. "Shall we just go and knock, or sneak around a little first?"

"Let's sneak," I said. "Trouble told me the cats are in a pen with a sort of tarp over it. I assume that's out back behind the trailer. I'd like to actually see them before we barge in and start berating Stephanie. There's no danger of her taking off, at least not in her car. Lawrence has her blocked in."

The rain had stopped again, and the sky looked a bit brighter, but wet bushes brushed our legs as we made our way past the black Honda, past the trailer, to a small clearing behind it.

"Well, shit," I said, seething at what I saw as we stepped into what could optimistically be called the back yard. A six by ten foot chain-link dog pen had been set up a little ways behind the trailer. In it, on a wet plywood shelf, huddled two miserable-looking piles of Bengal cats. The spots. Even soaking wet they were beautiful. One of them looked up, opened golden eyes, saw me, and meowed silently. Another emulated the first, but voicelessly also. That seemed ominous to me. Pissed-off cats complain very loudly in my experience, but these poor things seemed exhausted, dispirited, hopeless. Just as Trouble had said, a plastic blanket – in actuality a blue tarp – had been thrown over the top of the pen, but it had blown mostly askew, giving the cats virtually no protection from the rain. Puddles on the muddy ground below the Bengals' shelf provided the only water I could see. And milk which Trouble had poured through the wires onto the shelf had pooled into curdled-looking globs here and there.

I stepped around to the front of the cage but the chain link door bore a sturdy padlock, effectively trapping the cats inside. One of the Bengals called to me quietly, plaintively, and I shook my head in anger. This didn't make sense. The Bengals were a valuable asset. Why risk their health like this? Not to mention that leaving them out in the rain like this was bloody inhumane. "Just a minute, guys," I told them. I was sure glad Jen wouldn't have to see this. Would these cats ever again be the loving, confident beauties whose photos, and blue ribbons, adorned the cattery walls at Wild At Heart?

A female voice yelled something loud and unintelligible from inside the trailer. Stephanie, I presumed. "Let's invite ourselves in," I called to Miranda who had a couple of fingers through the wires of the pen, trying to soothe the cats.

"Let's do," she said grimly.

We went back around to the front of the trailer and I pounded on the tinny front door.

"Con?" a woman's voice called. "Get in here and help me!"

"Oh dear, was that a cry for help?" I asked Miranda.

"Seems as though it was," she replied.

"So I guess we better render assistance," I said, turning the knob and kicking the door open. I stepped inside to see Stephanie sitting at a table in the trailer's makeshift kitchen, hands in the air. Standing in a far corner of the trailer, gun held on Stephanie, was Trouble. I might have laughed if the situation hadn't been so dire.

"Who in hell are you?" she asked me. Getting a good look at her, I was not impressed. Greasy brown hair, bad skin, bad teeth. I guessed Stephanie had never been a beauty, but hard living was swiftly catching up with her.

I said nothing and she gave me a bewildered look. "Whoever you are, take the gun away from that kid. Trouble, dammit," she said, in exasperation, addressing the kid in question, "give this lady your gun."

"Nuh uh," he said, pointing the gun at her unwaveringly. "Give me the key to the spots' cage."

Miranda had come into the trailer behind me and uttered one small smothered laugh. "Ah, a difference of opinion. In my experience, usually the guy with the gun wins the disagreement."

"Hey, you two need to help me," Stephanie said. She looked from Miranda to me. "Well?"

I ignored her. "What's up, Trouble?" I asked the kid.

"Stef won't give me the key," he said, agitated. "I'll make her. I'll shoot her."

"I understand," I told him. "I'd like to shoot her myself. But we need that key. So maybe stand down, soldier. Reinforcements have arrived."

Trouble hesitated, then slowly lowered his gun. Good.

"Who the hell *are* you two?" Stephanie asked again, lowering her hands.

"Oh shut up," I told her wearily. "Just hand over the key to the padlock."

"I don't have it," she said, but her eyes flickered briefly to her purse which lay on the trailer's small kitchen counter.

"You amateur thieves are such untalented liars," I told her, grabbing her purse and emptying it into the sink.

"Hey!" Stephanie shouted.

The usual crap fell out of the purse, along with a set of keys. I held the keys up and examined them: a Honda key, two different Schlage keys, presumably for front door locks, a tiny one that looked like a mailbox key, and a small, shiny, brass-colored one bearing a Yale logo. Betting that was the padlock key, I took it off the key ring and tossed it to Miranda.

"Will you go out back and try this?" I asked her. "If it doesn't fit, I may have to do some serious arm-twisting in here."

I looked at Trouble standing uncertainly in the corner of the trailer. "Hey Trouble, want to go with Miranda and check out the key?" His eyes lit up and he nodded. "You can put the gun away," I told him, giving him a wink. "I've got this now." He sidled past me and I realized that despite his tough talk, he was trying to keep as much distance as possible between himself and Stephanie. Even though he had downplayed Stef and Con's mistreatment, I guessed that Peter hadn't been his only tormenter. "Good work," I told him as he squeezed past me. Heck, better to tell him that I appreciated his help than berate him for running away. As for his penchant for brandishing a gun to solve problems, well, we'd have to talk about that. Now, however, I had another problem to deal with.

"You can't take them," Stephanie said, deciding to play the affronted property owner. "Those are my cats. They're worth a lot of money. You're trying to rip me off. "

"They are indeed worth a lot of money," I told her, poking through the rubble of stuff that had fallen out of her purse. It took me only a few seconds to find what I was looking for – the envelope containing the ten hundred dollar bills that I had given Lawrence to purchase the two Bengals this morning. I stuffed the envelope into my jacket. "But they aren't your cats."

"They are so my cats," she blustered. "You can't prove that they aren't. And that's my money you just took. You're stealing from me." He eyes darted to the spilled contents of her purse. "I'll call the police."

Fishing her phone out of my pocket, I told her: "But you'd need this. I liberated it from the junk I dumped out of your purse."

"Who–" she started again, but I had had enough.

"Oh, cut the crap," I told her. "Norma Carruthers hired me to get her cats back. My friends and I are taking them out of this hellhole. I don't have time to fool around with you. The cats are sick, Stephanie. Shit, you haven't even fed them. The kid tried to do that. Whatever made you think you could stash them in a dog pen and leave them outside in the rain? They're not *things*. They live, breathe, feel. They're just like us."

"Con and Peter just stash them," she said indignantly, as though their model of animal cruelty was something to be emulated.

Miranda and Trouble came back into the trailer. "It's the right key," she told me. "Shall we start loading the cats? We have four carriers and there are eight cats, so–"

"Wait," I told her. "Eight cats? There should be nine cats. Eleven cats were stolen. Stephanie sold two to Lawrence and Aliya, so that leaves nine. Are you sure there are only eight out there?"

Miranda nodded. "Yes. I'm sure."

Furious, I turned to Stephanie. "You piece of shit. Did you sell another one?"

"No, I swear," she said, evidently frightened by the expression on my face.

"It's the baby spot," Trouble broke in. "He's so small he walked through the wires."

"Walked through . . . do you mean he got *out?*"

Trouble looked as though he might cry. "Twice," he said, his voice breaking. "I put him back. But he wouldn't stay."

I turned on Stephanie. "And you didn't notice this? That one of your pieces of stolen merchandise was missing?" Now I felt as though I might cry. Because Trouble's 'baby spot' must be Wild Thing, the smallest of the three-month-olds, the kitten Jen had been working with, her favorite, the one she wanted to adopt. And now he was where? Wandering around in the woods? Jesus. How could I show my face at Zee's without him?

"Trouble, go on out to the driveway, will you? Lawrence and Aliya are there in Lawrence's car. Ask them to bring the cat carriers. You can help them." He nodded and hurried out the door.

"As for you," I told Stephanie in a fury, "you're coming with us. I'm so goddammed mad at you I can't see straight. But I'm sure as hell not leaving you here so you can rush off to Con and Peter and tell them what happened."

I went into the trailer's small bathroom. There were some towels there and I grabbed them, opened the door, and threw them at Stephanie. There was a sweater hanging over the back of my chair and I threw that at her too. "Get on out there and help with the Bengals. You can make yourself useful by drying them before they go into the carriers, you asshole."

Stephanie seemed paralyzed. "I'm sorry," she blubbered.

"Don't you fucking talk to me," I told her. "You're only sorry that you got caught. This little cat caper you pulled is felony theft. And crawling through Norma's doggie door is still breaking and entering. That all adds up to lotsa jail time, sweetie. So think about that while you're helping. Get out of my sight."

When she made no move to get up, Miranda grabbed her by the collar of her denim jacket and hauled her out the trailer door. I could hear Miranda talking to Lawrence and Aliya in the driveway, and I closed my eyes, willing myself not to scream, or cry, or start ripping the trailer apart. There'd be time for screaming and ripping later. Right now my friends and I had eight sick cats to deliver to Zee. There was no time to search for Wild Thing. We had to focus on the ones we could save.

And as for me? I had to figure out what the hell I was going to say to Jen, who was back at Zee's, waiting, believing that I would find them all, as I told her I would, and bring them all back.

Chapter 22

I CALLED ZEE to tell her to expect us and calculated we were twenty minutes out. Lawrence, Aliya, Trouble, and two carriers of Bengals were in Lawrence's Range Rover just ahead of us on the highway. When the Range Rover sped away, Aliya and Trouble were in the back seat, tending to the remaining three-month-old Bengal who was clearly suffering, Aliya showing the kid how to tuck it under his sweatshirt to warm it up. The adult Bengals seemed much better off than the kitten, which was to be expected, but Lawrence was taking no chances and had put the two carriers on the front seat with the heater turned up to high. I was certain everyone would be toasty by the time they arrived at Zee's.

Miranda, Stephanie, two carriers of Bengals, and I were in Miranda's van, bringing up the rear. Why had I brought her along? Because I didn't dare let her out of my sight. But Stephanie's petulant silence had quickly turned to tears and wailing, which was fast becoming tedious.

"You can't do this!" she shrieked from the back seat. "This is kidnapping!"

"I can do this," I told her. "Consider it a citizen's arrest."

"There's no such thing as a citizen's arrest," Stephanie screamed. "You're making that up!"

"I'd listen to her if I were you," Miranda said calmly to the shrieking young woman. "Kieran used to work for the Crown Counsel's office. She knows what she's talking about. You're in a lot of trouble. But she told you that back at the trailer, didn't she? Felony theft. Breaking and entering." She tut-tutted and shook her head to emphasize the gravity of the situation. "I sure wouldn't want to be you."

"But you got the damned cats *back*!" Stephanie screamed. "So I took them. I made a mistake. Everyone makes mistakes. What do you want from me anyhow?"

When neither of us answered, she began weeping again. "I can't go to jail. I just can't!"

"Or for God's sake, it's prison, not Mordor!" I snapped at her. "You'll get a couple of years. Maybe more. So what? At least you'll get free cable. What are you so damned afraid of? Ruining your resume? Not getting your favorite shampoo behind bars?" She lapsed into silence and suddenly the reason for all this screaming and fear smacked me in the head. I got it. Actually, Trouble had given me the reason hours ago when he told me that the three of them – Peter, Con and Stef took green pills and passed out soon afterwards.

"You're a user," I said. "An addict." I turned to look at her. Of course she was. How could I ever have thought anything else? "A fentanyl addict. Was that why you stole the Bengals? To pay for your habit? Or was it something else?"

She averted her face and said nothing, retreating into silence once again. But I wasn't going to let her stay there.

"Talk to me," I said.

"What's in it for me?" she demanded. "If I talk to you, what do I get?"

I shrugged. "You want to stay out of jail, don't you? Tell us how all this fits together – the theft of the Oak Bay pets, the Bengals, you, Peter and Con, the greenies."

I could see hope, calculation, and the desire to just tell me to go to hell warring in her eyes.

"C'mon, Stephanie," I said, spinning a spiderweb of fiction for her. "Not everyone has to pay for this. Is the lucky person going to be Con? Or Peter? Or is it going to be you?"

Stephanie still said nothing.

"Probably this was Connor Malvern's idea," I said conversationally to Miranda. "He seems like a smart guy from what you told me about him."

Miranda looked sidelong at me, blinked once, and nodded. "Yeah, for sure," she said. "We should maybe offer him the chance to walk away from this."

"Con? He's a fuck-up!" Stephanie screamed at us. "A loser! Him and his father and that Blanchard creep. All they know how to do is steal animals for labs and dogfights. And where does it get them? They're *poor*! They almost got caught up-island a couple of years ago, after I set up that thing at Going To The Dogs for them. They almost screwed that up. Brother, did I hear about how scared they were that the Mounties were going to figure it out and arrest their asses."

"Yes, I think maybe that might have been in the news," Miranda commented in an even voice.

I had surreptitiously taken my phone out of my pocket and hit the Record app a few moments earlier. I certainly wasn't going to rely on my memory for this. Had Stephanie just admitted her part in the up-island animal thefts? The ones the RCMP blamed on coyotes?

"So I guess the Oak Bay pet thefts weren't Connor's idea? Or the Bengals?" I asked disingenuously. "I heard he was a genius."

Stephanie laughed and, as I hoped, rushed to incriminate herself with misplaced pride. "Genius? Con? I told you: he's a fuck-up. I got to know who had animals in the neighborhood and told him. All he and Peter had to do was pick them up. But taking the Bengals was my idea."

"Why would he object?" I asked her. "There was more money to be gained from the sale of the Bengals than from the sale of stolen pets."

"Because that's the way they always did things, him and his stupid father. Wait for a call from the dealer or the dogfighter, steal some animals, get paid, rinse and repeat." She laughed again. "I had a better idea – a way better idea – but because it was *my* idea and not his, or Peter's . . ." She fell silent.

"But you were willing to split the money from the Bengals with those two," I said, remembering what Trouble had told me. "That cash would have lasted you guys for quite a while. That's what you told them, wasn't it?"

"Who . . ." Stephanie began, then shook her head. "Trouble. That little shit has a big mouth. But just for your information, no way would I have split the money with Con and Peter. I had plans to leave as soon as the last cat was sold."

I laughed. "Getting tired of pimping for Con and Peter, were you? Oh, well. It's all water under the bridge now, isn't it? The old Robbie Burns line again," I said.

"I don't know what the hell you're talking about. Listen," she said, returning to her earlier theme. "Listen, I really need to not go to jail. Have I said enough?"

Miranda pulled the van off the highway onto Zee's little road.

"Oh, you've probably said enough," I told her, noting a white Oak Bay Police cruiser sitting in Zee's driveway.

"Okay," she said in evident relief. "Then you'll let me go?"

"Well, that will be up to Detective MacLeish," I said. "You'll be riding back to town with him."

"But you said . . ." she started as the truth suddenly dawned on her. "You lied to me."

"Did I really?" I said. I shrugged. "Hmm, I might just be rusty on the law. After all, I've been retired for a number of years."

"I'll die in jail!" she screamed.

"Nah. You won't," I said unsympathetically. "You'll just think you will."

"It's fine for you," she shrieked at me. "You don't know what it's like! To need to . . . oh, you don't know!"

"Actually, I do know, Stephanie. You're not so fucking special. Lots of us have gone down the rabbit hole." Indeed, I knew all about it. I knew how it was to stare at the Method and Madness bottle on the kitchen table at night, bargaining with myself that I'd just take one drink. Or two or three. Four, tops. Headaches the size of New-foundland in the mornings. The shakes. Yeah, I knew all about it, unfortunately.

"The Bengals were my *chance!*" she screamed. "My way out. I was going to get away! From Con, from Peter, from cleaning houses . . . I . . ." She fell into disconsolate weeping. "I was going to be *happy.*"

"Oh, boo hoo," I told her uncharitably. "A new life built on one big theft? That's a pretty shaky foundation, Stephanie. And besides, happiness is greatly overrated. Whoever said the goal of life was to be happy?" I got out of the van and went to meet Mac, who was standing in the driveway beside the police cruiser.

"Here's someone who's dying to talk to you," I told him as I opened the back door of Miranda's van and Stephanie flounced out. "Superintendant MacLeish, meet Stephanie Walters. The cat burglar."

"Pleased to meet you, miss," he told Stephanie. "Have a seat in the back of the car." He opened the back door for her. "Watch your head."

"I wouldn't let her go to the restroom alone if she says she has to stop at, say, McDonald's," I told him. "She no doubt has running on her mind."

He winked at me. "That's why I brought young Erin along," he said, gesturing to the astonishingly young Constable in the cruiser's driver's seat.

"I'll e-mail you an interesting audio file," I told him. "Stephanie and I had quite a chat on the way here."

Miranda rolled down the van's window. "Hey, Mac," she said. "Nice to see you again."

"Miz Blake," he said with a smile. "You and Miz Yeats retrieved the cats stolen from Wild At Heart, I hear."

"Well, most of them," she replied.

"Listen, Mac," I said seriously. "Stephanie is going to start to feel really bad really soon. She's hooked on, well, I'm not sure what. Fake heroin . . . street fentanyl . . . whatever's in greenies."

"And you know this how?" Mac asked, tilting his head and looking down at me from the thicket of his eyebrows.

I thought guiltily of the bag of greenies in Miranda's anorak pocket. "I can't tell you that right now. Later, for sure," I said enigmatically.

Mac sighed. "I'll let the jail know. There's not much we can actually do, but they'll keep an eye on her. Forced detox is never a picnic."

"Thanks," I said.

"Should I keep my cell phone close by tonight?" he asked.

I nodded. "It might be a good idea. Things seem to be, ah, coming together."

"I thought that might be the case," he said. "Take care, now." He got into the front seat of the cruiser with Erin, and the now-silent Stephanie glared at me from the back seat. Ah well. As Mac said, they'd do what they could for her.

On a whim, I motioned to Mac to roll down Stephanie's window.

"Say, whose kid is Trouble, anyhow?" I asked her.

She gave me one hate-filled look. "Bite me," she said.

❦

Trouble met us at Zee's front door.

"That girl Jen says I'm to show you where to bring the cats," he said, brimming with seriousness. "She said the ones Aliya and Lawrence brought look pretty good." He closed the door carefully behind us. "She cried a little when I told her we didn't have the baby spot, but she wasn't mad at me."

"No one's mad at you, Trouble," I said. "You did the best job you could guarding the Bengals. It's Stephanie's fault they're sick and the little one is missing."

"His name is Wild Thing," he told me solemnly, his blue eyes wide and sad. His blond hair had dried in curls around his face, giving him the look of one of Raphael's angels. Hmmf, I thought. An angelic, fifty pound gunslinger.

"Well, Miranda and I are going back for the dogs and the other cats," I told him. "We'll look for Wild Thing. He's probably just scared and hiding," I said with more confidence than I felt. "Lead on, kiddo."

"We're going to have pizza," he informed me. "Will you come back for that? We could save some for you," he said hopefully. "For when you come back."

I looked at him and frowned. Was he asking me something else, something that had nothing to do with pizza, I wondered.

"I wouldn't miss it," I told him. "Nothing stands between me and pizza. So you darn well better save me a piece."

He grinned. I noticed that he had shed his camo jacket and now had his oversized navy sweatshirt sleeves rolled up above his elbows. Ominously, the remnants of the burn he said Peter had caused on his arm stood out red and ragged-looking. I'd have Zee take a look at it.

I followed Trouble down the hall to the makeshift ICU. He held the door open, and as Miranda and I walked in with a carrier apiece, Jen called to us:

"Hi, you guys. Just put the carriers on the counter over there." Although I knew she knew better, her eyes darted to the carriers of Bengals from which Wild Thing was absent. I felt like a worm.

"Trouble, will you get four more needles out of the drawer over there? The big ones, like I showed you? Sixteen gauge," Donovan asked the boy. "Be sure to wash your hands first."

Trouble nodded and climbed up on a stool in front of the sink, evidently taking his vet tech duties very seriously. I was glad that Jen and Donovan were making him a part of the Bengals' care. He need-ed to feel included, I thought. It would give him a chance to feel worthwhile, to redeem himself. I wondered if that had been Zee's idea. Probably.

"It's getting pretty crowded in here," Jen told me. "Donovan, Trouble and I can handle this. Zee said to have you and Miranda go to her office." She gave me a small tremulous smile, "Thanks, Kieran."

"Hey, the day isn't over yet," I told her, forcing myself to sound cheerful.

"I know," she said, nodding. "Just . . . I know."

∾

Miranda excused herself to go to the kitchen and use her phone. I joined Zee in her office where she was sitting at her desk, reading some papers in a file. She closed the file as I came in, and swiveled her chair around to face me.

"I think the Bengals will suffer no permanent ill effects," Zee said in her precise way. "I have left Jen and Donovan in charge of their rehydration. And in charge of Trouble, that oddly-named child." She smiled. "Jen and Donovan are competent animal care technicians. Although I do not believe that either of them will want to pursue that profession. They are quite talented musicians. Have you heard about the opera they are re-imagining for their class project?"

I shook my head in amazement. "Re-imagining an opera? I remember Jen told me about a music project the morning she came to report the Bengal theft. But I had no idea she would be tackling something so ambitious. Which opera is it?"

She chuckled. "Something called *Tommy*. Jen and Donovan are uncertain what their music teacher will think of their choice, but they are working hard on it nevertheless. In fact they were at work on the aria last time I listened in."

"Wow," I said. "I remember that song: see me, feel me, if I remember correctly. Everyperson's plea for understanding."

"They are worried about performing it at school, so Donovan's sister is providing an opportunity for them to do a kind of rehearsal."

"Donovan's sister?"

"Apparently Celine – Donovan and his siblings were named after singers, so he informed me – works at a coffee house close to town. The manager has graciously agreed that Jen and Donovan can perform their re-imagined opera for coffee house patrons tomorrow night. They are hoping for some good feedback. That will let them make some changes in the opera before school next week". She looked at me shrewdly. "I am certain Jen would want you to attend."

"I'll be there," I said.

Zee smiled and changed the subject back to cats. "The Bengals were lucky they did not have to spend another night out in the rain," she said. "They had a closer call than I wanted to let Jen know. The kittens will take longer to recover, but I believe they will all be well."

"Thank God," I said.

"I doubt that God a hand in this," she said. "You found them in very short order."

I shrugged, uncomfortable with Zee's praise. "I had help."

"It's good you asked for help," she told me. "Too often we assume we have to attempt the hard things of life alone."

We sat in silence for a moment, then Zee asked: "The young woman who engineered the theft?"

"Stephanie. Mac has her. She's probably being booked right now."

Zee nodded. "Have you called Norma Carruthers?"

"I did. Just before I called Mac. She'll be in touch with you soon. She's eager to come see the cats."

"Of course," Zee said. "She may come whenever she likes."

"I noticed that Lawrence's Range Rover wasn't parked out front," I said.

"Ah, yes," Zee said. "Lawrence asked me to tell you that he had to take Aliya back to town and close up his shop. He said to call if you need him and the Range Rover again."

Miranda knocked at Zee's office door and joined us, leaning against the wall with her arms crossed.

"Everything okay at The Sanctuary?" I asked her.

"More or less," she said. "Felicity's still hiding. Jimmy's still singing. And swearing. And losing feathers. The bird vet made a call. Feather mites, he thinks. At least that's treatable, unlike his cursing. Listen," she said, "I was thinking . . . when we find them, and if it's okay with you Kieran, we can take the dogs and cats from Malvern's to The Sanctuary. Connie can set up caging for the dogs. All I have to do is call her. The cats can go in several of the unoccupied cottages. Depending on their condition, though, they may or may not need vet help." She looked at Zee meaningfully and cleared her throat.

"Of course," Zee said. "I would be happy to help. It might be late, but I will certainly be available."

I sighed. *Okay, Yeats, get up and go, I told myself. You're so fond of quoting things: once more unto the breach.* I realized that the longer I sat there, the more reluctant I had grown to get up and at 'em. I wondered if Miranda was feeling the same, what . . . fatigue? Despondency? Trepidation? Something unpleasant had laid its hands on me, that was for certain. Maybe it was sadness about the kitten I'd had to leave behind. Or maybe it was just low blood sugar. I mentally shook myself. Once more unto the breach indeed. Time to go.

"Shall we?" I asked Miranda, getting to my feet.

She nodded. "Let's shall."

"What about the boy?" Zee asked me as she walked us to her front door. "To whom does he get returned?"

What about the boy? Wasn't that a line from one of the songs in Tommy? I asked myself. "Damned if I know," I told her. "I'll figure it out. But for the time being, can I park him here?"

"Of course," she said graciously.

As Miranda and I walked to her van, she said: "My van won't hold all the pets you've told me are being held at Con and Peter's place. Do you have, well, a plan for that?"

"Great minds," I chuckled. "Yes, I do. Have a plan that is. Remember what Roy Scheider said in *Jaws? 'We're gonna need a bigger boat'.* So if you drive to Starbuck's, and make a stop at the hardware store next door to it, I'll make some phone calls. About a bigger boat. Or two."

Chapter 23

W E HADN'T SEEN the sun all day, so when God, or The Caretaker (a Star Trek conceit that I liked a lot better), turned
the dimmer switch down another notch, I realized this day must be
coming to a close. Fie on the romance of the gloaming anyhow: this
was simply bloody inconvenient. At least the rain hadn't started up
again. I'd had a few moments' misgivings about the wisdom of fetching the Oak Bay pets tonight, but a little interior voice urged me on.
I've found that ignoring my inner nag is rarely a good idea, so here we
were, boots wet again.

After fortifying ourselves with coffee, Miranda and I left her
van in Larsen's parking lot and just started walking, slogging our way
through the mud down the narrow road that wound between tall evergreens, past Stephanie's trailer, to . . . this place. What Trouble had
referred to as "the big house" looked like the misbegotten offspring of
the Bates Motel and the Hotel California. The living quarters seemed
to have originally been a small, tan, three bedroom shake-roofed house
which had spawned a myriad of radically different dwarf dwellings all
connected by decks and breezeways. It was a marvel of wacky architec-

ture and, no doubt, DIY construction. Frank Lloyd Wright beset by reefer madness. I was willing to bet no building permit had ever been posted on these premises. The main house as well as the anaconda-like sprawl of serial outbuildings had fallen into serious disrepair – indeed, the shake roofs all bore fuzzy topknots of moss, and in places, alarming swathes of siding had simply gone AWOL, leaving exposed plywood and support beams patched with black mold and damp.

Between the big house and the dog pens was a parking area, and a muddy black Jeep was parked there beside a grey pickup. Presumably Con's and Peter's vehicles. So they were both inside, somewhere. Good. That made our job less nerve-wracking.

However what interested me most was the kennel structure. Thoughtfully, for the comfort of the pets the kennel once housed, a slanted metal roof covered the dog pens, of which there seemed to be about three dozen. In its heyday, as Jan Larsen had explained, it had catered to pet owners who dropped Fritz or Fanny off here on their way to the ferry, and picked them up after their return trip. But that had evidently been some time ago. According to Miranda, Malvern junior and senior, as well as the malevolent Peter Blanchard, had been conducting their animal theft business up-island three years ago and for who knew how many years before that. So this place had probably been deserted for decades. Until now. Until the gang of four moved in and brought their illegal bunching business here.

The dog pens were deserted no longer, though. Even in the gloom of fast-approaching night, I was able to make out shadowy forms, excited by our arrival, eerily rushing about in their ten by six chain-link prisons in total silence. And yes, each dog's neck bore one of Trouble's "necklaces." Shock collars. That of course was why they weren't barking joyously, scenting rescue, bringing Con and Peter on the run out of the big house. I mentally apologized to the dogs, but my plan depended on their silence. Even in the near-dark I recognized some of the dogs from the photos Finn had sent me: Mara's nine month-old German Shepherd puppy, Dutch's old beagles, Marv and Patty's yellow lab. In a separate pen I recognized the missing cats: a calico, two Siamese, the peripatetic Baxter, and several more. Alarmingly, however, there were dogs who were not pictured in Finn's photos – a Springer spaniel, a Doberman, a Spitz and several others – and

I realized with horror that we had many more pets on our hands than the Oak Bay fifteen.

"Shit, look here," Miranda said in a low voice.

I looked at the pen to which she was pointing and said: "Oh, for God's sake."

It was the body of a dead dog. A long dead dog, therefore not one of the Oak Bay pets, I reassured myself, and quickly felt guilty for my partisan feelings of relief. It was little more than a skeleton covered by a mangy brown fur coat, once a floppy-eared, mixed-breed dog of mostly hound forebears. A dog someone had undoubtedly loved. Questions crowded my mind. Whose pet had this dog been? For how many nights had its owner sat in the dark in her living room, weeping, wondering what had happened? How had it fallen into the hands of the Malverns? And how had it died? Had it gotten sick and received no vet care? Had it starved to death? And why the hell was it still here in its pen? I bent down on one knee and saw, around its neck, a red collar its owner had undoubtedly placed there. BRUNO, it said in now-dirty white letters.

The desire to see the Malverns pay for this dog, and all the other animals they had mistreated, burned hot again in my soul, but I tamped it down. Because Miranda was right. I knew the law. We wouldn't be able to bring the Malverns and Blanchard to justice for animal theft or animal cruelty or neglect or any other kind of crime against animals, and that was beyond frustrating. I had to hang onto her alternate plan for dispensing justice. The greenies she had found in Thomas Malvern's trailer undoubtedly came from the big house. Maybe Con and Peter had stashed them in the old man's trailer for safekeeping? Maybe they were his ration? Who knew? We could simply return them to the source from which they had undoubtedly come – the big house. And with luck, when the police descended on this place, they would discover more. It really didn't matter. The possession of one hundred greenies constituted felony drug trafficking in Canada and, as far as I remembered, the bootleg fentanyl presently circulating in Canada was a Schedule I drug, akin to heroin. Con and Peter would go to jail for a crime the law did punish, and we would have to be content with that. For Miranda, the circle of the Malverns would be closed.

For me, however, things were a little different. I liked the idea of poetic justice as well as anyone. Hell, any justice for those disenfranchised by the legal system was fine. But for me, another end was served by my maverick career choice. Some philosopher said that for those of us who served justice with a small j, our job was not simply to bandage the wounds of victims caught beneath the wheels of injustice, but to drive a spoke into the wheel itself. Sometimes, especially times like this, I believed I was one of the spoke drivers. Other times, the times when I wrestled with the siren song of the Method and Madness bottle, I despaired that the wheels were too numerous, and those of us with spokes and the will to drive them, too few.

"Will you get a photo?" I whispered, tears of rage in my eyes. I wanted documentation of this dog who lay here in unlamented death. Maybe, somehow, we could arrange for its owner to identify it, claim it, connect it to its name, and thereby close their circle of loss. That was probably a fond hope. Most likely, when all this was over, I would have to come back for it, take it away to some green field, and bury it.

"Got it," Miranda said quietly.

I forced my thoughts back to the situation at hand and took out my cell phone. "All right. Time to make some calls."

⁂

As I waited at the far side of the dog pens, Olga appeared out of the gloom, Ellen at her side, a couple of leashes in their hands. Both women wore dark clothing, and Olga's bright hair was tucked up under a black watch cap.

"Did you have any trouble finding the road?" I asked quietly.

Olga shook her head. "Nope," she whispered. "Leaving glow-sticks to light the way was an inspiration."

"I thought they'd be helpful," I said. "How much transportation did you round up?"

"Five vans. Seven people. We're going to bring the dogs out two at a time on leashes, load them into vans, and drive to The Sanctuary. Are the pens here locked?"

"No. Just latched."

192

Her teeth gleamed in the near darkness in a grin and I realized that she was relishing this adventure. "It's a pity we can't shoot a video," she said. "Open The Cages could really make use of the footage."

I shook my head. "No. The light would bring Con and Peter out of the house and I really want them to stay inside. But I want you to take individual photos of the dogs. With their shock collars on. Who knows, if we need more charges against the animal thieves, we might be able to use them. But if everything goes well, your people will have spirited the animals away and the bunchers won't know what happened. Until it's too late."

"Ha, then it'll be who let the dogs out, arf, arf, right?" she said merrily. Olga was plainly giddy with delight. "So what's the story? Are they drunk in there? Stoned?"

"Something like that. But don't worry. You're in charge of animal liberation. Miranda and I will take care of the guys in the house."

"And if they decide to come out?"

Now it was my turn to smile. "Well, we'll just have to reason with them. They're not going to interfere with your people. We'll see to that."

"Okay," she said. "We've done this kind of thing under riskier conditions. I'll call you when the last animal is loaded."

"Say, did you bring carriers for the cats?" I asked her.

"Sure did." She gave my shoulder an encouraging pat. "We're old pros at this. Don't worry. We'll have everyone tucked up at The Sanctuary before you know it."

I met Miranda in the tiny parking area, just in front of the ramshackle deck surrounding the big house. She was leaning against the grey pickup and straightened up when she saw me.

"All quiet inside?" I asked her.

"Strangely, yes," she said quietly. "I tiptoed up onto the deck and looked in the lighted window there at the end of the house. That's the living room. The two of them are sacked out with the television going. That will help to cover any noise Olga's friends might make. Con's on the sofa and Peter's in an easy chair. Unbelievable." She put her hands in the pockets of her jeans. "This is too easy. Do you think we're going to be able to pull this off without Con and Peter interrupting us?"

"I sure hope so," I said. "If not, well, you know."

"Yeah," she said. "I know. But I prefer not to have to do that."

"Me too," I said. "So let's go hunker down by the front door and play Cerberus."

"Cerberus?"

"Yeah, the horrible many-headed dog that the Greeks believed guarded the gates to hell. It was his job to make sure none of the dead got out."

"You know the weirdest things," she said.

"I do," I agreed.

⁊

We almost pulled it off undisturbed. For about an hour, things went pretty smoothly. Then, something – a noise, a voice in his head, the realization that Stephanie hadn't returned – brought Con to the door. The first we knew about it was when an outdoor light which I had neglected to notice went on, flooding the dog pens with dismayingly bright illumination.

"Oh crap," I muttered.

A skinny, short guy, long, greasy light brown hair, three days growth of stubble on his face, baggy jeans, and a brown T-shirt opened the door and stepped out onto the deck.

"What the fuck?" he said, as two dark-clad figures led the last of the dogs on leashes around the corner of the dog pens into the sheltering darkness. "Hey, you, stop!" he yelled.

The dark figures and the dogs began to run. He started across the deck, clearly intending pursuit, forgetting he was in his socks, and Miranda stuck out her foot. He fell down the stairs into the yard with a desperate cry of "Shit!" and the door slammed shut behind him. Miranda jumped off the deck after him, hauling him upright by the neck of his T-shirt and twisting an arm up behind his shoulderblades. When he opened his mouth to yell again, she rapped him hard on the back of his head with her knuckles.

"No noise, asshole!" she hissed at him.

I heard the door to the house open behind me and turned to see the other buncher backlit in the doorway. He took one step out onto the deck and I shoved him hard with one shoulder, knocking him back into the house. He scrambled, lost his balance, and fell backwards over the coffee table, smashing it to bits, landing on a fusty-looking old green sofa, where he lay for a minute, stunned. Then he did what I didn't expect: with a roar, he came off the sofa and lunged for me. He was bigger and stronger than me, but not faster, and I danced out of his way. The ruined coffee table was a problem for him, and he tripped over its splintered remains, falling to one knee.

"Get up," I told him, keeping a respectful distance between us. I saw him measuring the space for a lunge, and realized that he would have charged me again except for my .38 which was pointed at his head.

"Just sit there," I told him. "On the sofa." He did.

"So now what?" he asked, looking at me with pale, expressionless eyes. No 'what the fuck?' for him. Something told me this was Peter Blanchard, the guy who liked to burn kids' arms, the guy who liked dog fighting, the guy Miranda had described as being a piece of work.

"Now we wait," I told him.

He looked at me unblinkingly and I had a chance to study him. Shaved, bullet-shaped head, pale, reptilian eyes, long scruffy brown beard, camo T-shirt, dirty cargo pants. He looked like a refugee from the Grateful Dead, or someone itching for the end of civilization. I wondered what the hell had drawn him to animal theft. Easy money, I guessed.

"What are we waiting for?" he asked coolly.

"The Oak Bay police: the jurisdiction from which the animals were stolen." I told him. I thought of the phone call I'd made to Mac just before my call to Olga, and said a silent prayer that the cavalry would arrive soon. I somehow doubted my ferocious presence would detain Blanchard for long.

"I don't see any stolen animals. So I think you'll have to prove that," he said.

"No, we won't," I told him. "Stephanie gave a statement this afternoon. And Con strikes me as the kind of guy eager to walk away from this crime, too. So I'm afraid: tag, you're it."

He snorted in derision. "You'll have to do better than that. We didn't steal animals . . . they were wandering around the streets. Strays.

There's no law against picking up strays. No one will press charges against us. Hell, no one knows who to press charges *against*. And even if someone did file a complaint, do you think a judge would hear the case? Dream on. The courts are too busy. And one more even if . . . even if the case did go to court and we were found guilty – which would happen about the time pigs fly – the most we'd get is a fine. You need to brush up on the law."

No, I didn't need to brush up on the law. Depressingly, I knew that most of what he said was right. Pets roaming the street were targets for many risks, not the least of which was bunchers, although that was a particularly horrifying fate. I opened my mouth to make a snappy comeback, but a noise behind me broke my concentration. I turned my head for a moment, fearing that Con might have broken free of Miranda and be coming back into the house to help Peter, and in that moment, Blanchard came off the couch at me. He slapped my right hand, hard, and I dropped my gun. Then, repaying the favor I did him, he shoved me backwards toward the front door. I more or less fell into Miranda who was on her way in, and we went down like a couple of Keystone cops. We heard a window break somewhere in the back of the house, and when we had untangled ourselves, Blanchard was gone. I swore loudly and colorfully, because, dammit, so was my gun.

THURSDAY

Chapter 24

MIRANDA AND I sat on the steps of the big house in the dark, trying our best to ignore Con who was curled up, pleading, in his temporary place of incarceration in one of the dog pens. I had no doubt about what was going through his mind: in a couple of hours he was going to start shivering and sweating and generally feeling as though he might die. Too damned bad.

"This feels a bit anticlimactic, doesn't it?" I said, imagining how Miranda must be taking this. "I was hoping we'd have wrapped things up tonight. Landed all the fish so you could write *finis* at the end of the Malvern and Blanchard story."

"I hoped the same thing," she said glumly. "Ah well. By the way, sorry about your gun."

"Well, we got three of the four bad guys we were after. And retrieved ten of the eleven Bengals," I said, trying to cheer her up with a summation. "Plus all the Oak Bay pets. Hell, we got even more pets than we knew were missing. At least five dogs and several cats I didn't recognize. We'll have to get their photos circulating on the internet."

"Yeah, I noticed they were big dogs," she said. "I'm afraid they were destined for dogfighting rings. Godammit, when will these bastards ever get put out of business?"

I said nothing because the answer, or one of the answers, was when people got smarter and started keeping closer track of their pets. When they didn't just open the door, go back to Netflix, or Facebook, and forget Rover out watering the neighbors' flowerbeds. I bet the Oak Bay pet owners would hold their pets a little closer to their hearts after this scare.

"Did you, um, repatriate the bag of greenies?" I asked her.

"I did," she said. "Just shoved them down behind a sofa cushion. I'm guessing the cops will have a field day in there. That one bag will be enough to put Con and Peter away. But I imagine that's not the only bag of pills they'll find. Or worse."

"Worse?"

"Yeah, I bet Con and Peter were dealing. The internet has made that all too possible. Anyone wanting to go into business can order powdered fentanyl from illegal labs in China. Where do you find the merchandise?" she asked rhetorically. "On the dark web. All you need is an account, a credit card, and a delivery address. Canada Post can't open packages weighing less than one gram, and a sample gram costs thirty-five bucks. Bloody cheap, yes? Cut it with fillers and it could make 100 pills. Or, if you don't want to get into the pill business, given that pill presses are now illegal, just sell tiny baggies of adulterated powder. Or if you really have balls, you can order a kilo of fentanyl for twenty grand. That will net you over two million bucks in adulterated sales on the street." She ran a hand through her hair in frustration. "Does it shock you to hear that I really don't care about all this any longer? Maybe I'm unpatriotic. Maybe I lack compassion."

I shook my head. "Well, I don't think you're guilty of either of those things, but no, it doesn't shock me. You've done your time in the trenches."

She grimaced. "Maybe I have at that. I come from a law enforcement family. My father was a tough Vancouver cop. One of my brothers went into the army, even served in Afghanistan, and two are small-town cops on the mainland still. I was the youngest kid by quite a bit, and the only girl. My mother was a teacher, but she died when

I was seven – just about Trouble's age. I remember when I was a little kid I would bring small, wounded things into the house – sparrows with broken wings, injured squirrels – and my mother and I would try to fix them up." She hugged her knees and I realized these must be painful recollections for her. I listened in respectful silence.

"After my mom died, the injured birds and squirrels I brought into the house went right out the back door. The big, brave guys I lived with had no time for small, wounded things. Or pets. Yet when the time came, I, too, went into law enforcement. The RCMP. I decided I'd outcop them all. What stupidity, trying to be one of the boys," she said bitterly. "Trying to be something other than the wimpy girl who cried over broken-winged sparrows. You know, even before the time my squad got involved with the missing animals up-island, I'd become thoroughly sick of law enforcement." She shook her head.

I thought briefly of Trouble, wanting to have as a pet one of the stolen animals that Peter, Con, and his father had stashed in the big house's dog pens. As Trouble had told me, Peter nixed that, though. No pets for Trouble. The fifty pound gunslinger and the retired Mountie had a lot in common.

"After this," Miranda gestured to the ramshackle big house, "it's clearer than ever to me that I just need to run The Sanctuary. I'm still crying over broken-winged sparrows, but now I'm not ashamed of it.

"We did – you and I did – what we could to bring the Malverns and Blanchard to some kind of justice. I feel better that we tried, even though we didn't hit a home run. At least they won't be stealing animals any longer."

I wasn't sure about that, with Blanchard still unaccounted for, but I didn't want to disagree with her. "What's the best part of running The Sanctuary?" I asked her.

She thought for a moment. "Working with throwaway animals who come to us sick and injured. Making them well again. Then finding good homes for them. A cat rescue group I know in Bakersfield, California, has a friendly, supportive vet who describes their mission as turning forsaken felines into furry friends. I like that. Second chances for the forsaken. You know," she said, turning to look at me, "sometimes when people come to us, thinking of adopting a pet, they're wounded, too. They're hurting and they don't even know it. Or they have an empty place inside themselves. Then, they connect with an animal and, just like that, two hearts are healed. It's wonderful."

"Miranda, why don't you go," I said, realizing that of course she wanted nothing more than to be back at The Sanctuary. "I can wait for Mac. He'll run me home."

"No, I'll wait with you," she said. "I can't imagine that Peter went very far. I wouldn't be able to rest thinking that he might pop out of the bushes. I called Connie. She and our volunteers are getting everyone tucked up in cages and cottages, and given good square meals." She yawned. "But when we hand this piece of trash," she gestured to Con, huddled miserably in a corner of his dog pen, "over to Mac and go home, I may sleep for a week. Or until the re-imagined opera tonight. Zee asked me to come. I think she's recruiting an audience for Jen and Donovan." She chuckled. "Want me to pick you up? I know the coffee house, and the parking lot there is tiny."

"Sure," I said. "Thanks. I'm looking forward to hearing what the two of them have done with *Tommy*. I'm probably showing my age and my philistine proclivities, but it's still one of my favorite pieces of music."

"No worries," she said. "I like it, too. Thank God for rock and roll. Didn't some rocker say that music would save our mortal souls?"

"I think so," I said, looking up as twin beams of headlights illuminated the little road from Larsen's. "Superintendant MacLeish has arrived. Again."

❧

Quite a few hours later, I waved goodbye to Miranda and climbed the steps to my front door. We had left Mac and a gaggle of cops salivating over what they were finding in the big house: as Miranda had suggested, there was much more than a baggie of a hundred greenies inside. I tucked the brown bag containing Trey's longed-for cans of Fancy Feast under one arm and put my key in the door, feeling, as some ancient rock song aptly described it: half past dead.

The cats were nowhere to be seen, but I didn't hold it against them. I hoped Trey was sacked out in my bed, buried under the covers where I intended to be just as soon as I shed my shoes and clothes. In my dark, cold house, I tossed my jacket at the sofa, dropped the cans of Fancy Feast on the kitchen table, kicked off my boots on the way to the bedroom, and collapsed on the edge of the bed, hauling off my jeans and peeling off my sweatshirt. Turning down the covers, I found a warm, soft, cat-sized lump at the foot of the bed.

"Mmmf," said Trey softly.

"Mmmf yourself, fat boy," I told him, then, sighing, slid down into the black pit of sleep.

❧

I was on a hillside, knee deep in emerald summer grass, a humming shock of golden light around me. Over the crest of the hill came a woman in a dress so blue it hurt my eyes, skirt billowing out around her. She paused, light brown hair blowing around her face, and I realized this was no one I had ever seen before, yet I seemed to know her.

I heard him before I saw him, and so did she. We knew right away who was bounding across the field to meet us on that hillside in high summer, calling out joyously. He came loping through the grass — a floppy-eared, brown, mixed-breed dog of mostly hound forebears, with shining dark eyes — and as the woman reached for him, falling to one knee, he put his head in her hands. She put her face against his head, rubbed his ears, then stood up, laughing.

"Good boy, Bruno," she said. "Let's go home."

❧

Sometime around dawn, I came awake, tears on my face. Drying my eyes on my sheet, I lay there for a moment in the opalescent light, then got up, ignoring Trey's muttered complaints, and splashed water on my face. Dressing in yesterday's clothes, I made coffee, filled my travel mug, and opened two cans of Fancy Feast Turkey and Giblets, leaving full bowls for Trey and Vlad. From the garden shed in my back yard, I took a few things I needed, then went around the house in the pale morning to my car. It would be, *mirabile dictu*, a sunny day. Maybe T.S. Eliot's opinion of spring could be ignored. Maybe, as someone had pithily remarked, he was just a small dark cloud of a poet.

Lost in thought, I drove out onto Monterey, then south to Beach Drive, along the oceanfront. Had it been only four days ago that I had driven this same route with Jen? It seemed like months. I had a few tasks to complete, some files in my mind that were still open, and I realized that not until I dealt with them would I be able to rest. Then, later, when those jobs were finished, I could come back to bed. Why, I could sleep for the whole day – I wasn't due at the coffeehouse to hear Jen and Donovan's opera until seven. Miranda said she would pick me up at six, so I had the entire day to just . . . veg out. I was looking forward to it. Maybe I would even read a little, or listen to music. At the same time.

I worried all the way to Saanich that my Karmann Ghia would get stuck in the mud of the little road leading to Con and Peter's place, but it didn't. I made one stop at Stephanie's trailer, then carried on down the lane and pulled my car into the parking area between the dog pens and the big house. The dilapidated structure looked even worse in daylight, doubly so because it was now festooned with yellow plastic tape bearing the words CRIME SCENE – DO NOT CROSS in attention-grabbing black letters. I had no intentions of crossing.

I parked my car, got out, and walked towards a grassy spot under a little clump of wild rhododendrons, to the left of the big house, between the dog pens and the forest. The rhodies bore pink buds, and I realized that when they bloomed, this would be a lovely spot. Taking my bundle from the back seat and unwrapping it, I set it on the ground, then walked back to the dog pens. Bruno's body was light and insubstantial in my arms, and I carried him, wrapped in an old grey blanket I had brought from home, to the grassy spot I had picked out under the rhodies. I placed his body gently on the ground, then just started digging. The ground was still damp from the past few days' rain and yielded easily to my spade. I cut foot-square pieces of sod and piled them to one side, then applied myself to making the hole larger. The soil was almost black and smelled intoxicatingly spicy. When the grave was about three feet deep, I realized I'd gotten quite warm, and shed my jacket, tossing it on the ground beside me. Then I picked up the feather-light body of Bruno and laid him, wrapped in his blanket, in the dark earth.

At that moment, my phone rang. I looked up at the achingly blue early-morning sky where a few fluffy white clouds scudded like small ships under sail. Not for the first time, I cursed technology. I wanted to be alone with Bruno, the sky, and a poem I half remembered about dogs, but the intrusive clamor of my phone was yanking me back into the world. Well? A few days ago hadn't I told the world that I was once more available? So here it was, seeking me out in the middle of a ritual I wanted to perform in private.

"It's Jen," she said tentatively. "Sorry if I woke you up."

"You didn't wake me," I told her, looking closely at a rhodie branch, noticing how incandescently green the rounded leaves were, and how the bottom of the bud was a deeper pink than the top. It would be a beautiful flower when it opened. The edges of rhodie petals were frilly, I recalled, their throats speckled. I had a sideways thought about Lawrence and his newly-discovered passion for nature photography. The vole in the iris.

"Hey, you're up early, kiddo," I said, a little knot of worry forming in my stomach. "Everything okay?"

"No," she said. "It's Trouble. We put him to bed in the spare room, but when I went to get him for breakfast, Kieran, he wasn't there. He's gone!"

I closed my eyes. Of course he was.

Chapter 25

I SHOVELED THE damp earth back into the little grave I had dug, placed the pieces of sod on top, and tamped them down a bit with my sneakers. Leaning on my shovel, I thought about the poem I wanted to recall to honor Bruno – a poem called "Where To Bury A Dog" written by a long-dead poet by the unlikely name of Ben-Hur Lampman. I let the poem's lines flow through my mind like bright fish in a stream, and waited like a patient angler. I wanted something fitting, something that would help make sense of the fact that Bruno had suffered and died in that hell for dogs created by the Malverns and Peter Blanchard. Then I had it, the part I had been looking for, the best place to bury something beloved:

"If you bury him in this spot, the secret of which you must already have, he will come to you over the grim, dim frontiers of death, and down the well-remembered path and to your side again. For the best place to bury a good dog is in the loving heart of his owner."

And as I always did when remembering that poem, I wept a little for the beloveds I had lost. Their faces came to my mind just as Lampman had said they would, came over the grim, dim, frontiers of death – a black cat with white stockings and an astonishing spray of whiskers; a white cat with a heart-shaped grey spot on his shoulder; a ginger cat with a white bib and kiwi green eyes.

"Well, that's real nice," a harsh voice called out from somewhere close behind me. "Someone finally buried him. He stank all winter, you know."

I turned. Peter Blanchard stepped out from the forest and leveled a gun at my head. As far as I could tell, it was my gun.

"Yeah, it's yours," he said, putting an end to my wondering. He snickered. "So you might just have to dig that hole a little bigger, because I'm going to shoot you and bury you in it, you interfering bitch." I guessed the intervening hours had had put him in a testy mood, cut off as he was from his supply of greenies. Too bloody bad.

"Well, aren't you going to beg?" he asked. "If you do, I might let you go."

"Nah," I said. I certainly wouldn't beg, but I thought it prudent to point out that he really didn't have to shoot me. Who knew: he might just listen. "C'mon, Blanchard," I coaxed, "why do this? You could just walk away. Fade into the forest. Go on into town. Get whatever you need so you can stop feeling like this."

"Oh yeah?" he shouted, "and pay for it with what? Last night I had to leave my wallet behind in the house. And my car keys. The cops took them. Thanks to you, I don't even have a damned credit card!" He looked at me in fury. "I watched the house for hours last night, and the cops took everything away. Everything! And your friends took the dogs, so . . . " He blinked as his thoughts skittered away in another direction. "Those damned dogs. I hated them, but they were our bankroll. This was going to be the last time we had to steal dogs. And cats. Why in hell do you think I teamed up with the Malverns? They were a couple of losers but they had a sweet animal theft business going. The only smart one was Con's girlfriend Stephanie, but Con could never see that. Stealing the Bengals was inspired."

I thought this wasn't the time to tell him that Stephanie had had no intention of sharing her windfall with anyone, so I said nothing.

He muttered something unintelligible, and I suddenly decided to hell with it. I would just say what I wanted to say.

"Peter, for God's sake, you brought this on yourself. It's hardly my fault. In your stupid, greedy plan to be The Greenie Kings, you and the Malverns did something so horribly wrong it's beyond description. You sentenced hundreds of animals to fear-filled, miserable, unnecessary deaths. You're just as responsible for their suffering as the researchers at the end of this sorry chain. And now? It's payback, you asshole. Malvern senior is dead, probably from an overdose, Stephanie and Con are in jail, and you –"

"Shut the fuck up!" he yelled. "Those animals were just begging to be stolen. There's no such thing as payback. Is that something out of a philosophy book? Like a punishment for being bad? There's no such thing."

I shouted back at him: "There *is* such a thing as payback . . . and you're feeling it right now. Are you sweating? Feeling dizzy? Crampy? Pukey? Unless you bugger off out of here and go get yourself another fix, you're going to cold turkey your own fentanyl. Tell me that isn't payback. Why it's such poetic justice I might laugh." I knew I was walking a tightrope, but I wanted him to get so angry that he forgot himself and took that damned gun off me for a moment. I needed more ranting and raving. I needed him to get careless.

Instead, he cocked the hammer of the revolver, my revolver, and raised the gun to point squarely at my head. I stared down the opening in the end of the muzzle, which seemed huge enough to swallow me up. "Fuck it," he said. "I'm just going to shoot you."

"No!" a small voice called out. "You're not! Hands up!"

Clad in his ridiculous too-large camo jacket, face clenched in determination, Trouble stepped out from the forest behind Blanchard.

A look of rage passed over Blanchard's face and I realized in horror that Trouble might well be the first shooting victim here today. As Peter turned his head to look at this annoyance behind him, his gun hand moved off me just a little and I realized this was my chance. I planted my feet, wound up, and swung the shovel at his head. The force of the blow might well have killed him on the spot, but something – a noise my feet made, a half-glimpsed motion – made him throw his right arm up defensively. The full force of the shovel connected with his right arm with a horrid *crack* – I heard bones break. A millisecond later, the blade collided with the side of his head. He dropped like a felled tree, discharging his gun as he fell, then lay motionless, eyes closed, gun tumbled out of his hand into the bright spring grass.

"Oh shit," I said, tossing the shovel aside. I dropped to one knee and felt for the carotid in the side of his throat. In relief, I felt it pulse strongly. Why in hell was I relieved that he was still alive? Then I looked up at Trouble, who seemed frozen, gun pointed at Peter's head.

"Hey, Trouble," I said. The kid gave no indication that he had heard me. Again, I called to him, louder this time: "Trouble!" but again he didn't hear me.

I could see from his face that he was gone inside his own head to someplace *else*, someplace where there was only rage and the desire to punish, to kill. Trouble was about to deliver his own payback. At last he had his nemesis, his tormenter, at his mercy. I knew where he had gone because I'd been there a a few times myself. The place where Trouble now found himself was a dark, soul-destroying place, a labyrinth, and there was only the Minotaur waiting at its end. I couldn't let Trouble go there. I was not the clever Ariadne who could hand him a ball of string. He wasn't Theseus, he was just an eight-year-old kid and he might never find his way out.

Despite my shouting his name repeatedly, Trouble did not look at me – he seemed lost, determined, his gun trained unwaveringly on Peter's head. In a moment he would pull the trigger and keep on pulling it until the gun's magazine was empty. At this range, even an air pistol would surely kill Blanchard. And if he did kill, I didn't know how the kid would be able to recover from it, how many times he would replay the scene in his head, how it would scar him. I searched frantically for something to say, something that would bring him back to here and now. Nothing bright occurred to me, so I said to him what I had said yesterday in Stephanie's trailer: "Stand down, soldier. I've got this now."

He looked up at me, blue eyes wide, pupils huge and dark, and I saw the fear and rage begin to trickle out of them. He let his gun hand fall to one side.

"He was going to kill you, Kieran," he said, and then the tough little kid cracked and he began to cry, barely coherent words tumbling out of him. "I couldn't let him do that. I tried to guard the spots, but Stef took two of them. Then the little one, Wild Thing, got lost. But you knew how to save Wild Thing. You said so at Zee's. So I had to find you and guard you."

Then he started to shake. His teeth chattered, and heedless of whether this was the right thing to do or not, I just grabbed him and hugged him hard. "Oh, Trouble," I said, "oh, Trouble."

❧

My shovel blow had indeed broken Blanchard's right arm, which he now cradled defensively against his body. It bulged alarmingly, and I realized the break must be a compound fracture. I'm sure it hurt like hell. As well, his head was bleeding – his right ear had also been a casualty of my shovel blow, and was now only nominally part of his head. Too bad. I had stripped off his shirt and used it to roughly bandage his head, which seemed only humane, but I hadn't a shred of pity for him. With only a little urging from me, and some prodding with my .38, Blanchard had stumbled into one of the dog runs, where he now sat in a corner in the dirt, looking ill and clutching his arm. It struck me as pretty damned fitting that both Con and Peter had ended up in the very pens that had held who knew how many stolen pets. What was that Shakespeare had said in *Hamlet*: hoist with his own petard? Indeed.

"Aren't you going to call someone?" Peter demanded. "My arm's broken. And shit, my head's bleeding."

"Yeah, I can see that," I said, not bothering to keep the scorn out of my voice. "For the time being, though, try to be a big boy about things. I'll call for help shortly, and you sure won't like how that's going to end up. In the meantime, you won't get gangrene. So shut up. I'd offer you a painkiller, but, oh dear, it seems the cops took all those away."

I left Peter and went to sit on the steps of the big house, in pretty much the exact spot I had sat with Miranda the night before, this time beside the still- weeping Trouble, who affixed himself to my left arm.

"Sssh, it's okay," I told him. "You saved me. You did. You risked your life. You distracted Peter. You made him look away from me so I could hit him. You were very brave, kiddo."

I handed Trouble a tissue I discovered in my jacket pocket and as he blew, I pulled out my phone and called Mac.

"Morning, Mac," I said, when he answered "Remember the old Meat Loaf song, "Two Out Of Three Ain't Bad"?"

"Hmm, this must be Miz Yeats," he said. "It's unseemly of me to admit it, but I do remember. Just shows you what misguided youths we both had. But I take it your call is not just to reminisce about bad rock music?"

"You take it correctly," I told him. "We can rewrite that song and call it "Three Out Of Three Ain't Bad.""

"You got him, didn't you?" Mac said, satisfaction in his voice. "You got Blanchard."

"I did," I said, wishing I could share whatever jubilation he was feeling. Maybe it was the fact that I had escaped death by a whisker, or that Trouble had almost blown holes in Peter's head that sobered me, but I felt decidedly downbeat.

"What happened?" Mac asked.

"Blanchard made the mistake of coming back here to his house. He's had a bad morning, I'm afraid. Apart from trying and failing to shoot me, he's had a small gardening accident. A run-in with a shovel."

"Ouch. Sounds uncomfortable," Mac said.

"It is, judging from the volume of his complaints," I told him. "I rendered a little first aid, but I think you'd better bring professional medical help along with your fearsome self."

"I can do that," he said. "With pleasure. We'll be there in half an hour."

"And, Mac, I need to ask a favor."

"Anything," he said.

"Well, wait 'til you hear it," I told him. "I know I need to come in and make a statement, but there's something else important I need to do right now. I might not get to the station until quite a bit later today. Or even tomorrow."

He was silent, clearly thinking this over, then said: "All right. I'll cover for you. Go do what you need to do. You can tell me about it later."

❧

I put my phone away and Trouble asked, wiping his nose and stuffing my Kleenex into a pocket of his jacket: "Can we go and find Wild Thing now?"

"Well, here's the thing," I said. "He's probably hiding. I may have figured out where he is, but we have to give him some more time to feel safe. And while he's seeing if things are safe, you know, looking around, I think we need to leave him alone."

We sat in silence, Trouble still pressed up against my left side. I put my arm around him. It seemed the thing to do. He sighed.

"How would you like to go and have blueberry pancakes?" I asked him after a few minutes.

"Then we can come back and check for Wild Thing?" he asked, with the single-mindedness of the very young.

"Hmm, maybe not right after pancakes," I told him, "But soon thereafter. I have something else in mind for you, kiddo."

❧

Stuffed with pancakes, we stood in the boys' clothing section of that huge superstore we all love to hate. Trouble looked up at me in perplexity.

"We're going to buy you some new clothes," I said, hoping this would go over well. Who knew: maybe he was sentimentally attached to his camo jacket, dirty navy sweatshirt, and muddy jeans. I hoped not. "You can pick them out. After all, we're going to an opera tonight and we have to look spiffy."

"What's an opera?" he asked.

"Hmm, well, it's a story told in songs. You'll like this one. It's about a little boy named Tommy. Jen and Donovan are performing it."

He nodded, absorbed in a study of the shelves packed with bright T-shirts, folded jeans, packages of underwear and socks. "Kieran, maybe you should pick out something spiffy for me," he said at last, clearly overwhelmed.

I smiled. "Okay. Black is always spiffy for evening wear. We'll start there."

Chapter 26

I PARKED MY Karmann Ghia in front of Stephanie's trailer, closing my door gently. Trouble did the same with his, and I held a finger to my lips for silence as we made our way from the driveway around the back of the trailer. I'd set my humane trap up there a few hours ago and I was fairly confident that if Wild Thing was still in the vicinity, he'd be in it.

"Check underneath," I whispered to Trouble. He nodded, getting down on hands and knees, crawling until his head disappeared under the trailer.

"Kieran! He's here! In the wire cage!" he called in a hoarse whisper.

I said a prayer of thanks to the God of Cats and joined Trouble kneeling in the muddy grass. Sure enough, in the trap was a small cat, bronze, spotted with black rosettes. Wild Thing, the last of the missing Bengals, looking not at all perturbed. In fact, he looked mighty pleased with himself. An empty, well-licked can of tuna was on its side in the back of the trap, and he was gently biting Trouble's fingers as the kid stuck them through the wires to soothe him.

"He remembers me!" Trouble exclaimed.

I wasn't so sure about that, but I didn't disagree. No need for silence now, though. The kitten was safely trapped. Zee had told me many years ago how to catch a feral cat. Pleading, coaxing, soft words, blandishments, I had wondered? No, Zee had said firmly. Tuna and a humane trap. It had worked then, and it worked now.

"Can we put him in the carrier?" Trouble asked.

"Sure," I told him. "I'll hold the trap open, and you take him out and put him in. Be sure to hang on to him." I placed the carrier I had brought on the ground, and Trouble made the transfer, kissing Wild Thing on his head as he put the kitten safely into the nest of fake sheepskin I had made for him.

"He likes his bed!" Trouble exclaimed. "He's singing!"

"Hmmf," I said, impressed by the fact that Wild Thing looked pretty darned good. He'd probably spent a couple of hungry but dry days under the trailer, not shivering in the rain under a bush as I had initially feared. I had been afraid he'd be in terrible shape, but really, apart from being ravenous, he looked, well, fine. I shook my head. Cats.

"Can you call Jen?" Trouble asked. "She'll be happy. Should we take him there now?"

"Sure," I said. "Let's go."

As we headed off down the highway to Zee's, Wild Thing's carrier on Trouble's lap, I asked him: "Say, sprout, how did you get back to the big house from Zee's last night?"

"Oh, I called the taxi lady and used the old dog man's plastic card," he said matter-of-factly. "I've done it before. When he wanted me to go to the bank in the wall for him."

The bank in the wall? The ATM, I guessed. Of course. Call a cab and use a credit card. How else would an eight-year-old get around in Victoria late at night?

"But I wasn't running away from Zee's," he told me solemnly.

"No? What then?"

He frowned, saying nothing, and I decided not to press him. There'd be time for answers later. Answers to all sorts of questions. Wild Thing purred in his carrier, Trouble hummed a little tune to him, and I became suddenly very sad. Because Wild Thing was going to be Jen's cat. Trouble would soon have to give him up. How many stolen pets had the kid seen pass through the Malverns' dog runs while he watched, dreading the time the man in the white van came for them, distressed, unable to do anything about it. Undoubtedly he had sensed something was wrong. And when he'd asked to have one of them as a pet, thereby saving its life, Peter had burned his arm and laughed at his pain. No pets for Trouble.

And I was sad, too, because when I thought about it, I had actually wrecked Trouble's life, miserable though it was. My quest for the Bengals and the Oak Bay pets had led me to Malvern's enclave in the forest, and to Trouble. Sure, the animals would all go back to the people who loved them, as Trouble liked to put it, but what about him? In the three days I had known him, he had lost four of the four people he knew, plus the roof over his head. Malvern's trailer was condemned, the big house would be systematically taken apart by the police in their continuing search for drugs, and Stephanie's trailer had been only marginally habitable in the first place. What would become of Trouble? It wasn't as though I could return him, like a stray cat, to the people who loved him. Were there any, I wondered?

We turned into Zee's driveway and Trouble said to Wild Thing: "You're home now. It's all okay."

I thought I might cry, because in that moment it became clear to me that it wasn't honor, or compassion, or kindness, or even love which might hold first place as the most powerful concept in the English language. It was home.

"Can I carry him in?" Trouble asked me.

I cleared my throat, which had, unaccountably, tightened a little. "Sure, kiddo."

Zee met us at the front door and Trouble beamed up at her. "We got him!" he announced. "Kieran's trap caught him. I helped."

"I'm sure you did," Zee said indulgently, kindly not mentioning the kid's late-night flight and the worry that had probably produced. "Why don't you take him on into the cat hospital? There's an empty cage. You can put him in there."

"Is he sick?" Trouble asked. "He doesn't look sick."

"He's probably okay," Zee said. "I'll check him over, though."

As Trouble disappeared down the hall, Zee said to me: "Jen and Donovan are in the other room. Last-minute jitters. They've been practicing for days, though, so everything will probably go off without a hitch." She raised an eyebrow. "I am now very familiar with that rock opera."

When I responded with just a noncommittal murmur, she looked at me shrewdly. Zee has always been able to sense when something might be amiss with me, and this was no exception. "How are you?"

"Me?" I said breezily. "All's well that ends well. Twenty-six of twenty-six animals recovered. Three out of three miscreants put away. End of story."

"Hmm," Zee said. "Why am I not so certain of that?"

"Don't go all inscrutable on me, now, Zee," I said irritably. "And no Confucianisms. I'm not in the mood."

"Very well," she said. "I'll try to be plainspoken, as that is what you've requested." We took seats at the kitchen table. "I'm having tea. Would you like to join me?"

"No thanks," I said. "I'll sit for a minute, but Trouble and I are on our way to my house for some scrubbing before the opera. We're kind of grubby. What do you need to be plainspoken about?"

Zee looked into her tea mug, then up at me and said: "Norma called today."

"Today?" I asked. "Wait. I called her yesterday, as soon as we delivered the Bengals here. I left a message. I would have thought she'd have called you a lot earlier." I thought for a minute. "She ought to have been pretty darned excited to hear about the Bengals. A little worried about their health, but still excited that they'd been found. Hmmf. Miranda, told me that Mara and Marv and the others started calling her for updates at six a.m. They were deliriously happy. That seems like a normal reaction. What's up with Norma?"

Zee took a sip of her tea. "She says she won't be able to come and see the cats until tomorrow."

"What? I don't get this."

"Kieran . . . apparently she's going to dispose of them when they're well and she's taken them home. She's decided to close the cattery. She intends to sell the prize winners to other Bengal breeders then sell the remaining cats as pets. Some of the females will need to be spayed, she thinks, as she can't be sure who bred with whom while they were out of her care."

I was stunned. "I . . . are you sure?"

"Very sure. I was as shocked as you are now."

"But I don't understand this," I said. "I mean we got them *back* for her. All of them. Trouble and I could have had our heads blown off rescuing Wild Thing. So she's worried about inbred litters. Really? I mean those cats were so cold and ill I'm sure they didn't have their minds on canoodling. And besides, isn't there a feline morning-after pill?"

Zee smiled. "Something like that, yes."

"Then?"

Zee shrugged. "If you want to know the answers, you will have to ask her those questions."

I groaned. "Oh, crap, why bother? If she's decided, she's decided. But this seems so . . . extreme. And unnecessary. What? She now looks on the Bengals as damaged goods because they got URI and Giardia and spent a few days in the rain? But that's only some of them. The two she took to the cat show are fine." Maybe it was inappropriate, but I found myself feeling quite aggrieved with Norma. Or maybe I was feeling defensive. At any rate, I felt as though I'd failed her somehow.

"So that's why you didn't high-five me when I said all's well that ends well," I said to Zee.

She nodded.

"Huh," I said finally, trying to let all this sink in. "It's up to Norma, of course, what she does with the cats. I did my job. I found them."

"Still, it is somewhat of a surprise," Zee said.

"Oh well. Norma will come for her cats when they're better. I'll present my bill and that can be the end of the story. Clients hire me to put Humpty Dumpty back together again. Restore the status quo. It just didn't happen with the Bengals." I fell silent, still feeling aggrieved. "Speaking of Bengals, did Norma agree that Jen could adopt Wild Thing?" I asked.

Zee nodded. "Yes. In fact she doesn't want an adoption fee from her."

"Good," I said. "At least that's settled. But whatever the reason, it's sad that Wild At Heart will cease to exist."

"Norma's cattery may go out of business," Zee said, "but there will be other Wild At Hearts. There is a small percentage of cat lovers who long for the wild look. They yearn for that which is not tame, tailored, predictable. Consider the wild crosses that have been bred: Savannahs, Ocicats, Toygers, and five or six more in addition to Bengals. It's as though breeders are artists painting with DNA, not oils or watercolors."

I was surprised at Zee. She didn't usually take flights of fancy.

"Anyhow," I said, "I'm glad Norma is letting Jen have Wild Thing. I'd better go. Trouble definitely needs a bath and I need a shower. And I'm thinking of stopping by a haircutter's to get his mane trimmed. He has new clothes, too. We bought some a little earlier today."

"What an adventure for him. He will be quite splendid tonight." She looked at me and raised her eyebrows. "And then?"

I groaned.

Hmm," Zee said enigmatically. "I'll tell Trouble you're ready to leave."

ↁ

I left Trouble at the haircutter's in the little strip mall on the way to my place in Oak Bay, and dashed next door to Starbuck's to pick up coffee for me and a hot chocolate for him. My phone rang while I was waiting in line. It was Miranda.

"Hey," she said, "I'm glad I reached you. Sorry I couldn't talk longer with you when you called earlier. So I thought I'd check and see how things were going. Did Mac pick up Peter Blanchard?"

"I imagine so," I told her. I had called Miranda between stuffing Peter in Bruno's dog run and going off to look for Wild Thing. She had been in the middle of reuniting some of the Oak Bay pet owners with their pets. "It's good to know that's all over. As I said to Mac, three out of three ain't bad. Now you can close that file in your mind."

"It's a relief," she said. "I used to think about the Malverns and Peter Blanchard and seethe. Listen, I thought I'd come by your house about five instead of about six, if that's okay."

"Sure," I said, curious.

"I have some things you need to see," she said mysteriously.

"I need to see them before the rock opera revival this evening?" I asked her, puzzled.

"Yeah, I think you'll want to see what I have to show you."

"Okay," I said, mystified. "I'll see you about five. Should I order some dinner?"

"Sure," she said. "I've been too busy to sit down and have a proper meal. These reunions have kept us rushed off our feet. All that joy is exhausting."

Not to mention the barking, I imagined. I put Trouble's and my drinks in my car, then returned to haircutter's where a whole different kid awaited me. He had been shampooed, shorn, and blown dry and now looked more than ever like a Raphael angel, with a mass of short blond curls. I paid his cutter, added a generous tip, and we walked together to my car.

"I've never been to a place like this," Trouble said. "It smelled like flowers. The lady was nice. She told me her name was Tiffany. I was a little scared, though," he confided.

I was amazed. The kid who had held his gun unflinchingly on Peter Blanchard, spooked about a haircut? "I promise not to tell anyone," I said solemnly. "Sometimes getting a haircut freaks me out a little, too."

He nodded, plainly relieved to think he was not alone in trepidation of grooming rituals. I wondered how he would react to the fact that he absolutely had to take a bath. Well, we'd see.

Chapter 27

"So I live alone here," I told Trouble as we pulled into my street and parked in the driveway beside the house. "Well, not completely alone. There's a lady who lives upstairs. Her name's Helen. And I have two cats."

He had been inspecting the house but turned to me eagerly. "Two cats? They're yours? What are their names?"

"Trey and Vlad," I told him.

"Are they kittens like Wild Thing?"

"No, they're grown up cats. Trey lies around the house and Vlad lives in the rafters in the back porch. Then at night when Trey and I are sleeping, Vlad roams the premises at night, patrolling for rodents, although he's never found any. Grab a couple of those bags from the back seat, will you?"

Burdened with my own bags full of kids' clothes, I unlocked the front door. I found that I was a little nervous. I wanted the kid to like my house. Why was that, I wondered?

"Let's put the bags in the spare room," I said. "Through here."

He followed me into the spare bedroom, looking around at my library as we passed through it.

"You sure have a lot of books," he said in wonder.

"Yeah, I do." All that wisdom, and most days I was sure none of it had stuck inside my skull.

Trey was snoozing on the bed in the spare bedroom in a patch of spring sunshine. He looked up as we came in.

"Mmnnow?" he said.

Trouble laughed. "He's saying hello."

"He is," I told him.

"He's a big cat," Trouble commented. "Can I pet him?"

"Sure. Let him sniff your fingers, like you did with Wild Thing in the cage. Maybe take your jacket off first, though."

Trouble shed his camo jacket and handed it to me. I felt the weight of the gun in its pocket but hung the jacket in the closet, saying nothing. The jacket was pretty filthy, as were his jeans and sneakers, so I thought it a fine time to broach the subject of a bath.

"I'm going to take a shower and change clothes," I told him. "These are the same things I wore yesterday and they're getting a little ripe. I was thinking you might want to change into some of the clothes we bought. Probably you'd like a bath first, though."

A look of apprehension came over his face. He blinked furiously and his eyes travelled from mine to his camo jacket, hanging in the closet. His gun, I thought. He won't go into the bathroom and take his clothes off unless he has his gun. Ai yi.

"You can take your gun into the bathroom with you," I said quietly. "You probably won't need it here in my house because it's really pretty safe, but I understand." I took his gun out of the camo jacket's pocket and handed it to him.

He looked down at the air pistol in his hands, clearly miserable, and I wondered what else I could do to make him feel safer.

"Why don't I start the bath," I said. "You could take your sneakers and socks off in the meantime."

I got some towels and put them in the bathroom for him, started the water, then went back into the spare room where he was sitting on the edge of the bed, gun in hand. His sneakers and socks were still on his feet. I got it. Gun or no gun, not a stitch of clothing was coming off until he was in the bathroom.

"Let's pick out some clean clothes for you for after the bath," I said breezily. "You can take them in with you. How about these?" I held up a plain light blue T-shirt, a dark blue quarter-zip fleece top, and some jeans. I removed all the tags, put socks and underwear with his new sneakers, and presented him with the pile.

"Are they spiffy enough?" he asked. "For the opera?"

I laughed. "They're plenty spiffy. I'm going to put them in the bathroom and shut off the water. They'll be on the floor with the towels. Just go on in when you're ready. I have some work to do on my computer. I'll be in the kitchen."

From the kitchen I heard the lock being turned on the bathroom door. Okay. Probably Trouble considered himself safe now. I shook my head. What in hell had happened to this kid?

I turned on my computer and settled down with Google. There was something I needed to know.

೪೨

Time flies when you're on the Internet. And also when you're in the bath. I touched back down in Victoria from cyberspace and realized I hadn't heard splashing from the other room for some time. Knocking on the bathroom door, I called: "You okay in there, kiddo?"

"Yes," a muffled voice said. "I'm just putting these clothes on."

"Well, c'mon out and let's see how you look," I said. "Trey was thinking you might have drowned."

The bathroom door lock turned, and Trouble came out, fully dressed, right down to his socks and sneakers. It was the first time I had seen him out of the oversized clothes that were probably Con's cast-offs, and I realized how damned small and skinny he was.

"Let's give your hair a wipe-down with a dry towel," I said, ruffling up his hair. "There. You're perfectly dazzling. There's a full length mirror in the hall. Go look at yourself."

He did, smoothing his fleece top down a little, and looking critically at himself. "Will I have to give these clothes back?" he asked. "After the opera?"

"Give them back? No, sweetie. They're yours."

He nodded solemnly, but something else was clearly on his mind. I thought I knew what it was, but now wasn't the time to broach the subject.

"Miranda's coming for dinner," I said. "Would you like Chinese food?"

He looked at me in evident confusion, and I realized he had no idea what I was talking about.

"No problem, I said quickly. "I'll just order something. I think you'll like it. I still have some work to do in the kitchen, kiddo. Would you like to go into the spare room with Trey? You can lie on the bed and play with him. I can find a couple of books you could look at. You could read to him," I suggested.

He went in to join Trey while I walked to my library and selected a book for him: "He Wakes Me", a picture book about a little girl and her cat that was meant for a slightly younger reading age than Trouble's. I collect kids' books and books about cats and hoped this one would please Trouble. I found him propped up on the bed with pillows, Trey under one arm, and handed him the picture book. As I left, he was setting the scene for Trey: "There's a little girl sleeping in her bed and her orange cat's there beside her," he told him. He continued: "The story says: 'He wakes me with his feet. His toes are soft, with hidden needles'." Trouble laughed a little at that, and Trey, always appreciative of good literature, purred loudly. I tiptoed away, back to the kitchen.

After another half hour, I shut off my computer and sat back in my chair. On one Bengal cattery website, a prizewinning breeding female was being offered for sale for five thousand dollars. At a conservative estimate, Norma's Bengals were worth upwards of thirty grand. So Norma would realize quite a bundle if she sold the cats to other breeders. But cat breeders were not in that business for the money, as she had told me. It was for the love of the breed, for the love of the cats. It surely would make more sense to just hold onto all the cats, see who became pregnant with unplanned litters, sell those kittens as pets, then carry on. Wouldn't it? Why in hell was she doing this?

I got up and paced around the kitchen a little, checking to see that I had clean dishes for the Chinese food, then decided screw it, I'd just phone Norma. Maybe she could make me see what wasn't at all clear to me.

She answered on the third ring.

"Kieran Yeats," I told her. "Norma, I'll come right to the point. A young friend and I delivered your missing kitten to Zee's this morning. She tells me that you're going to break up the cattery. That seems such a shame. Can you tell me why?"

"Yes. I can tell you," she said after a moment's silence.

More silence, then: "Do you have any children, Miss Yeats?"

"No, I don't."

"Then I don't know if you'll be able to appreciate what I'm about to tell you."

I bristled a little at this. Mothers often tend to invoke a mysterious maternal understanding, a wisdom peculiar to those who have offspring, when they attempt to explain to us childless and presumably heartless others, some egregious act committed by their bairns. *Oh, you can't possibly understand because you've never had children.* Fooey. I had a feeling something like this was coming. I wasn't wrong.

"I think I owe you an explanation, Kieran," she said, "so I'll be straight with you. I know you've worked hard for me and I appreciate it. The thing is, I have a son who is in legal trouble." She uttered a little mirthless laugh. "Actually he's been in legal trouble most of his adult life. And I've always bailed him out of it. At considerable expense to myself. I know it was wrong of me, but I was always there for him. With my checkbook."

She continued: "Ever since I opened the cattery he's been, well, draining me dry. I've sold cats I never intended to sell, just to keep him out of jail. What was once a joy for me – developing the Bengal breed – has become instead a chore. I worry about cat shows; I worry about winning Best Kitten or Best Cat; I worry about how much money a prize-winner might bring me. So I've made a decision. The theft of the Bengals was really the deciding factor. I'm going to close the cattery, sell the cats, and be done with all this. I'm going to send him a lump sum, tell him to take control of his life, then do what Heather has been urging me to do for years. Travel. Take a cruise. I'll probably sell this house, too."

My heart sank. But if she thought selling everything and sending Carruthers Junior a lump sum of money to change his life would be the end of everything, she was mistaken. My parents had had a blood-sucking leech for a son, and no matter how much they gave, he needed more. They always do. So unless Norma intended to change her name and go live in Bora Bora, her son would find her and continue to put the screws to her for money. I wondered if in her heart she didn't know that. Far better to stiffen her backbone and tell junior to go to hell. It wasn't too late.

But I didn't say that. Nor did I say: "Is that what you really want to do, Norma? I thought you loved seeing the cats who weren't show-stoppers go to good homes, loved seeing the breed improve, loved going to cat shows, loved competing." Why didn't I say anything? Because it would have been cruel. Whoever he was, whatever he'd done, Carruthers Junior's needs trumped Norma's dreams. Well, she'd given me the truth. Another person who'd lived down to my expectations.

"I'm sorry to hear that," I said honestly. "I hope things work out for you. Thanks for letting me know." Then, not knowing what else to say, I ended the call.

I was thinking balefully of mothers and sons when the doorbell rang. I paid the Chinese food delivery person and put the boxes in the oven, on low.

Miranda's van drove up just as the food delivery car was leaving, and she came in, a familiar black garbage bag in her hands. I recognized the bag as the one into which she had tossed Thomas Malvern's computer, his cell phone, a fat accordion file marked "Important Papers", a box of cartridges for Trouble's air pistol, his book about Bomba The Jungle Boy, and some lined notebooks. That seemed months ago.

I hung her jacket up on the coat tree and we went on into the living room. The promising spring afternoon had turned cold and grim, as they so often do, and I had made a fire, which now crackled cheerily in my fireplace.

"Trouble?" she asked.

I motioned for her to follow me into the hall and pointed into the spare room where Trouble lay sleeping, snuggled up with Trey, book open beside him, and she chuckled.

"He cleans up nicely, doesn't he?" she commented as we went back into the living room.

"Do you want a drink?" I asked her, realizing in amazement that I didn't. Could it be that March Madness was over?

"No, thanks," she said.

"I'll go make tea," I said. "We're having Chinese food, so that seems like the thing to do."

She came into the kitchen and leaned against the counter as I filled a kettle and put it on the stove, then found a teapot, teabags, and mugs. "This afternoon I was kind of trapped in my office waiting for the Oak Bay pet owners," she said, an odd look on her face. "So I took a look through Thomas Malvern's file of important papers we took from his trailer."

A bubble of alarm rose in my mind. "Oh? Anything interesting?"

"Plenty. I think we'd better go and sit down."

Chapter 28

"YOU'LL WANT TO read all this when you have time," Miranda said, piling Thomas Malvern's accordion file on the coffee table. "But I can hit the high points for you."

"Okay," I said, studying her face for clues.

"Well, first off, Trouble's a Malvern," she said. "His father was Thomas Malvern's younger son, Andrew, apparently the favorite son. Andrew served in the army and was killed in Afghanistan. He received the Star of Military Valour. It's a pretty high honor. The medal itself is here in Malvern's file."

Aha. That maybe explained the old guy's weeping over war poetry, a couple lines of which Trouble had recited to me when we were trudging to Larsen's in the rain. And his assertion that his father had been a soldier. I had thought it just a piece of fancy on his part. "So, Thomas Malvern, as unlikely as that seems, really is . . . the kid's grandfather?"

"Yup."

"Wow. Who was his mother?"

"A woman named Kerry Adair. It seems that she and Andrew Malvern married in secret. Thomas never wanted Andrew to marry Kerry. Trouble was born while his father was in Afghanistan."

"So Andrew's dead," I said, trying to get all this straight. "But what about Kerry, Trouble's mother?"

Miranda shook her head. "Dead too. She died in a car accident when Trouble was three or four."

"Crap. What a hard-luck kid."

"Tell me about it," Miranda said. "There are some newspaper clippings in the file, some photos, and many pages of writing that Malvern left, along with a will. A kind of end-of-life confession, full of regrets. Seems Malvern was angry with Andrew for marrying Kerry, angry with Andrew for going off to Afghanistan, angry with Andrew for getting killed, and then angry with Trouble."

"That's a lot of anger."

Miranda sighed. "Yeah. After Kerry died, Trouble became, well, an inconvenience. Con certainly didn't want to be saddled with him. And grandpa was still mad at Andrew, so he didn't take him in. Apparently he lived with Kerry's mother for a while, but the old lady passed away too. So Trouble ended up being shuffled around among who-knows-who until he finally came to live with Malvern senior."

I shook my head. "I bet during the shuffling is when he started to be called Trouble."

"Maybe," Miranda said. "It sure wasn't his given name. Fortunately Thomas Malvern makes it clear in his will that Trouble is the kid's nickname, his aka."

"Yeah, that's important, legally. Go on."

"Anyhow, the kid finally came to live with his grandfather when he was four or five. The old man says regretfully that he pretty much ignored him, though."

"I can imagine what happened," I said. "The kid ended up bouncing back and forth between his grandfather and Con. Between the big house and the old guy's trailer depending on who he felt safe with that particular day. The son of father's favorite son. No wonder Con and his buddy Peter treated him like crap."

"Well, Trouble may end up having the last laugh," Miranda said.

"What do you mean?"

"Remember, I said there's a will?"

"Yeah, I do. Please tell me there's more than fifty cents in it for Trouble."

Miranda laughed. "Much more. For years it seems Malvern ran a legitimate kennel business on the property where we found the stolen animals. Called it North Island Kennels, but it was just one of his businesses. It seems he operated several, all under the umbrella of North Island Enterprises. The structures on that five acres, as well as his two vehicles were owned by North Island Enterprises."

"Ha!" I exclaimed. "That's why I couldn't trace the damned brown van, even though I had a DMV list. I didn't know about North Island Enterprises. I was looking for the surname Malvern. Fooey."

"He seemed to be a pretty well-organized and moderately successful guy. Until he fell off the roof of his kennel, fixing something. Then he started taking opiates for pain, couldn't run the kennel, and looked around for an easy animal-related business. It seems he knew plenty of people in the animal world."

"So he took up bunching? Jesus, what a come-down," I said bitterly.

She continued: "Apparently Con persuaded him that animal theft would be a lucrative business and that the kennel, which was nice and secluded, would be a perfect place to stash the animals. Malvern agreed – he writes that he regrets agreeing – and the two of them started stealing animals and passing them on to an animal dealer Malvern senior knew. Then Con's buddy Peter the dogfighter – yeah, Malvern knew about that – joined the business. He wouldn't let the two of them provide stolen animals for dogfighting – I guess even he had his standards. You know, if what Malvern did wasn't so despicable, I might have some pity for him. He fell down the slippery slope of opiates. He lost whatever feeling for animals he once had. If he had much."

We sat in silence for a moment and then I said. "Tell me about the will."

"Well, after Malvern ended up hooked on fentanyl and had some idea of where his life was headed, he got all his papers together – property deeds, titles to vehicles, and so on – and decided what he wanted to do with his assets. He had an attorney draw his will.

There's a business card stapled to a copy of it." She turned to look at me. "Trouble is a very well-off kid. Malvern essentially disinherited Con and left everything to Trouble except for a token dollar to Con. He had a pretty decent bank account, too. And just imagine what five acres on the ocean north of Victoria is worth."

"A lot, I would guess. But tell me one thing. What's Trouble's real name?"

"You won't believe it. The kid's birth certificate is right here." She pulled it out of the accordion folder and showed it to me. Sure enough it was an official birth certificate bearing the seal of the Province of British Columbia and listing the following:

Mother's name : Kerry Campbell Adair
Father's name : Andrew Thomas Malvern
Child's Name   : Tristan Kerry Malvern

"Tristan . . . you mean Trouble's real name is Tristan? For crap's sake . . . wasn't that the name of one of King Arthur's knights? Whoever names their kid *Tristan*?"

"Whoever does?" Miranda agreed. "But look at the middle name. I know this is all a shock, but tell me what it is."

"Kerry. Holy shit, but that's –"

" – the kid's mother's name. Focus in, Kieran. Look at what's written on the line under 'Child's Name'. Read it to me."

Oh my God. I had gotten so hung up on the kid's weird given name that I really hadn't read the rest. "It says 'Sex: F,'" I told Miranda.

"It does, doesn't it?"

"It sure does."

"And Trouble therefore is?" she laughed.

"Tristan Kerry Malvern," I said. "Trouble is a girl."

❧

Ah, coffeehouses. Why do we love coffee so much? Chemists would tell us that it's because the caffeine molecule displaces adenosine from its receptor, thereby keeping us alert; stimulates dopamine, making us feel good; and revs up adrenaline so we're ready for flights of creative fancy. As well, its more than 800 aromatic compounds make us swoon with delight. Poets have likened it to a warm hug from God. I wouldn't go that far – I just know that it smells wonderful and tastes fantastic. And a little revving up doesn't hurt things, either.

As Miranda, Trouble and I walked into the coffeehouse, I thought fondly of my undergraduate days at University of Toronto, and the seedy neighborhood just north of the University. During my time at U of T, in more evenings than were good for my GPA, I'd thrown over my study of philosophy and the thorny question of whether Heraclitus could step into the same stream twice, for coffee and music in Yorkville.

Alas, the wave of famous coffeehouses and the singers they introduced had receded by the time I was an undergrad, but we all knew their history: the Riverboat was where that strange folk singer from Saskatoon named Joni Mitchell sang nightly, as well as some lanky guy from Orillia named Gordon Lightfoot, and the Toronto kid with the wavery tenor named Neil Young. How I wished I had been born years earlier. The Riverboat and The Purple Onion, the most famous of the coffeehouses in the so-called "festering sore" of Yorkville were shuttered by the time I was a folksinging and coffee-drinking afficionado, but I and my fellow coffeehouse mavens all secretly hoped that Ian and Sylvia might make a surprise return visit to one of the now respectable establishments. Of course, that never happened. Nevertheless, we swore that the strains of "Four Strong Winds" still lingered in the streets of Yorkville.

I have to confess that I was still in a bit of a daze as the result of Miranda's revelations to me about Malvern's will, Trouble's father and mother, and most all, his gender, or rather her gender. Holy crap. Had I taken her to the wrong section of that superstore to buy clothes? Would she rather have had a pink T-shirt? And oh my god, what about the underwear? Not to mention, which pronoun would I now have to use in thinking about him or her? How did the kid think about herself? Everything had changed, right down to the kid's name. Tristan. This would all take some talking to Trouble, and some getting used to.

The audience at the coffeehouse seemed to be composed of people about my age – ageing hippies still unaccountably fond of tie-dye, former folk music aficionados, people who remembered the rock opera *Tommy* and were curious about how two young musicians might re-imagine it. I was glad to see that there was a pretty good crowd – Donovan's sister Celine had evidently advertised the event. We picked up coffee, tea, and hot chocolate and found a table where Zee, Lawrence, Aliya, and a couple who Zee introduced as Donovan's parents were seated. We chatted, and then it was time for Jen and Donovan to perform.

After a brief introduction, Jen and Donovan walked onstage. She was wearing a plain black T-shirt and black jeans, and Donovan wore the same. I grinned. I guessed that was what serious young coffeehouse musicians wore these days. Jen's hair was spiked and gelled into immobility, and Donovan's light brown dreadlocks were tied back behind his head. They looked terribly young and terribly nervous. For crap's sake, they were thirteen and fourteen. I would have been quaking in my sneakers too in their place. They smiled briefly at each other and Jen took a seat at the coffeehouse's piano, while Donovan arranged himself behind his cello – I hadn't known which instrument he played until that precise moment – and simply began to tell us in song the story of Tommy, the child abused and trapped by his family within his family – the dark, disturbing heart of The Who's rock opera. As they began playing, I realized how effective Donovan's cello was going to be as a counterpoint to Jen's piano work. This re-imagining would be a quiet, thoughtful, somewhat melancholy trip through Tommy's life. It began in a minor key.

Tommy Walker's mother, believing her husband to have been killed in the war, had begun an affair with Tommy's uncle. And why not? Optimistic about the future, Mrs. Walker sang to her lover about how '21 was going to be a good year, especially if the two of them saw it in together.

However, in the mysterious, tragic ways of opera, Tommy's father is not dead. He returns, to spoil the lovers' plans, and things go to hell as Tommy's father and uncle fight, Tommy's father is killed, and Tommy sees it all. The lovers are rid of the intrusive presence of Tommy's father, but frightened by the presence of a witness. What about the boy, they ask themselves, what about the boy? He saw it all.

Determined to make the crime vanish, Tommy's mother and uncle begin to gaslight him, but Tommy resists, clinging to the truth.

Every time they say he didn't hear it, his voice asserts that he heard it; every time they say he didn't see it, his voice asserts that he saw it.

But eventually, they badger Tommy into agreement. He agrees that he won't tell word of what happened to anyone, won't tell a soul what he knows is the truth. And so Tommy becomes deaf, dumb and blind to protect himself from remembering what he witnessed.

I think it was this point at which my epiphany began, if epiphanies can be protracted. I suddenly thought of Trouble. I was vaguely aware of Jen and Donovan progressing through the separate songs that made up the rock opera, but I had stopped really listening. I was absorbed in my thoughts.

What if something akin to what had happened to Tommy had happened to Trouble? Not witnessing his father's murder, not that – Andrew Malvern had died a hero in Afghanistan, after all. But something else, something personal, something so profound and frightening that Trouble also had had to deny reality? Had someone said to him: "You didn't hear it, you didn't see it, you never heard it, not a word of it"? Had someone told him: "You won't say nothing to no one, never tell a soul what you know is the truth?" Had something so bad transpired that he had changed genders in his mind, become a boy because it was too damned frightening to be a girl?

I sipped my now-cold coffee and looked over at Trouble watching Jen and Donovan in open-mouthed absorption. What if?

The story progressed, Tommy retreating into the prison of his mind.

I have only had two epiphanies in my life. One happened when I was in English class in high school when I suddenly understood poetic meter: pentameter, heptameter, hexameter – I got them, all of them. It was as though I had been given the key to poetry. It was a true light bulb moment. The other happened when I met my first love. Just like the corny old song said, my heart stood still.

My heart stood still again as Jen and Donovan began the opera's last song, Tommy's aria. It is preceded by an ugly scene of rejection in which those who had previously loved him turn against him, telling him that they forsake him, intend to rape him, and finally, vow to forget him. Then Tommy, deserted and alone, speaks from his heart to those who have not seen or heard him. Jen stood up from her piano, walked out to the front of the stage, and began to sing, *a capella,* arguably the first of the four most moving lines in rock music: see me, feel me, touch me, heal me. Donovan left his cello, joined her, and sang the second line, a repeat of the first. Then they sang the third and fourth lines together.

I get it, I said to the universe. I get it. I see him. I see Trouble. I see the abandoned kid, the soft-hearted animal champion, the brave-hearted little gunslinger. The child no one wanted. The child who was just . . . trouble.

The audience was silent through the first four lines of the aria, but then Jen and Donovan took their places at their instruments again and began the final verse. The audience came to its feet and sang along, sang just as joyously as Tommy's followers who had finally seen and heard and felt Tommy. We all knew the words: "Listening to you, I get the music, gazing at you, I get the beat."

And then it was over. Donovan's parents rushed to congratulate the two young people, Zee, Lawrence, and Aliya had drifted away and were talking animatedly among themselves, and Miranda, Trouble and I were left alone at our table. He looked up at me uncertainly.

Miranda looked from him to me, then said: "I'll go warm up the van."

I handed Trouble the navy down vest I had bought him at the superstore and he put it on, zipping it up, putting his hands in the pockets.

I looked down at him and smiled. He smiled back.

"Let's go home," I said.

Author's Note

ALTHOUGH THIS BOOK is a work of fiction, animal theft, bunchers, and the use of companion animals in research laboratories are, sadly, facts. People wishing to learn more about these subjects are encouraged to contact the organizations listed below for more information, and for ways they can help. But the most important way they can help is by keeping their pets indoors.

Animal Alliance of Canada
#101 – 221 Broadview Avenue
Toronto, Ontario M4M 2G3
Canada
www.animalalliance.ca

People For The Ethical Treatment Of Animals
501 Front Street
Norfolk, VA 23510
www.peta.org

Last Chance For Animals
8033 Sunset Blvd #835
Los Angeles, CA 90046
www.lcanimal.org

To My Readers

I HOPE YOU enjoyed reading Stolen. And if you did like it, I'd be grateful if you would go to amazon and give me a review. It would be tremendously helpful. In these brand-new days of indie publishing, amazon reviews helps authors immensely. We have no big marketing department at a traditional publishing house to boost our sales – we rely on word of mouth, so to speak. I'm relying on you to spread the word. Thank you in advance for this favor.

Linda J Wright

www.lindajwright.com

CPSIA information can be obtained
at www.ICGtesting.com
Printed in the USA
LVHW012300080119
603253LV00006B/215/P